A PLUME BOOK

THE NAMES OF OUR TEARS

Madonna Gaus

PAUL LOUIS GAUS lives with his wife, Madonna, in Wooster, Ohio, just a few miles north of Holmes County, where the world's largest and most varied settlement of Amish and Mennonite people is found. His knowledge of the culture of the "Plain People" stems from more than thirty years of extensive exploration of the narrow blacktop roads and lesser gravel lanes of this pastoral community, which includes several dozen sects of Anabaptists living closely among the so-called English or Yankee non-Amish people of the county. Paul lectures widely about the Amish people he has met and about the lifestyles, culture, and religion of this remarkable community of Christian pacifists. He can be found online at www.plgaus.com. He also maintains a Web presence with Mystery Writers of America at www.mysterywriters.org, and a blog at http://amish-countryjournal.blogspot.com.

Other Amish-Country Mysteries by P. L. Gaus

Blood of the Prodigal

Broken English

Clouds Without Rain

Cast a Blue Shadow

A Prayer for the Night

Separate from the World

Harmless as Doves

THE NAMES OF OUR TEARS

AN AMISH-COUNTRY MYSTERY

P. L. GAUS

A PLUME BOOK

PLUME
Published by the Penguin Group
Penguin Group (USA) Inc., 375 Hudson Street,
New York, New York 10014, USA

USA | Canada | UK | Ireland | Australia | New Zealand | India | South Africa | China
Penguin Books Ltd, Registered Offices: 80 Strand, London WC2R 0RL, England
For more information about the Penguin Group visit penguin.com

First published by Plume, a member of Penguin Group (USA) Inc., 2013

LIBRARY OF CONGRESS CATALOGING-IN-PUBLICATION DATA
Gaus, Paul L.
The names of our tears : an Amish-country mystery / P.L. Gaus.
pages   cm
ISBN 978-0-452-29819-4 (pbk.)
1. Amish—Fiction. 2. Drug traffic—Fiction. 3. Amish Country (Ohio)—
Fiction. 4. Mystery fiction. I. Title.
PS3557.A9517N36 2013
813'.54—dc23   2012045399

Printed in the United States of America
10 9 8 7 6 5 4 3 2 1

For Kathy and Tim. We don't get to choose our siblings, but once in a while, when genetic roulette is combined effectively with such character as derives from life, someone like me gets lucky.

Preface and Acknowledgments

WHEN I started searching for an authentic location for the opening chapter in this story, I used the county engineer's Highway Map of Holmes County, Ohio, which is still the best map available for people who want to explore the lesser known regions of Amish country here. It can be purchased for one dollar in the engineer's office across the street from the old red brick county jail, on courthouse square in Millersburg. I used the map because I wanted to set the opening scene in one of the most remote and difficult places to find in all of Holmes County. But with the map unfolded on the passenger's seat and a GPS locator parked on the dash, it still took me nearly an hour to find the spot I had chosen. It is on the way to nowhere at all, and it proved to be the perfect choice. The glade is just as I described it in the book, with a rocky stream and a clearing where a private rendezvous might reasonably be arranged. In that respect it served my purposes well. Unexpectedly, though, when I first found the clearing, the location further proved itself to me as the perfect spot for a murder, because at the edge of the clearing near the stream, an open grave had been dug. I was surprised to say the least. I have since learned that it was an animal's grave and not a person's, but still the impression that the open grave had on me has remained strong throughout all the months since I first started designing and writing what became the present novel. I hope readers will appreciate the surprise and astonishment that I experienced when I first went to that location with my map in hand, hoping only that it would serve the story well.

I wish especially to thank the editors at Plume and specifically Denise Roy, senior editor, who has believed steadfastly in this series and whose support has been of great encouragement and benefit to me. I am also grateful for the fine work of the publicity manager at Plume, Mary Pomponio. Last but never least, I thank my literary agent, Jenny Bent (the Bent Agency, New York), who has given strong support for this story (and for the other seven novels in the series) while expertly guiding me through the transition to a new publisher.

The righteous cry out,
and the Lord hears them;
He delivers them from all
their troubles.
The Lord is close to the
brokenhearted and saves
those who are crushed in
spirit.

Psalms 34:17–18

THE NAMES
OF OUR TEARS

THE NAME'S
OF OUR TEARS

1

Monday, April 4
7:45 A.M.

IT WAS Coblentz chocolate that had Mervin Byler awake so early that morning—fine Coblentz chocolate, and the artful widow Stutzman who made it. This would be his seventh trip this spring up to the heights at Walnut Creek, and he knew the best gossips in the valley would be making sport of him again today.

What could draw old Mervin out so early, they'd be asking each other so delicately. Was it really the Coblentz chocolate? Was he just a retired old farmer out for a drive? Maybe he just liked to show off his high-stepping racehorse. Or could it be the widow Stutzman?

Oh, how they'd sure be buzzing today, Mervin thought. *Why yes*—he smiled—*it looks as if he's washed his best Sunday rig again.*

Mervin stepped out into the cold air in a new Amish-blue denim suit and stood on the front porch of his white clapboard Daadihaus, set back twenty paces from the wide gravel drive that curled around the back of the big house. A cool breeze tugged at his white chin whiskers, and a gust caught under the wide brim of his black felt hat, nearly lifting it from his head. He settled the warm hat back into place and stood to enjoy the familiar sounds of the farm—all the family, parents and kids alike, at work since well before dawn.

In the woodshop behind the barn, that was his oldest son Daniel he heard, running lumber through the tabletop saw. Lowing as they nipped at the hay in the feeders, the milking cows were back on the hillside pastures beyond. The youngest kids were bringing baskets of eggs out of the henhouse. And beside the big house, an older grandson was starting a gasoline generator, charging the marine batteries for the several electric appliances the family kept—a phone in a little shed out by the road, a secret radio for severe weather, half a dozen lightbulbs where safety called for something other than kerosene lanterns, and an electric butter churn that Mervin had brought home on a whim from Lehman's hardware in Kidron.

Standing on his front porch, Mervin listened with satisfaction to the familiar sounds of morning chores, the rhythms of family life on the farm. In his day, when the farm had been theirs, he and his Leona had been accustomed to early rising, too. They had owned the farm for forty years, and then they had lived together for seven more happy years in their little Daadihaus, watching Daniel and Becky raise their own, in the same home where Mervin and Leona Byler had raised their twelve. It's fitting, Mervin thought. The old move aside for the young, who in turn honor their parents with the gift of a new home.

Byler sighed and thought about Leona, gone for nearly three years. So fine a woman; so many good years. Now their little Daadihaus was a lonely place for him, and Mervin had fallen into slack habits. Most would say it was shameful, the way he ignored the chores. He slept in, and he got up when it suited him. Mervin Byler figured he had earned his rest.

Truth be told, Leona might say it was a bit much. When they had retired, she had insisted that they rise with the others and tend to their share of the chores, too. But now Mervin gladly let the sons plant and harvest the crops, tend to the livestock, handle all the duties on the farm. Mervin Byler was retired, and he had fun and suitable places to be, never mind what the gossips might say about the widow Stutzman. He felt young again, and he knew with the wisdom of age that that feeling was not to be squandered.

With great satisfaction over his prospects for the morning, Byler noted that the stiff breeze was snatching a thin gray line of smoke from the chimney of Becky's kitchen stove, at the back of the big house. The fire is still going, he thought. As late as it was, there would still be hot coffee in her pot. Maybe he could take some of Becky's biscuits, too. Wrap them in a towel for the trip. Byler considered it briefly.

But his best mare was already hitched and waiting on the drive, shuddering from the energy bottled up in her limbs. Just like Mervin, she was eager to begin.

Mervin clipped down the wooden steps on his new leather soles and climbed into his Sunday buggy, laughing at himself. Thinking that he could already hear the chatter. Knowing what the valley gossips would say if they ever got a look inside his cupboards, stuffed full to bursting with Coblentz chocolates of every kind. They would be asking themselves why an old man needed to be driving back to Walnut Creek again when his cupboards were already shamefully overstocked with more sweets than any sensible man could eat.

For the fun of it, he ought to drop a hint somewhere along the line. Put it out there among the talkers that he didn't really like chocolate that much. Truth be told, he favored salty chips more than sweets. Wonderful, crunchy, salty chips of every kind.

Just tell one of them, he thought, and soon they'd all be a-chatter. He'd make a few trips into Walmart for a dozen bags of Ruffles, and that news would be singing like electric in the wires. *Why, don't you know? Mervin doesn't really like sweets at all.* Then he could enjoy the sparks. He couldn't remember a time when he had felt so young.

But don't kid yourself, Mervin smiled. Today I'll just tap the glass. See if she'll come around to the tourists' gallery for a chat. Maybe he could visit on Sunday with the North Walnut Creek Lehmans, and stay after services for the social. Then his valley would sure be all a-buzz. Was it the Coblentz chocolates or the widow Stutzman? A Sunday visit in old Ben Lehman's district would settle it for sure. They'd all be talking for over a month.

Mervin climbed up, took the reins, and walked his buggy out to the lane in front of the big house. He turned right to follow Township Lane 166 toward the north, thinking that maybe she'd give him a look today. Something to help him make up his mind. But hadn't she done that already the last time he had visited? Mervin wasn't sure. Was it a look, or was it a smile? Maybe it was just a glance.

Yes, at the time, he had thought it was just a glance. Now it seemed to him that it might have been more than that. Was it really encouragement for a suitor, or was she mocking an old fool?

Never mind, he told himself. I'll tap on the glass today. Then she'll give me one look or the other look, and I'll know if I should bother with any more chocolates from the Coblentz store. Not that there's room in my cupboards.

He set a good pace for his horse and took the reins in his left hand. With his right, he fished his money roll out of the side pocket of his denim trousers. It was a suitable sum, he thought. Four hundred and eighty-seven dollars, most of it in tens and twenties. He wouldn't need nearly that much. Still a man ought to be prepared. Maybe after he stopped in Walnut Creek, he'd run up Route 39 to the Walmart in Millersburg. That'd put him home after dark. Smiling broadly, he thought how that news would spread itself around among the folk. Up to Walnut Creek for the widow Stutzman and way over to Millersburg just for chips? There'd be no end of the talk.

At the intersection with Township 165, Byler turned left and took the gravel lane where it cut a gap in the remote southeastern corner of Holmes County. Exhausted from a brutal winter, most fields lay bare on the rolling hills, but some had been plowed already, their tidy rows of newly turned earth looking eagerly dark and moist for planting.

On the slope to his left, he saw the new shoots of winter wheat promising the harvest in July. Ahead on his right stood the stubble of feed corn cut last autumn, the arching rows of blunted shafts curving gracefully over the crest.

Take the back roads today, Byler thought. No sense getting out on SR 39, where the traffic is so crazy. When had the tourists discovered Walnut Creek? Twenty years ago, there hadn't been anything at all in the little town. Now it was overbuilt for commerce, and the traffic was incessant, with out-of-state plates and buses from all the big cities.

Mervin frowned. He gave the reins a determined slap. Back roads will take longer, he told himself, but the trip will be safer, and you'll get there in one piece, you old fool. So stick to the backmost roads.

The narrow wheels of his buggy cut fine, wavy lines into the gravel and mud of the lane, and he gave the reins another slap to encourage his horse. The whisper music of his buggy wheels running in the wet gravel and the clipping rhythm of his horse's hooves spoke peacefulness to him. Coblentz chocolate and the widow Stutzman. Who could ask for a better morning?

Following the creek that was fed by the spring on the Yoder farm, he traveled generally north and west, and made the sharp right turn where the road curved to the north. The glade that lay ahead to his left was lined by sycamores whose old roots sank deep into the rocky cut of the creek. A stand of barren maples beside the road sheltered the little glade from view at first, but soon he reached the clearing beside the road, where the Yoders maintained a service road for an oil well. Behind the low knoll, Byler could see the top of the wellhead where the Yoders took off their natural gas feed, and beside that stood a green tank for the oil that was being pumped slowly out of the ground.

As he skirted the glade, however, Byler saw a horse and buggy standing at the back of the clearing, beside the bend in the service road. The horse was tethered to a sapling, and it was bucking wildly in its harness, its head popping up and down and back and forth as it whipped the leather reins that were tied to the tree.

Byler stopped, climbed down from his rig, and circled around through tangled brush to reach the front of the horse, not wanting to agitate it any further by coming up on its rear. As he approached, he called out to the horse, "Hey there! Hey, big fella! Whoa!"

But as he pushed through the brambles, his feet crunching twigs and fallen branches, the horse bucked and danced all the more, its hooves striking strangely to the right and left, as if it were trying to sidestep a rattlesnake. As if it couldn't bear to let its footfalls touch the ground.

And that's when Byler first saw the girl lying underneath the rear hooves of the horse. An Amish girl in a forest-green dress, wearing the black denim jacket of a man. Sprawled under the hooves of the frantic horse. Trampled facedown in the mud beside the spring. Clothes caked with bloodied mud, arms and legs sprawled to the sides like broken twigs. The hair at the back of her head matted with blood from a gaping hole in her skull. The frightened horse pounding out its terror on her back.

Byler stepped up to the sapling and drew his pocketknife. He cut once at the reins wrapped around the trunk, but failed to sever the hold. He cut again with more force, and the leather gave way, but still held. Then he slashed with his blade a third time, and the reins snapped free, sending the horse bolting off to the side, dragging the wheels of the buggy sideways over the body of the girl, flipping her onto her back. The horse and buggy disappeared around the curve of the lane. Staring down at the trampled body of the girl, Byler could hear the plaintive cries of the horse as it struggled to free itself from the harness. He knelt to brush mud from her face and felt a round wound in her forehead.

*   *   *

Each time the buggy bounced out of a chuckhole, it seemed to Byler that it actually flew. He whipped the horse again and tried to keep his seat as he raced back home to the phone booth beside the road.

Thirty yards out, he started slowing the horse, but he overshot the phone. Not bothering to steady or tether the horse, Byler hopped down beside the picket fence in front of Daniel's house, let the horse pace forward to stop on its own, dashed into the phone booth, pulled the receiver to his ear, and tried to turn the dial. His fingers were shaking badly, and it took him three tries to swing the dial around to get 911.

Groaning as he waited for an answer, Mervin's feet marched out a manic step in place, inside the tight confines of the little shed. When the operator answered, he shouted, "Dead girl!" as loud as he could, and repeated it, saying, "I found a dead girl!"

He dropped the receiver, pushed back through the door, and ran for the house, shouting, "Daniel! Becky! Get help!"

Then he remembered the phone and ran back to the booth. When he picked up the receiver, the operator started asking him questions, and he answered them as best he could.

"Beside the Yoders' spring.

"Yes, it's Holmes County. At the big bend of Township 165 and 166.

"She's dead, I tell you. Get the sheriff!

"Because I felt a hole in her forehead! When I tried to brush the mud out of her eyes."

Then, with his thoughts muddled by adrenaline, Mervin answered several more questions, while Daniel and Becky stood outside the phone booth with anxious questions in their eyes.

Mervin finished his call, laid the handset back on its cradle, and stood alone inside, trying to understand how he could manage to do what the man on the phone had asked him to do—to go back, to wait there, and to talk with the deputies when they arrived.

He turned in place, opened the door, and stepped outside to tell Daniel and Becky what he had seen. But several of the children had gathered with their parents, so he drew Daniel aside to whisper.

As he did so, Mervin Byler couldn't remember a time when he had felt so old.

2

Monday, April 4
8:40 A.M.

DETECTIVE SERGEANT Ricky Niell followed a circuitous route to meet Mervin Byler. When the call had come in, he had been in Berlin, to the north, taking a statement from a local who had been knocked down by an impatient tourist hurrying to park his car in a prized spot at the curb. The injured man was sitting on a bench in front of the old Boyd and Wurthmann Restaurant while paramedics splinted his ankle. All around him flowed the early morning circus of a society gone hideously commercial, with English tourists thronging the sidewalks, cars and tour buses clogging the main road and all of the side streets, and garish music playing from loudspeakers outside the trinket establishments that so many English folk considered to be authentic country treasures.

Frustrated by the spectacle, Niell left Berlin abruptly. He followed SR 39 south and east out of town, dropped down off the crest at Walnut Creek, pushed around the long, sweeping curve, and turned south on TR 420. He needed to hurry, but the country lanes were narrow, pitched steeply, and curved dangerously. With mounting urgency, he forced his cruiser around a series of sharp turns and switchbacks, traveling deeper into the secluded hillside pasturelands north of Baltic. TR 420 to County

140, then TR 141, TR 164, County 70, back onto TR 164, and finally left and south again on TR 165, driving ever slower as the lanes constricted and turned to gravel and mud.

After another tortuous quarter mile of frustration, Niell stopped, punched up a wider view on his GPS display, and studied it to see how deeply into the isolated countryside he had managed to penetrate. Once he had confirmed his location, he rolled his cruiser forward with guarded satisfaction, came over a rise, and dropped into a pocket between the hills.

Directly ahead he saw a black buggy parked on the road, with a short, round, white-haired Amishman holding the bridle of his horse. The man waved to him somberly, and Niell rolled forward and stopped ten paces from the nose of the horse. Then Niell called in his location on his radio and got out of his cruiser, zipping up his duty jacket out of a habit grown to ritual after a long and hard winter. But once out of his cruiser, he realized that the cold spring breezes that were stirring over the high grounds at Berlin and Walnut Creek weren't reaching into the deep draw where he had parked, so he unzipped his jacket, took it off, and tossed it onto the front seat.

As fastidious as ever, Niell was dressed in designer slacks, with a coat and tie. He had his badge clipped to his belt in front. His black hair was longer than he liked and parted on the right, the way his wife, Ellie, preferred. His mustache was still black and pencil thin. Otherwise, he was clean-shaven. His shoes were polished and fashionable, and unsuited to the terrain, so he sat on the edge of the driver's seat to change into a pair of work boots.

As he did that, Mervin Byler marched forward and offered his hand. "I'm Mervin Byler and I called about the girl," he said in a rush and pointed into the clearing where the body lay.

Niell stood up, shook hands, and walked over with Byler to stand between the buggy rig and the glade. "Did you move the body, Mr. Byler?" he asked.

"No," Byler said nervously. "No, I just turned her head a little."

"So, really, you did move her."

"I just turned her head, Deputy, to see if I could help. Other than that, she's right where I found her."

Niell studied the glen and judged the clearing to be thirty yards wide and forty yards deep. It sloped back to a stand of tall, barren trees, where a creek coursed over jagged rocks, showing patches of ice and snow in the shaded crevices.

To Niell's right there was a small knoll, around which a service road curved and disappeared. Beyond the top of the knoll, he could see the round metal dome of an oil tank.

Between the creek and the road to his left was a field of tangled weeds, dead shoots, and wild grasses. Half a dozen saplings stood as a boundary between the grasses and the clearing where the girl lay. Frowning at the body, Niell pulled a new spiral notebook out of his hip pocket.

As he sketched the scene in his notebook, Niell heard voices behind him. He stepped around the rear of the buggy and looked up the rise to the crest of the hill beside the lane. There he saw a half-dozen Amish kids and half as many adults, standing out in the wind on the high pasture, watching from a height of thirty feet.

Niell shook his head, annoyed by the curiosity of the locals. Death, it seemed, was a draw for them. He shrugged, thinking it a shame that they had gathered so quickly. But it had always been like this, even in the most peaceful, quiet corners of the county.

But there was nothing he could do about it, so he turned to Byler, flipped to a new page in his spiral notebook, and asked, "Has anyone gone after the horse, or is everyone up there—you know—just *watching* us?"

Niell felt awkwardly tall beside Byler, and he quickly regretted his sharp tone. He was constitutionally even tempered, but the onlookers on the high pasture behind him had touched a sensitive nerve. It was not that long ago that a similarly annoying crowd had gathered outside the ranch home of Darba Winters to watch the investigation into the murder of an Amish neighbor south of Fredericksburg, and then the curiosity of the crowd had bothered him equally. Not as much as it apparently had bothered the gruff Sheriff Robertson, but enough all the same. Then, with her husband dead, Darba Winters had disappeared, raising the sheriff's ire all the more. And while it often had fallen to Niell to smooth over the ruffled feathers left in Sheriff Robertson's powerful wake, Ricky was now a detective, and he figured that he had advanced enough in rank and seniority to let the other deputies worry about Robertson's short-fused insistence.

So today, with the locals already gathering to watch, Niell didn't much care to think about Robertson's eventual appearance at the scene. Truth be told, the sheriff didn't always help. Besides, Niell mused, we have a detective bureau, now, and the sheriff really isn't needed here. Let Captain Newell manage the details for once, Niell thought. Let the detectives run this investigation.

The detectives in the bureau consisted so far only of Ricky Niell and Corporal Pat Lance, she with air force training in detective work, and he with only one more state certification still to earn. Bobby Newell had come out of retirement to serve as captain of detectives, and Robertson had promised to appoint another deputy to detective status. More to the point, he had promised to let the captain and his detectives take the lead on murder investigations.

Niell pulled himself away from his thoughts, reprimanded himself for the distraction, studied the little man beside him, and asked again about recovering the horse. But Byler didn't respond. Perhaps he hadn't heard. He was staring intently at the body of the girl, and Niell had to tap his shoulder to get his attention. "Mr. Byler, has someone gone after her horse and buggy?"

Absently, Byler answered, "I sent one of my grandsons after it."

"Because I need to see them both," Niell added. "I wouldn't want the horse unhitched before I got a look."

Byler nodded and marched back around the rear of his buggy. Niell followed. Byler called out to one of the lads standing on the high pasture, and the boy scrambled down the slope directly. Then Byler instructed the boy using the authoritative Dietsch dialect of the region, and the boy ran down the road, heading north.

Byler nodded his satisfaction and said to Niell, "He'll catch up. They'll leave the horse hitched when they bring it back here."

Niell studied his position in the deep pocket between the hills. "You can't see anything down in here, Mr. Byler. How will they know where the horse is?"

"Oh, it's probably just over that hill behind the creek. Horses don't like running much on their own. The lads will track it down."

"Will this new fellow get there in time to tell your grandson not to unhitch the horse?"

Byler shrugged and smiled weakly. "We'll have to wait and see. They are brothers."

Niell considered that, walked back to stand between Byler's buggy and the glen, and asked, "Mr. Byler, do you know who she is?"

As Niell spoke, another cruiser came around the curve and rolled to a stop behind Byler's rig. Corporal Stan Armbruster got out with a camera, and walked up to Niell and Byler. He was in a trim-fitting uniform, with a duty belt loaded heavily with gear. His black hair was military short, and his round face showed a fair complexion and a ready smile. As he came forward, he said, "I came in through Farmerstown, but I took a wrong turn. Should have gotten here first."

"I haven't been here very long," Niell said. "Is Lance on her way?"

"She's coming down from Mt. Hope. Might be a minute, yet."

"OK," Niell said, "I'm sketching the scene, so you walk a circuit around it, taking pictures from a distance. We'll go in closer when Pat gets here."

Armbruster nodded and started walking a wide circumference around the glade, taking pictures from various angles. Niell called out, "Be sure to get shots from up on that little knoll," and Armbruster nodded.

Turning back to Byler, Niell asked, "Do you recognize her, Mr. Byler?"

Byler shrugged. "I didn't get much of a look, since her face was so muddy. But I think she's a Zook. I think she works at a bed-and-breakfast over on 557, just this side of Charm."

"But are you certain?"

"No," Byler said. "But I think she's one of the Zooks from out that way."

Niell called Armbruster back and said, "Stan, let me take the camera. I need you to check at a B and B on 557."

Niell turned to question Byler, and Byler offered, "It's the Maple Valley B and B. If she's a Zook from over there, she lives across the road, and down about a quarter mile."

"But we're not sure," Niell said to Armbruster. "So just go over and ask at the B and B. See if a Zook girl is working this morning, or if she's supposed to be but hasn't showed up. Call me when you get an answer, but don't say anything about this murder."

Armbruster nodded, climbed back into his cruiser, backed up, backed around in a wide patch of road to head out, and drove away, swinging over to the right to let Pat Lance's cruiser pass by on his left, coming in.

Lance parked behind Byler's rig and got out. She was a blond, Germanic woman with close-cropped hair. She had large, round blue eyes, set far apart. A strong nose and prominent chin mixed with her determined attitude about law enforcement, causing some to conclude that she was too formal, perhaps somewhat too severe. As she walked up to Niell and Byler, she asked, "Where's Stan going?"

Niell handed the camera to her and said, "He's gonna check at the B and B where Mervin, here, thinks this girl worked," and then he introduced Lance to Byler.

Lance offered her hand, but Byler hesitated to take it. She held it out farther, smiling, and eventually Byler took it bashfully. Then Lance leaned in to study Niell's notepad and said, "You've been sketching?"

Niell nodded. "I've got the clearing sketched, but we'll need measurements of everything, once we go in closer. I've also got these tracks sketched."

Lance took the notebook, compared Niell's sketch with the tracks on the ground, and handed the notebook back to Niell.

Niell said, "OK. We've got the track of one buggy wheel, going in first. Then these tire tracks overlie that, and must have covered over the track of her second buggy wheel. Then another buggy circled around over all of the other tracks."

Byler offered, "That'll be where I swung my rig around, to go back to the telephone."

"The tire tracks go in, curving right," Lance said, "and back out, curving left. Someone drove in behind her, and then came out to head back north, the way they came."

"You recognize the tires?" Niell asked Lance.

"I saw a lot of those in the air force. It's a Humvee."

"That's what I thought," Niell said.

"Excuse me," Byler said, "but what's a Humvee?"

"It's a military vehicle, Mr. Byler," Niell said. "But probably a civilian version."

"Like a Jeep?" Byler asked.

"Bigger," Lance said.

Nervously, Byler asked, "What was an Amish girl doing with a soldier?"

"It might not have been a soldier," Niell said. "They make Humvees for civilians, now, too."

"But why would anybody want one?" Byler asked.

"They're big," Niell said. "And powerful. It's a status thing."

Byler shook his head. "I can't stay if there are going to be soldiers."

"I'm sure it wasn't a soldier," Lance said, intending reassurance.

But Byler ignored her, shifting nervously from foot to foot, disturbed very deeply by this new revelation. He studied the tragic scene in front of him and tried to reconcile himself to soldiers. He thought it so very sad that he had already reconciled himself too easily to violent death.

The dead girl still lay where he had left her, faceup with the mud swiped across her brow from when he had tried to clear her eyes. He had tried to get a look at her face. To see if she was still alive.

From the edge of the clearing, he could see the hole that he had felt in her forehead. Her dead eyes stared an accusation back at him, as if his disturbing her had been a sin. At his feet, the big, knobby tire tracks curved back out onto the gravel lane. He hadn't noticed them before. A soldier? Military? War. It all washed through him as a nervous flush of sorrow, and he realized he had stayed too long.

Looking up, he saw his grandsons in the distance beyond the barren trees, leading the horse and buggy over the saddle between two hills. He pointed them out to Niell and said, "I can't stay here anymore."

Niell asked, "Where will you be, Mr. Byler?"

"Third farm around there," Byler said, pointing back down the lane. "After you hit 166." He paused and then said—thinking of it as a confession—"We've got a white shed out by the road, with a telephone in it."

"You'll be at the house?" Niell asked.

"In the little Daadihaus at the back."

Sorry for the man's distress, Niell asked, "What are you going to do, Mervin? I will need to talk with you again."

"I'm going to sit with some chocolates," Byler said as he climbed up to his buggy seat. "Sweets will have to do, Deputy. Because"—he hesitated sadly—"today I'm just fresh out of chips."

3

Monday, April 4
9:25 A.M.

FROM THE perimeter of the clearing, Niell and Lance finished taking photographs of the scene and then approached the body of the girl by circling left through the brush where Byler said he had walked. Beyond the brambles, a maple sapling stood at the edge of the clearing, and Lance took several photographs of knife marks on the trunk of the tree, where Byler had cut the reins to free the horse. Then they stepped forward, carrying Ricky's evidence kit in a large tackle box, and studied the body more closely.

The ground around the girl was trampled extensively with hoof prints, and it was clear to them as they approached that the body had been trampled, too. She lay mostly on her back, but her right arm, obviously broken above the elbow, was twisted unnaturally behind her shoulders. Her left leg had been snapped midshin, and it lay hideously out of alignment, somewhat bent up under the opposite knee. Lance circled around the body shooting photos at every angle, not watching the placement of her feet too carefully, because it was apparent that if footprints or evidence had been left in the dirt and weeds beside the body, it had all been obliterated by the pounding of the horse's hooves.

Wearing blue nitrile gloves, Niell used a plastic spatula to take scrapings from the area around the girl's forehead wound, and he bottled them up in a small evidence jar. Then he ran a swab directly across her wound and bagged that evidence, too, saying, "Byler said he wiped mud from her face, so it may be hard to tell if there was gunpowder residue on her forehead."

Lance swung her camera strap over her shoulder and knelt beside Niell at the side of the body. She lifted the girl's left hand using forceps to clutch the sleeve of her jacket. It was a man's black denim jacket, and Lance pointed that out. Then she said, "Ricky, she's missing a finger on her left hand."

Ricky used an evidence swipe to clear mud from the stump of her ring finger, and the swipe came away bloody. "So, where's the finger?" he asked, as he helped Lance lay the hand and arm back into position on the ground. The swipe went into another evidence bottle.

Lance asked a question of her own. "How did she lose it? The finger, I mean. It could have been cut off by the sharp edge of a horseshoe."

She snapped her hands into a pair of nitrile gloves, moved over to the girl's head, and felt the back of the skull with her fingertips. "Exit wound, Ricky," she said. "A big one. A gunshot wound."

Niell stood up. "OK, she was shot. But how did she end up under the hooves of the horse?"

Lance stood, too, and followed Niell back through the brambles and brush. "Maybe she was standing close to the horse when she was shot," she said to Ricky's back.

When they reached the lane, they bagged their nitrile gloves, and Ricky said, "There's no way to tell where anyone was standing."

"And no way to tell how many people were here," Lance added.

Down the gravel lane came the slow rattle of an empty buggy. It was hitched to a horse in high lather, one Amish lad leading the horse by the reins, while the shorter of the two walked beside him. The horse was still somewhat agitated, blowing froth from its nostrils and lips, and lifting its feet in an awkward, irregular gait.

The boys stopped the horse behind Ricky's cruiser, and Niell and Lance walked up to them.

The older of the boys said, "She's hurt. Hind legs are bloody where she's been kicking at the shafts."

Niell stepped to the flank of the horse and saw that one of the hickory shafts had been cracked and splintered near the rear. The left edge of the whiffletree was nicked and scratched. Several of the straps comprising the harness had been loosened by the exertions of the horse, and the breeching was stretched out of place at the rump of the horse.

Lance asked, "Will she be OK?" and the younger of the boys said, "We think so."

The older boy spoke with more assurance. "She needs leg wraps with a poultice, and new shoes. She'll be fine."

Niell and Lance stood at the front of the buggy and studied an ugly splatter of red blood that had coalesced and bled down the front of the buggy's dash. The splatter ran across the back of the buggy's seat. Despite his training and experience, Niell was appalled by the crimson spray. He said as much to Lance, and she answered grimly, "This is where she was shot."

Wondering about the Amish boys who had obviously seen the blood, Lance turned around to check on them. Apparently uninterested, they were helping each other bend and lift the left front leg of the horse to inspect the hoof. They paid scant attention to Niell and Lance.

Leaning in beside the buggy's dash, Niell found a hole punched into the leather seat back, roughly in the center of the blood splatter, and he asked Lance for a pair of long forceps. She went back to her cruiser, took out her kit, opened it on the hood, and brought Niell a long pair with blunted tips. Distracted by the boys, she handed the forceps to Niell and nodded toward the youngsters. With their penknives, they were cleaning mud from the horseshoe. Lance gave Niell a bewildered shake of her head, and Niell shrugged fatalistically. Obviously the lads weren't disturbed by what they had seen, and Niell said softly to Lance, "I think they'll be OK."

Turning back to the buggy, Niell had Lance take several photographs of the dash and of the damaged buggy seat, then he eased the tips of the forceps into the round hole in the leather. He felt something solid, opened the forceps wider to acquire the object, closed gently, and pulled back on a straight line with the path into the hole. It was a bullet, spread by impact to a wide and ugly star shape in front. It had been black coated originally, but now it was abraded along its flank by the lands and grooves of a gun barrel to reveal striations of shiny copper where its heavy base hadn't expanded. The star blades fanning out and back at the front of the bullet were blood- and flesh-encrusted, but the sharp tips were bright metal, though jagged, as if they had been cleansed by passage through the leather of the buggy seat.

Niell looked at Lance and groaned, "It's a Black Talon, Pat. A forty-five-caliber Black Talon."

"I thought those were illegal. Pulled off the market a long time ago."

"Yeah," Niell said. "Since the Clinton administration. Looks like someone kept one."

Lance said, "It's a really big wound that I felt at the back of her skull. And it would have to have been a hollow-point that made it."

Niell dropped the slug into an evidence jar and screwed on the lid. He studied the hole in the seat back and took a position wedged between the dash and the rump of the horse. "If she was shot in the head, and the bullet ended up here, she must have been standing in front of her buggy like this, right here, tight against the rump of this horse."

"OK, but forty-five autos throw brass," Lance said. "Where's the brass?"

Ricky shrugged. "Over there in the mud somewhere?"

"And where's her finger?" Lance asked.

The boys spoke up, then. One of them had a folding knife open in one hand, and with the other he held up a silvered brass bullet casing between his fingers. The second boy displayed a handkerchief with mud on it, saying, "We cleaned it up for you," with a satisfied smile.

The lad with the brass casing said, "We found this wedged under the horseshoe. It's probably why she wasn't walking so good."

Lance took the casing, said, "Thank you, boys," and showed the shiny brass to Niell, saying, "Won't be any fingerprints left. But it's a forty-five, Ricky."

She carried it over to her evidence kit at the front of her cruiser and dropped it into a jar. Niell followed with the forceps and the bullet.

As he reached Lance's cruiser, Ricky's phone sounded the captain's tone, and he answered the call, handing his evidence jar and forceps to Lance.

Captain Newell asked over the phone, "Making any progress, Detective Niell?"

Ricky mouthed "More photos," to Lance, and said to the captain, "We've finished with the preliminaries. She's ready for Missy."

"Our ME's not there yet?" Newell asked.

"Not yet," Ricky said, walking back to the front of his cruiser with Lance.

Newell humphed into the phone. "I got a call from Stan. I told him I'd call you."

"He was supposed to call me," Ricky said.

"I think he would have, Detective," Newell said. "But he was standing out on the front porch of that B and B, getting ready to call you, when he heard an explosion from down the road."

"What kind of explosion?"

"A big one. Smoke and dirt thrown into the air behind a house. It was down at the Zooks'."

"What'd he learn about their daughter?" Ricky asked, nervous about the explosion.

"She just got back from Florida. Came home on the bus over the weekend."

"Has she showed up for work?"

"No."

"Does anyone over there know where she is?"

"No, Detective. But Stan's waiting for you at the Zooks'. And they're asking if we know where she is."

"Are you going to meet us out there?" Niell asked.

"Oh, no," the captain said. "This is a job for the sheriff."

Niell felt a tug on his sleeve, and when he looked down, one of the Amish boys was pulling a small red leather wallet out of the side pocket of his denim trousers, saying, "We found this under the seat."

Niell thanked the lad and said to Newell, "Wait a minute." He handed the phone to Lance. From the wallet, he pulled a folded check stub from the Maple Valley B and B, with Ruth Zook's name on it. It was dated nearly two months earlier.

Niell took the phone back from Lance and said to Newell, "We've got a wallet here, Captain. There's a check stub in it, from the B and B, written to a Ruth Zook, address on 557."

"OK, Niell, meet the sheriff at the Zooks'. You can call Stan, too. And bring your camera. We'll have them look at her picture."

"OK, but if she's their daughter, they won't like seeing her this way."

"Is there a way to get a picture that isn't so hard to look at?"

"Not without disturbing evidence."

"Then we can't do anything about it."

"OK," Niell said again. "But what was that explosion?"

Newell laughed. "Old Man Zook, the grandfather, used *about a ton* of dynamite, from what Stan tells me, to breach the dam on his farm pond. Stan says that there's mud, water, and dead fish spread for about a quarter mile downstream from there, and it wasn't the explosion that killed the fish."

"What do you mean?"

"All the fish in the Zook pond were killed sometime last night, Ricky, before the explosion this morning."

* * *

Before he left, Ricky gathered the boys on the far side of his black-and-white cruiser. Except for their difference in height, they could have been twins. Certainly they were dressed like twins. Shiny blue denim pants, with large slit pockets in the sides. Brown work boots, somewhat new. Long-sleeved blue shirts under black wool vests that were fastened in front by hook-and-eye closures. On each of their heads sat a new straw hat, butter yellow in color, with a thin black hatband. The crowns were shaped like fedoras, but the brims were built wide to ward off the sun, more practical than fashionable.

Ricky leaned over to them and said, "You've been a big help. Thanks."

Each lad gave a mature and sober nod of his head.

Ricky wanted to smile, but he knew it would be misinterpreted. Instead, he said, "You've seen a lot here. You're very brave."

The older of the two said, "We've seen blood before."

The younger added, "And we've seen dead bodies."

Niell acknowledged that. "You've handled yourselves well."

The lads straightened a bit, seeming to Niell to be curiously martial in their postures. "Maybe you should head for home," he said. "Someone needs to check on your grandfather."

"He's seen dead bodies, too," the older said.

"I'm sure he has," Ricky said. "But I think he's going to be sad. Maybe you could check on him."

The younger lad looked up to the older, and the older said, "We can do that."

Ricky said, "Why don't you tell me your names, so I can ask for you when I visit your grandfather."

"John."

"Mahlon."

"John and Mahlon, OK. Now, before you go, can you tell me if you've seen this girl before?"

The boys' eyes turned in the direction of the glade, but Ricky had positioned them on the far side of his cruiser. The body wasn't visible to them.

The little fellow, Mahlon, looked back at Niell, considered the question with eyes that seemed to be searching his memory, and said, "I don't think so."

John said, "We talked about that when we were bringing the horse back. We don't think we know her."

"Maybe you don't know who she is, but you remember seeing her once or twice," Ricky led.

The lads shook their heads in unison.

"OK," Ricky said, standing up straight. "Please check on your grandfather. If I get a chance today, I'll come by your house and check with you, to see how he is doing."

The lads nodded sternly, turned, and walked down the lane. As they passed the glade, their eyes turned compulsively toward the body of the girl.

4

Monday, April 4
11:05 A.M.

WHEN RICKY Niell got to the Zook residence on 557, there were seven buggies parked on the gravel drive. They were clustered beside a sprawling, yellow-sided, two-and-a-half-story farmhouse, with a gabled roofline and a wraparound front porch. Nearly two dozen Amish folk—men, women, and children—had gathered on the porch of the home, and they watched Niell intently as he got out with his camera and walked up to Armbruster and Robertson on the driveway. On the lawn off to the side stood an Amish man in black denim, about fifty years old, with a white-haired grandfather in uniformly similar dress standing next to him. Each man wore a wide-brimmed, round-crowned black felt hat, and as Niell approached, he read apprehension in their expressions. Word had passed, it seemed. The family had gathered itself to hear bad news.

Ricky pulled Robertson aside and whispered, "Are you sure about this, Sheriff? None of these photos is easy to look at."

Sheriff Bruce Robertson was dressed in a gray business suit, white shirt, and blue tie. He had managed to lose a few pounds over the winter, thanks to a diet and exercise program that Melissa Taggert, his wife, had devised for him, but the sheriff was still as broad through the shoulders as he ever was, and still somewhat round at the belly. He turned to study the two Amish men on the front lawn, then turned back to Niell, saying, "They already suspect it's her, Ricky. They've been getting news about this for nearly half an hour, and when I pulled in, they asked about the dead girl over on TR 165. They've got a description of her from someone, and they're expecting the worst."

Niell looked up to the porch and saw that many of the people there had faces lined with tears. The children shifted nervously beside their parents, aware that something was dreadfully wrong, if not completely certain yet what it was. As if to honor hope while it was still possible, few words were spoken among the people. What needed to be said was most plainly visible in the grim countenance of a middle-aged woman standing in plain Amish blues and blacks at the front edge of the porch, watching Ricky advance with his camera, as if to accuse him personally for a loss she couldn't possibly bear.

Niell turned back to Robertson, and the sheriff said, "I called Cal Troyer to come out."

Feeling an awkward hesitation about what Robertson wanted him to do, Ricky asked, "Then, don't you think we should wait for Cal? Before I show them any pictures?"

Robertson shook his head. "We need to do this, Ricky. The father and the grandfather are the only ones who need to look."

Ricky nodded solemnly. He switched on his camera, selected a photograph that plainly showed the girl's face, and walked over to the two Amish men. When he showed the LCD display on the back of his camera to the men, the father cried out and jerked his head away reflexively as a shudder of anguish washed through him. The grandfather calmly took the camera, studied the face of his granddaughter, and nodded wordlessly. Then he turned to walk up the porch steps, to give the news to the family. The father stayed with the lawmen, head hanging down, tears coursing his cheeks and wetting his chin whiskers.

Zook lifted his hat slowly off his head and brushed the tears away. Robertson and Armbruster flanked the man, intending to steady him if he buckled at the knees or lost his balance.

Drawn by the sorrow he saw on Amish faces, Niell stepped compassionately toward the porch and helplessly watched the people file back into the house. They ushered their children along in front of them, trying in whispers to explain to the youngest what had happened.

After all the others had gone inside, one young girl, maybe ten years old, stood on the porch in her plain lilac dress and white head covering, studying Niell as he looked up to the porch. His eyes turned to hers, and he saw that she was struggling not to cry. Bravely, or maybe angrily, he thought, she stood rock still, with her fingers curled up into little fists, seeming to deny herself the release of tears that would force her to confront her sorrow.

Niell took a few steps toward her, not really knowing what he might say, but she cast him an angry scowl, as if accusing him for her loss. He took another step toward her. She glared both determination and isolation down at him, and then she turned and walked back into the house without speaking.

* * *

By the time Cal Troyer arrived at the Zook residence, Stan Armbruster had returned to the murder scene on TR 165. He was to assist Melissa Taggert, who had phoned Robertson to say that she had gotten her ME's crew out to the location. Pat Lance was still there, too, retaining the horse and buggy for Taggert's inspection.

Cal pulled in behind Niell's cruiser. In front of it sat Robertson's blue Crown Victoria. Beyond that, on the long drive back to the biggest of three barns, black buggies were parked in a neat row. There the horses had been tethered to a picket line strung from a maple tree out front, back to the nearest corner of the barn. Cal counted nearly a dozen buggies as he walked forward.

Niell and Robertson stood with a slender, white-bearded Amish fellow about sixty-five years old. As Cal walked up, the man was saying to Robertson, "The fish were all dead when I got up this morning."

Cal listened and started to ask a question, but Ricky pulled him aside and said, "They took it badly, Cal. But one little girl seems worse than the others. Ten years old. Lilac dress and white cap."

Grandfather Zook turned to Niell and Troyer, and said, "That's little Emma Wengerd. Ruth was the only one of us that she was close to."

"Why's that?" Cal asked. He held out his hand and said, "I'm Pastor Cal Troyer, Alvin. We met at a barn raising a couple of years ago."

Alvin Zook nodded a confirmation. "Swinging hammers on the peak."

"She's a Wengerd?" Cal asked.

"Yes, but she's adopted," Zook said. "Her family—all six of them—was killed when a truck ran over their buggy, over near Farmerstown."

"I remember the crash," Troyer said.

Zook lifted his hat and ran a wrinkled handkerchief across his brow. "Emma hasn't been able to adjust to her new family. Except that she took to Ruth. She followed her around everywhere. They used to talk about all sorts of things. You know, life. Like real sisters. So Emma is probably going to take this as hard as any of us."

5

Monday, April 4
11:50 A.M.

WITH CAL and all the Zooks headed inside, Robertson asked for the memory card from Ricky's camera. Niell pulled it out of its slot in the camera and opened the rear door of his cruiser to take an evidence bag from his kit. He dropped the memory card into the plastic bag and attached a voucher slip to it. Then he signed and dated the voucher slip and handed it to Robertson. While the sheriff signed the slip, Ricky loaded another memory card into the camera's slot.

Robertson said, "I'll get these photos up on our computers while you go back to help Lance and Missy. Call me if Missy finds anything I should know about."

Ricky stowed his camera in its case on the backseat and turned back to Robertson. "Are you going to call in Rachel Ramsayer, to help with the photos?"

"She's already there," Robertson said. "I asked her to help with dispatching, when your wife went home."

"Why'd Ellie go home?" Ricky asked.

"Upset stomach. She said she'd be fine in a little while."

Ricky nodded and held his peace.

Curious to know why Niell hadn't asked more about Ellie, Robertson asked, "Is there something I should know, Detective?"

"It's probably just the stomach flu," Ricky said. "I'll lead you over to the murder scene. If we go through Farmerstown, it's not too far."

"No," Robertson said. "You handle things over there, with Missy and Lance. But send Armbruster back to Millersburg. In the meantime, I want to have Bobby Newell look at these pictures with me. Are they all on this one card?"

"Everything I have so far," Ricky said. "I'll get more."

"Anything unusual that I should know about, before we go through these photos?"

"Well," Ricky said, "she's a mess. Trampled by her buggy horse. I think she was shot. With a Black Talon. And there are Humvee tracks that overlie her buggy wheel tracks. She's got an entrance wound on her forehead, and she's got an exit wound at the back of her head. We found the bullet embedded in the backseat of her buggy. And she's missing the ring finger on her left hand."

Robertson frowned. "It's too far out of the way for her to have stumbled onto something. You know, she wasn't just *in the wrong place at the wrong time*."

"I think she must have gone there to meet someone," Ricky said. "So the question is, who would want to meet her there?"

"Meet her there," Robertson nodded, "with a Humvee and a Black Talon."

* * *

While Ricky and the sheriff were talking on the Zooks' driveway, Cal Troyer climbed the steps to the front porch and knocked on the door. Alvin Zook answered the knock, held the screened door open for Cal, and let the pastor into the front hallway.

To Cal's right, the parlor was filled with Amish folk, sitting wordlessly on several church benches. Two older ladies flanked Mrs. Irma Zook, who was Alvin's daughter-in-law and the mother of Ruth. When Cal entered, the men looked up with unanswerable sorrow, then turned their heads down to resume their meditations. Of the women there, none looked up as Cal came through.

At the back of the hallway, the large kitchen was filled with a half-dozen Amish women cooking food in the oven and on the stovetop. All of the available counter space was being used for other preparations. From the back porch, two more Amish ladies carried cloth bags filled with groceries into the kitchen, then turned around and went back down the steps to get more bags out of a buggy parked at the back of the house. Alvin led Cal down the back steps and pulled him aside, so that the women could pass up the steps again with more groceries.

Whispering, Alvin said, "We know death, Cal. We know it well. But murder? Who knows anything about that?"

Mindful of all the people inside, Cal whispered, too. "Alvin, why would Ruth head over that way? Did she know anyone there? Because it's not on the way to anywhere."

"I don't think so. Not in particular. But you know how it is. Amish people know everyone. In one way or another. We know all the Amish families, and they all know us."

"Do you need any help?" Cal asked.

"We know what to do for the family," Alvin answered. After a moment's hesitation, he said, "Maybe you could try to talk with Emma."

"Of course," Cal said, turning back toward the steps.

Alvin turned him around with a light touch on his elbow. "She's not in there, Cal."

"Where, then?"

"She'll be in the barn. She's got a secret place where she goes to be alone. I'm sure she's there now, and I'm sure she's alone. Someone needs to talk with her."

"Shouldn't someone in the family come with me?" Cal asked.

"Normally, yes," Alvin said. "But Emma doesn't talk to us very much. I really don't think she likes us. I'm sure she doesn't like living with us."

"How long has it been since her family was killed?"

"Almost two years."

"Is she still sad?"

"Not really," Alvin said. "It's more like she's angry. She acts like she never got past the anger."

"Doesn't she talk with anyone, Alvin?"

"With me, I guess. A little bit. Sometimes. Mostly she talked with Ruth."

"She doesn't speak otherwise?"

"Oh, she talks about regular things. Everyday conversations. Doing chores. School and such. But she doesn't really let anybody get close to her thoughts. She's private, and sometimes I fear what she's thinking."

"Like what, Alvin?"

Zook hesitated, cleared his throat, and said, "I'm afraid she's going to hurt herself."

"Then what makes you think she'll talk to me?"

Zook shook his head sadly, and puddles of tears appeared in his eyes. He pulled a handkerchief out of his pants pocket, wiped his eyes, and blew his nose. "She has a secret name I use. When no one else is around. I call her my stratus flower. It makes her smile."

"Stratus flower? Like in the atmosphere?"

"Right. She's a flower. And she holds herself far apart from the rest of us. She's withdrawn, like she's as far away as she can get, and still be here. You know, like she's up in the stratosphere. So I call her my stratus flower, and when I've said that, I think I've seen her smiling inside. I think those are the only times I've ever seen her smile."

6

Monday, April 4
12:25 P.M.

WHEN SHERIFF Robertson pushed through the front door of
the jail, Rachel Ramsayer—a dwarf lady, the daughter of Cal
Troyer—was standing to Robertson's right, on her stepped plat-
form behind the dispatcher's long wooden counter. To the sheriff's left, a black iron door served as the sole entrance to the
first-floor gang cell, for prisoners who were not a danger either
to themselves or to others.

The dispatcher's radio and recording equipment, a tall and
wide battery of lights, dials, wires, and switches, was stacked on
the tables behind Rachel. The dispatcher's computers, keyboards,
and monitors sat on the tabletop below the radios. Underneath
were the new servers that Rachel had installed for the department. Today, between calls, Rachel had been finishing her efforts
to modernize the department's data and evidence logs and to
install new desktops and routers, a task on which she had been
working since coming on board full-time for the sheriff last
spring.

Robertson turned right inside the front door and pushed
through the wooden swinging door at the left end of the counter.
He handed Rachel the plastic evidence bag, with the SDHC

memory card from Ricky Niell's camera, said, "Thanks for coming in," and lumbered out of his suit jacket.

Rachel signed and dated the voucher slip on the bag. "It's been quiet, Sheriff. Except for Mervin Byler's 911."

Robertson laid his suit jacket over an arm. "Niell, Lance, Armbruster, and Taggert are all still out at the murder scene. There's preliminary photos of it on that card."

"The usual with the photos, Sheriff?"

"Yes, then please voucher the card over to Captain Newell. We'll both look at the photos, once you have them uploaded and backed up."

* * *

When Robertson had left for Millersburg, Ricky Niell headed back to the kill spot by circling up through the heights at Farmerstown and dropping down again on a sharp angle onto TR 164. Then as he descended lower into the cuts east of town, he swung hard right into the draw where TR 165 led south. Soon he had reached Melissa Taggert's medical examiner's panel truck, parked beside the clearing, nose to nose with Pat Lance's cruiser. Farther down the lane, Pat Lance attended Ruth Zook's horse and buggy while talking on her department cell phone.

Missy had a team of two medical assistants working to lay the body of the Zook girl on a body bag that had been spread open on the ground beside her. Two Holmes County deputies stood back several paces, holding a collection of rakes, hoes, and shovels. There weren't any other vehicles parked on the lane, so Niell concluded that all four attendants had come out with Taggert in her van.

As the two assistants worked with Ruth Zook's body, Taggert met Niell at the edge of the clearing and asked directly, "Ricky, did you get a chance to search for her finger?"

"Not really, but we found a bullet and the casing."

They heard the finalizing rasp of a heavy zipper closing the body bag, and Niell and Taggert turned to look.

With equal parts anger and frustration, Missy complained,

"She's very small, Ricky. Tiny. That horse must have broken every bone in her body."

Surprised by Taggert's emotion, Niell said, "That doesn't sound like you, Missy."

"She's so young, Ricky. And small. It just tears me up to see young women like this. I need a vacation."

"The Zooks told me she was only nineteen," Niell said. "She had gone down to Pinecraft for February and March. Her first Florida vacation. Worked in a little restaurant there."

Taggert's assistants rolled a gurney into the clearing and loaded the body bag onto it. Then they rolled it to the back of Taggert's truck, lifted it forward so that the legs folded against the bumper, and slid it on its rails into the back of the truck. When they had closed the doors, they stepped over to Niell and Taggert, and one of them asked, "Find the finger?"

Missy nodded. "Start right where the body was lying, and work outward from there. It has to be here. Somewhere. Because the wound on her hand is fresh." Then Missy sighed out frustration and added, "What I mean is, she hadn't lost her finger earlier, so it still has to be here."

Thinking Taggert might say more, the assistants held to their place beside her on the lane. With uncharacteristic harshness, she waved them back to work. Eyeing Niell, they stepped away, took a hoe and a rake from the deputies, and began to work their way into the pulverized dirt and trampled weeds, where the horse had danced out its fright.

Once they had started their search, Missy drew a cleansing breath, motioned Niell along, and said, "Let's go talk with Pat."

Pat Lance finished her call as they approached. She flipped her cell phone closed and said, "That was Stan. Before he left the Zooks', he stopped to 'take a few samples.' He's on his way here, and he says he has something interesting."

"Like what, exactly?" Missy asked, sounding curt, almost disdainful.

Niell arched an eyebrow, and Lance said, "He didn't say."

Surprised again by Taggert's display of emotion, Niell asked, "Are we finished with this buggy, Missy?"

"For now," Missy said, and rolled her shoulders to dump frustration. "We've been all through the thing, looking for her finger. Under the seat, in the back, floorboards and crevices, and it isn't there."

"Can we have someone take it back to the Zooks'?" Niell asked.

Taggert looked to Lance and back to Niell. She laughed unconvincingly, rubbed at her temples, and said, "Detective, I don't think any of us knows how to drive a horse and buggy."

"I think I know someone who will help," Niell said.

"Mervin Byler?" Lance asked.

Before Niell had answered, Stan Armbruster pulled in behind the buggy and got out holding a small Ziploc bag with a blue liquid inside. As he walked up beside the horse and buggy, he held out the bag and said, "On a hunch, I took some water samples. This last one came from almost a quarter mile downstream from the Zooks' pond, but they all tested the same."

Taggert took the little test bag from Armbruster and gave it a shake. She recognized the classic color, a deep turquoise blue, and said, "That looks like a positive test for cocaine."

"It *is* cocaine," Armbruster said. "It's a very concentrated sample. It must have come from a batch that was close to pharmaceutical grade, and everything downstream from that pond is either dead or dying."

* * *

Back at the Byler farm, Ricky pulled in on the driveway, circled around to the back, and found Mervin Byler sitting out on the front porch of his Daadihaus. He was in a hickory rocker, but he wasn't rocking. His hat lay on the porch boards beside him, and in his lap he had an open box of Coblentz chocolates. Ricky climbed the porch steps, sat in a matching rocker beside the motionless Byler, and said, "You weren't kidding about the sweets."

Byler stirred wordlessly and took another piece out of his box. He put it in his mouth and offered the box to Ricky. Niell said, "Thanks," took one, and bit into a cherry center. "Good," he said, and eased back in his rocker.

36   P. L. GAUS

Byler held the box in his lap for a moment, then set the box on the floorboards between him and Niell. He rocked forward and back once, rubbed at his white chin whiskers, got up, paced a bit, and sat back down. "I'm eighty years old, Deputy," he said. "And she was dead before she even got started."

"I know," Ricky said. "Doesn't seem fair."

"It isn't fair," Byler said.

"Her folks say she was only nineteen."

Mervin picked up the box of chocolates, thought for a moment, and set it back on the floorboards. "You met little John and Mahlon?" he asked.

"Yes."

"So how many years will they get, Deputy?"

Ricky shook his head, ate the rest of his chocolate, and said, "They were brave."

Byler nodded. He pulled a handkerchief from his side pants pocket to dry his eyes. "Is there something I can do for you, Deputy? Something to make myself useful for a change?"

Ricky stood up. "Would you drive Ruth's buggy back to the Zooks'?"

"I can do that," Byler said, keeping his seat, eyes cast down.

"I'll follow you over to Zooks' and give you a ride back."

Mervin nodded glumly, but remained seated.

Ricky leaned back against the porch railing and said, "This isn't your fault, Mervin. Really, you didn't even know her."

Mervin growled restlessly, pushed his hat onto his head, stood up, and said, "Come on, Deputy, you'll have to take me back there."

"First," Ricky said, "tell me again how you found her."

Mervin dropped back into his rocker, tossed his felt hat to the floorboards, took up the box of chocolates, and said, "Do you know the widow Stutzman?"

7

BEHIND THE largest of three tobacco-red barns, Captain Newell stood with Grandfather Alvin Zook, on the high bank of the Zooks' mostly empty pond. The muddy bottom of the pond was strewn with dead aquatic animals—fish, turtles, snakes, and a few mud puppies. "Tell me again when you blew the dam," Newell said. "Before the sheriff got here?"

Zook answered, "Well, actually, it was before your deputy arrived. Maybe fifteen minutes before that."

"What time was it?"

"Around ten. Maybe ten thirty. But I don't keep a watch."

"And when did you discover that the fish were dead?"

"First thing this morning. Daylight."

"When did you decide to breach the dam?"

"Oh, right away, Captain. We had to let the bad water out. And it took us a couple of hours to drill the holes for the dynamite."

"How'd you know the water was bad?"

"Dead fish."

"Where did you get the dynamite?"

"My father had some left over from when they dug out the pond."

"Is there any of it left?" Newell asked.

"No, that was the last of it."

"Good," Newell said, and circled around the high edge of the pond to the deep V-shaped cavity in the wall of the dam. There at the deepest part of the pond, a wide oval of muddy water remained in the bottom, below the level of the breach. Zook followed and said, "I wish I had used more dynamite."

"You used plenty," Newell said. "Really, Mr. Zook, I wish you hadn't used any at all."

Zook shrugged his shoulders and smiled. "I had to release the bad water."

Below the dam, from the timbered valley where the creek flowed away, they heard the distant bark of a gunshot. Soon Stan Armbruster came into view in the muddy bottoms. He was carrying a large evidence bag. A deputy slogged along behind him, carrying the carcass of a dead raccoon by its tail. They climbed the steep bank to the top of the dam, and Armbruster displayed the evidence bag. Inside it, he had two wads of brown plastic wrapping, with edges that had once been sealed with packing tape. He thumbed the contents around inside, showed a ragged cut in the plastic wrapping, and said, "Here's where someone cut the packs open, Captain, to pour it all out. We'll be able to get some fingerprints."

Newell turned to Zook. "When did Ruth come home from Florida?"

"Friday evening," Zook said. "It's a twenty-four-hour trip, so the bus left Pinecraft on Thursday."

"The Pioneer Trails bus?"

"No, the other one. It's new. The Sugarcreek-Sarasota Bus Company."

"OK," Newell asked, "what did Ruth do the rest of Friday and Saturday?"

"Mostly she slept, I think. She said she had a cold and was tired from the trip."

"And Sunday?"

"Same thing. It wasn't a church Sunday."

"Did she really have a cold, or was it something else?"

"Like what, Captain?"

"Maybe she was crying and didn't want anyone to know."

Zook hesitated. "Could be. She didn't eat anything. Why?"

"Because I think she got mixed up in something," Newell answered.

Armbruster nodded his agreement. "Mr. Zook," he said, "there's a little plastic rowboat downstream from here, like it was flushed out of the pond when you blew the dam."

Zook nodded. "That's ours. It was floating in the middle of the pond this morning, capsized."

Newell turned to Armbruster. "How far downstream did you search?"

"Quarter of a mile, Captain." He hesitated, looking back into the bottoms. "Maybe a little more."

"I think we're going to need more men out here," Newell said.

"Why is that?" Zook asked.

Newell asked, "Mr. Zook, did Ruth bring home suitcases?"

"Yes, two."

"Is that how many she took down to Florida?"

"I'm not sure. Why?"

"Did they seem heavy to you?"

"I think one was, but she wouldn't let me carry it. Why?"

Armbruster said, "We'll find more than these two wrappings, Captain."

"So, let's find them all, Stan. I want to know how much there was."

Armbruster walked down the slope toward the barns to make a call, and the deputy with the dead raccoon followed.

Newell called after them, "Why'd you have to kill the raccoon, Stan?"

"It was already dying," Armbruster called up the slope. "Lying beside the stream, heaving from the gut."

"What's going on, Captain?" Zook asked. "Is this why Ruth was killed?"

Newell nodded, frowned, and studied Zook's eyes. Gently he said, "I'm just guessing, Mr. Zook, but I think Ruth brought something back from Florida that she regretted. Something that got her killed."

"But why?" Zook asked. "What was in those bags?"

"Cocaine, Mr. Zook. A lot of cocaine. And if Ruth changed her mind and poured it all out in your pond last night, then someone here in Ohio would have been very angry about it."

"So they just killed her?" Zook asked, incredulous.

"Mr. Zook, if it really was as much cocaine as I think, I'm surprised they didn't do worse."

* * *

Out front on the Zooks' driveway, Cal Troyer scowled renewed heat at Sheriff Robertson and barked again, "It's preposterous!"

"It fits the evidence, Cal," Robertson said with forced calm. "I'm getting tired of explaining that to you."

"Amish girls don't mule drugs!" Cal shot. "It's just preposterous."

Robertson broke off and turned out a frustrated circle ten paces away.

Cal advanced and growled, "You can't be serious."

"Those are Humvee tracks over there, Cal. Amish don't drive Humvees. And the bullet was a Black Talon. That's a city round, not something we have out here in the country."

"I don't care," Cal said. "This is a good family. They could no more be involved in drugs than you could turn down a meal. It's just not in their natures."

Angered even more by the insult, Robertson pushed past Cal and stepped over to the nose of his blue Crown Vic. He leaned forward and planted his palms flat on the hood of his car, drew several slow breaths, pushed away, and turned back to Cal. "You're not listening, Cal. She probably did this on her own. The family didn't have to know anything about it."

Cal followed the sheriff. "There has to be another explanation."

"Cal, it was cocaine that killed everything in that pond. We tested it. And they're finding plastic wrappings downstream. So Ruth Zook went to that clearing this morning to tell someone she had dumped it all out. The whole shipment. That's what got her killed."

Behind them, two deputies carried women's clothing and two old leather suitcases out of the front door of the Zook house. As they came down the porch steps, Robertson nodded at them and said to Cal, "That's all gonna test positive for cocaine, Cal. And Missy's gonna test her hands. If you come up with another explanation, let me know. In the meantime, I'm gonna run an investigation that assumes she was transporting drugs up here from Florida."

As he spoke, Ricky Niell pulled in behind the sheriff's Crown Vic, and soon he was followed by Mervin Byler, driving Ruth Zook's horse and buggy. Frustrated by the sheriff, Cal turned angrily for the house and went up the front steps.

Ricky parked and got out, and Byler swung the rig around them and drove on down the driveway, stopping beside the house. Robertson waved Ricky forward and marched ahead toward the buggy, calling out, "Wait just a minute."

Ricky trotted up behind the sheriff and asked, "What's the problem?"

Robertson turned back to him and asked, "Did we test this rig for cocaine?"

"Stan and I already did that, while Missy was finishing up with the body."

Robertson waited for more, and Ricky added, "There's cocaine on the reins, and on the brake handle. Some on the harness, too, but not anywhere else."

Hearing that, Byler dropped the reins and groaned, "What's going on around here?"

Robertson stepped up beside the buggy and said to Byler, "Are you Mervin Byler?"

"Yes. This is crazy talk, cocaine. What's going on?"

"Mr. Byler," Robertson said, "I think you stumbled onto something much bigger than a murder."

Laboriously, Byler climbed down from the buggy seat. He shook his head sadly and asked again, "What's going on out here, Sheriff?" Then he walked slowly back to stand beside the passenger's door of Ricky's cruiser, gazing skyward, as if he needed more answers than any man could provide him.

To Robertson, Ricky said, "While I was talking with Mervin Byler, over at his house, Missy found the finger in the dirt at the clearing."

"Has she taken the body back to Millersburg?" Robertson asked, eyeing Byler. "And do you have everything you need from Byler?"

"Yes, to the first, and yes—I have everything I need from Byler. For now. I'll come back down tomorrow and talk with him again."

"What did Missy say about the finger?" Robertson asked. "Did someone torture her? You know, cut it off?"

"She says she can't tell yet."

Cal came back out of the house, eased slowly down the front steps, and walked up to Robertson and Niell on the drive. "I wanted to talk with Emma again," he said, sounding defeated.

"What have you been talking about?" Robertson asked with a conciliatory tone.

"We haven't been talking about anything, really," Cal said. "She's just been listening. At least I hope she has. And I'm sorry I called you fat."

Robertson shrugged it off, saying, "I know what I am, Cal."

"Sorry," Cal muttered.

"OK," Robertson returned. "What's going on inside the house?"

"They're praying for the man who killed Ruth."

"You're kidding," Robertson said.

"No. They've agreed to forgive him."

"Just like that?"

"No, Sheriff, not *just like that*. But yes, they're praying for him, and for Ruth."

Robertson said, "It sounds to me like somebody needs to be praying for Emma Wengerd."

8

Monday, April 4
4:00 P.M.

ON THE second floor of the Millersburg jail, Captain Newell
led Ricky Niell and Pat Lance into his corner office. He took a
seat at a black metal desk, with his back to a tall window with
white venetian blinds. During recent expansions in the sheriff's
department, new offices had been created on the second floor of
the jail for the captains and for Chief Deputy Wilsher. With seniority, Newell and Wilsher had been given corner offices. The
chief's windows faced the courthouse square, like the sheriff's on
the first floor. Newell's, when his blinds were open, gave a view
of the parking lot for the bank next door. Most of the time,
Newell's blinds were closed.

As Ricky pulled a second memory card out of his camera,
Captain Newell switched on his monitor. Sheriff Robertson came
into the small office, and Niell and Lance shuffled forward to
make room for him. Then the captain took the memory card
from Niell and put it into his desktop computer.

Once the captain had his photo program running, he reached
over to switch on the wall monitor, and when he opened the
proper folder on the memory card, the murder scene photos appeared as small thumbnails in a grid display. Newell focused his
attention on his desktop monitor. To watch the wall display,

Ricky and Pat stood together at the left front corner of the captain's desk, facing the wall to Newell's right. Robertson watched from a position just inside the doorway, leaning back against the frame.

As a preliminary screening, Newell worked through full-screen displays of the first dozen photos and then started again at the beginning. First was a wide-angle photo of the entire glade where the body had been found, and Newell asked, "Is this your establishing shot? The overall scene?"

"Yes," Ricky answered, "but we also have those wide-angle views from positions all around the clearing."

As Newell advanced through the photos, Ricky narrated for the captain and the sheriff. There was the clearing where the dirt had been trampled in the middle of the small glen. There were the brushes and dead grasses at the south edge of the clearing, and the hillock on the north boundary. The rocky cut lined by barren trees to the west. The gravel of narrow TR 165, lining the eastern edge.

Newell paused on a photo of the knoll and asked, "Is this just a big pile of dirt?"

Lance answered. "Captain, it looks as if someone had piled dirt there twenty years ago and forgot about it."

"Excavating for the well?" Newell asked.

"Probably," Lance answered. "I'll check, but it's not really part of the natural terrain."

Next, Newell paused on a photo of the trampled earth and asked, "This where she was lying?"

Again Lance answered. "Yes. And it's where Dr. Taggert found her finger, once they had moved her body."

On a photo of the bullet hole in the buggy seat, Newell paused and said, "Black Talon, right? Spread out wide?"

Ricky said, "Yes. We figure it was mostly spent when it exited the back of her skull."

Newell nodded and stared grimly at the ragged hole in the leather. Then he moved backward and forward to review other photos.

There were shots of the wrecked buggy parts and of the lathered and injured horse. There were shots of Ruth Zook lying bent and broken in the dirt. Photos of the tire and buggy tracks, showing either their overall pattern or close-up detail, followed by photos Niell had made as Lance poured a rubber mold into the depressions made by the Humvee treads.

Robertson stood silently and watched the display on the wall behind Newell. When the captain had finished his first pass through the photos, Robertson stood straight in the doorway and said, "Good work," nodding to both Niell and Lance. He turned to the captain and said, "Bobby, you let me know if there's anything on the first memory card that isn't duplicated here."

Then he motioned to Niell and Lance, pulled them out into the hallway, and said, "Ricky, I need a report from Missy. It'll be preliminary, and she won't want to give us much detail yet, but get what you can from her, and come back here."

Niell acknowledged his orders and left.

To Lance, Robertson said, "Pat, I want you to show up at the Zook farm about six or six thirty this evening. Ask a lot of questions, and try to get the grandfather—Alvin—to tell us more of what he knows."

Lance hesitated. "I don't know, Sheriff. Old Order Amishmen don't care at all for women detectives."

"Oh really?" Robertson smiled.

Lance studied the sheriff's expression and said, "Of course, you knew that."

Robertson nodded. "I'll be coming out myself, about an hour after you get there. So call when you first arrive. I want to question the father and the grandfather *after* you've gotten them nervous. Or maybe a little resentful."

"Why do you want them resentful?" Lance asked.

"I want them to be relieved to have a man asking the questions, Lance. I think I'll learn more, once they're happy to be finished with a woman in charge."

"You'd exploit a stereotype?"

"Of course. It is what it is, Lance. They've been like this for decades, maybe centuries."

"What do you think you'll learn?"

"I think someone out there knows more about this. I don't buy it that Ruth Zook came home after two months in Florida and didn't speak to anyone at all."

* * *

Once Lance had left, Robertson stepped back into Newell's office and eased himself onto a sturdy wooden chair. Newell was still clicking through crime-scene photos. Robertson watched for a while, studying Newell's expression.

The captain was solid in build. For most of his adult life, he had trained in his spare time as a bodybuilder. Then, in retirement, he had worked to take off the extra weight that he had carried in competition. He had two grown children living in Columbus, but after his wife died of breast cancer, he hadn't had much contact with them. Several years earlier he had taken retirement, ostensibly to devote himself to his sport, but after little more than a year, Newell had begun showing up in the sheriff's office, asking about jail business, patrols, old cases, and personnel. When Robertson had offered him the position in the fall as captain of detectives, Newell had taken the post gladly. Robertson had thought all along that Newell's retirement wouldn't last.

Now Captain Newell sat facing the sheriff in his new office, the defined muscles in his neck, shoulders, and arms straining the fabric of his white shirt. He wore his usual attire, a plain blue tie, loosened, with the collar of his shirt unbuttoned, and black slacks that matched a pair of black horn-rimmed glasses that greatly magnified his brown eyes for anyone standing in front of him. His brow was heavy, and his chin was squared under thin lips and a Roman nose. In build, temperament, and command style, he was the antithesis of the heavy and mercurial sheriff. In his devotion to law enforcement, though, Newell was the sheriff's equal.

"Bobby," Robertson said eventually, "you think we're right about this?"

Newell looked up from his monitor. "That she brought drugs up here from Florida?"

"Yes, but I mean that she didn't want to do it. Or at least she changed her mind."

"Sounds reasonable."

"So what would make her do it?" Robertson asked.

Newell shrugged his shoulders. "Or *who* would make her do it?"

Robertson stood. "Drugs have been finding their way into northern Ohio for decades, Bobby."

Newell switched his monitor off and stood behind his desk to face the sheriff. He pushed his heavy glasses higher up on his nose and said, "I heard you tell Lance that you were going back out to the Zooks' place, later this evening."

The sheriff smiled. "To talk to the men."

A grin spread across Newell's thin lips. "They're not going to be happy that you sent a woman out to question men."

"You wouldn't play it that way?"

"Probably not. They're in mourning. Deserve some peace."

Robertson shrugged an apology. "We need to know why an Amish girl brought suitcases of cocaine up to Ohio."

"What if nobody knows why?" Newell asked.

Robertson laughed, "I'll be gentle, I promise." He turned in the doorway to leave and said back over his shoulder, "Right now, we don't have much drug use in Holmes County, and a suitcase of cocaine just showed up on our doorstep."

Newell followed the sheriff out into the second-floor hallway and said, "Amish girls don't mule drugs for dealers, Bruce. When you go back out there, keep that in mind."

9

Monday, April 4
5:15 P.M.

AFTER AN early supper at a restaurant in Charm, Cal searched downstairs at the Zooks' for Emma, but he didn't find her with the other mourners. People were seated in the parlor and the first-floor sewing room, all silent as he passed through the house. In the long hallway from the front door to the kitchen at the back of the house, friends, neighbors and relatives sat on wooden deacon's benches, used bimonthly for Sunday services. These were the same benches that the men carted from house to house whenever they were needed for long visiting, mostly at weddings and funeral vigils.

Cal walked slowly down the hall, between men and older women as sober as a stern lecture and as still as death itself. Most eyes were closed, heads bowed in prayer, but some people sat staring at their hands in their laps. One old fellow gave a silent nod as Cal passed by, and then bowed his head again to pray. Cal knew they were praying both for Ruth and for the man who had killed her. He hoped they were praying also for little Emma.

At the kitchen door at the back of the house, Cal stepped aside to let two women in plain dress come up the steps from the drive below. One woman carried a basket of eggs, and the other held two loaves of bread in metal baking pans. The women eased past Cal as he held the door for them, and then, without speaking to him, they went into the kitchen to help other women working at the sink and stoves. An English neighbor lady standing at the sink, dressed in black slacks and a red knit sweater, looked up and gave Cal a sad smile before she returned to her work peeling potatoes.

Cal walked down the back steps and headed across the drive toward the barn where he had earlier that day found Emma Wengerd hiding. On his way, he passed two small groups of kids in Amish dress, standing outside to whisper. As he drew near to each group, the kids fell silent and watched him closely as he headed for the largest of the tobacco-red barns.

Inside, Cal's eyes adjusted slowly to the dim light. He stood a moment on the wide avenue down the middle of the barn, and his senses registered the classic sounds and aromas of the farm. There was soft lowing from a cow tied to a post inside the first stall on the right. A Standard Bred buggy horse lifted its head over the gate slats of the second stall. The musty aroma of wet hay and manure filled his nostrils. A flutter of wings sounded in the rafters high above him.

Cal worked his way down the right side of the avenue, looking in each of the stalls. At the far end of the barn, he searched in the right stall, where he had found Emma earlier that day, but she wasn't there. He called her name, but she did not answer. When he circled back to the line of stalls on the left, he found Emma in the first one, sitting on the straw floor beside a stack of hay bales, with her arms wrapped tightly over her knees. When he pulled the gate open to enter, she looked up briefly, then put her head down to hide her face.

Plainly, Emma was a girl in distress. Her white head covering had become somewhat dislodged from the bun of her brown hair, as if she had started to pull it off and had forgotten it. Her long lilac dress was spread carelessly over her knees; its hem lay in the straw around her ankles. She had taken her day apron off, and it lay crumpled at her feet.

Cal pulled a heavy bale of hay from a tall stack beside her and set it down to Emma's left. He sat there and studied her, small and alone, in a place he knew she had considered private. She turned her eyes up to him once, and he saw that they were red and swollen. Hoping she would talk, he pulled another hay bale into place beside his and asked, "Emma, can you have a seat with me? Can we talk a little?"

With her face buried between her knees, Emma gave a muffled but determined answer. "I'm not crying."

"No," Cal said, "I can see that now. Can you sit up here with me?"

Emma didn't answer, and she didn't move.

Cal tried again. "I know that you're sad about Ruth."

"I don't want to talk about it."

Cal nodded, but she didn't see. He leaned over to lay a hand on her shoulder, but she buried her face deeper between her knees, jerked away from his touch, and remained seated. Cal eased off his hay bale and knelt in the straw beside her. "Emma," he said, "I can see that you've been crying. If we talk a little, it might help."

"I could talk to Ruth," Emma said with a whisper. "Only Ruth. But I'm not crying."

"I can see that," Cal said.

"I don't want to cry for her."

"Why, Emma? It might help if you did."

"If I can't be strong for her, then I'll know she's really gone. And I won't really know she's gone until they bring her home in a coffin."

"Then I think you must be the strongest girl I know," Cal said. Again he tried to lay his hand on her shoulder, but again she wrenched away and kept her face buried between her knees.

Cal waited in silence for several minutes beside her. Eventually, Emma offered, "Ruth is the only one I could let see me cry."

"Did you cry when you lost your family?"

"Only Ruth saw that," Emma said, looking up.

"Oh, Emma, God sees all our tears."

Emma ignored that and said, "She's the only one I could trust with my tears. The other kids teased me if I was sad."

"Kids can be cruel, Emma. You're lucky you had Ruth."

"Is she really dead?"

"Yes," Cal answered softly.

She turned her face back into her knees. When Cal reached out for her shoulder, she pulled away again.

"If Ruth is really gone," Emma whispered, "then I can't cry anymore. Not ever. Or if I do, I can't ever let anyone see me do it."

"God knows all our tears, Emma."

She looked up briefly and buried her face again. "Ruth was the only one I could trust."

"You can trust me, Emma. I wouldn't tell anyone. And you still can pray."

Emma shook her head and squeezed her arms tighter around her knees. Muffled by her dress, her voice seemed distant and weak. "I can't let anyone see me cry."

"You have to trust someone, Emma."

"That sounds like something Ruth would say."

Cal held silence, waited. Cautiously he said, "Your grandfather says you are his stratus flower."

Emma didn't reply. Instead, she stood up and brushed off the back of her dress. She retrieved her day apron and tied it on. She straightened her prayer cap at the back of her head.

Cal stood beside her, and she turned to face him, she so much smaller than the pastor, so much younger. With a determined struggle for bravery written in her expression, she declared, "I can't pray anymore, Pastor Troyer. And I can't cry."

Cal took a step toward her, but she backed away. Bunching fists at her side, she said, "If Ruth is really dead, she will never be able to tell me why she was crying last night. So, if God is watching, you just tell him that I can't cry anymore. And tell him that he doesn't have to bother with any more of my prayers."

10

Monday, April 4
6:30 P.M.

WHEN PAT Lance knocked at the screen door on the Zooks' front porch, she was dressed in a navy blue pantsuit with a plain white blouse buttoned demurely at the top. Her detective's shield was clipped to the lapel of her suit jacket, and she held her electronic tablet at her side, intending to type notes as she spoke with the men. A teenaged boy came to the door, looked blankly out at her, and turned back into the house. Wondering why he hadn't spoken, Lance nosed up to the screen and watched him walk down the long hallway to the kitchen. Lining both sides of the hall, she saw Amish folk seated with their heads bowed in prayer. None of them seemed to notice her.

Eventually, an older woman in a dark blue dress and white day apron walked forward from the kitchen at the back, drying her hands on a plain white linen towel. She came out through the screen door, and Lance stepped back to allow her to pass.

"I am Mrs. Zook," the woman said, glancing at Lance's badge. "Ruth was my daughter."

"I am sorry for your loss," Lance said earnestly.

Mrs. Zook didn't reply.

"May I use your first name?" Lance asked. She sat in a rocker and laid her tablet across her knees, fingers poised to type as she looked up to Mrs. Zook for an answer.

"Mrs. Andy Zook," the woman said.

"But your first name?"

Hesitating, Mrs. Zook held to a formal posture and replied, "Irma."

Lance typed her name. "I was hoping to speak with Alvin Zook, and to your husband."

"My husband is praying," Irma said with wooden weariness. "Alvin is in the kitchen."

"Can you ask them to come out?"

Irma hesitated. "I can speak with you myself, Deputy."

Eyes fixed on her tablet, Lance asked, "Did you speak with Ruth after she came home?"

As if deflating, Irma lowered herself into a rocker beside Lance. "I did not, Deputy," she confessed. "Her grandfather Alvin brought her home from the bus at Sugarcreek, and she went right up to her room. Alvin said she was tired, but I still should have gone up to her."

"I am truly sorry for your loss, Irma," Lance said. "If I can help . . ."

Irma shook her head and stared at her hands in her lap. Knotting her fingers into her kitchen towel, she whispered, "I should have gone up to her."

Lance lifted her fingers from her tablet and reached a gentle hand over to Irma's wrist. "Irma, I will do everything I can to find out who killed her."

Mrs. Zook looked to Lance and back to her hands. "What good will that do, Deputy?"

"It'll be justice," Lance said.

"Justice, in place of a life?" Irma asked. "How is that a fair trade?"

"It's all I can offer."

"I know. We understand the finality of death as well as any people do."

Lance let a quiet moment pass. Irma gazed out across the front lawn and seemed to watch traffic on 557 without seeing any of it. Gently, Lance asked, "Irma, may I speak with your husband?"

"I can only ask," Irma said. "He is praying."

"Really, Mrs. Zook, I need to speak with Alvin, too. Both of them."

When Irma Zook went back into the house, Lance typed a few notes on her tablet. After ten minutes alone on the porch, she stood and nosed back up to the screen. At the end of the long hallway, she saw short Alvin Zook standing beside a middle-aged Amish man seated on the last chair on the right. Lance knocked softly on the door, and Alvin looked up. The man he had been speaking with also looked up briefly, but bowed his head to return to his prayers.

Alvin came forward in the hall, pushed out through the screen door, and said, "Andy has asked me to speak for him."

"Does he know anything about Ruth?" Lance asked, holding her tablet across her breast. "Can he tell me anything to report to the sheriff?"

Alvin answered, "No," and led Lance down the front steps. They crossed the front lawn to the driveway at the side of the house, and Alvin added, "I think I am the only one of us who spoke with Ruth."

Tablet at her side, Lance asked, "You think?"

"Yes, but I wouldn't be surprised if Emma went up to see her last night."

"Then maybe I should talk with Emma."

"I can answer all of your questions, Deputy," Alvin sighed. "At least for now."

*   *   *

When Bruce Robertson arrived at the Zooks', Alvin was standing with Pat Lance on the driveway. Under the wide brim of his black felt hat, his face was ashen. He took a side step away from Lance, as if he were embarrassed to be seen talking alone with her, and as Robertson walked up to them, Alvin said, "Your deputy has been asking a lot of questions."

"She's a detective, Mr. Zook," Robertson said, holding out his hand.

They shook briefly, and Robertson added, "She needs to be asking a lot of questions right now, and I hope you'll answer all of them."

Alvin turned his face down and said, "I've told her everything I can."

To Lance, Robertson said, "Do you have everything you need, Detective?"

"Yes."

"Thank you, then," Robertson said, and Lance knew she had been dismissed.

She stepped back to her black-and-white cruiser, got in behind the wheel, and backed around Robertson's Crown Victoria to leave. As she was driving away, Robertson asked Alvin, "Is your son here? Ruth's father?"

"Yes."

"Then I have some questions of my own. Please ask him to come out."

Alvin turned for the front porch, and Robertson followed him up the steps. When both Alvin and Andy were out on the porch, Robertson led them down the steps to the driveway, to stand at the front bumper of his blue sedan. He sat back against the hood and asked, "So, who brought Ruth home from the bus?"

Alvin said, "I did. And I told that earlier to your Captain Newell."

"Did you tell that also to Detective Lance?"

"Yes, Sheriff. I told them both. Also your Detective Armbruster."

"He's just a deputy, Mr. Zook. Not a detective yet, so that's why he wears a uniform."

Both Alvin and Andy gave Robertson blank stares.

Robertson folded his arms over his chest and continued. "How many suitcases did she bring home?"

"Two," Alvin said.

"Did she take two down with her?"

"Only one," Andy said.

"You drove her to the bus?"

"Yes," Andy said.

"Only one suitcase?"

"Yes."

To Alvin, Robertson said, "Did you ask her why she had a second suitcase when she came home?"

"Why would I?" Alvin asked.

"Because maybe she acted strange about it."

"Well, she wouldn't let me carry it."

"But you told Captain Newell that she seemed tired to you."

"Yes."

"So, why didn't you offer to carry her suitcases?"

"I offered, Sheriff. She let me carry the one, not the other."

"Did it seem to you that the suitcase you did carry was too heavy?"

"Not really," Alvin said.

"Was the other suitcase heavy? As far as you could tell?"

"I think so," Alvin said. "She struggled with it."

"How about her clothes? Did she do any laundry on Saturday?"

Andy answered, "No. My Irma does laundry every day, except Sundays. Ruth didn't even come down from her room."

"Because she was sick?"

"Yes," Alvin said. "She told me she didn't feel well."

"When did she tell you that, Mr. Zook? Right when you picked her up?"

"Yes, but it's a long bus ride. I thought she was just tired from the trip."

"What else did she say?"

"Nothing, really."

"Was she talkative? I mean normally."

"No more than anyone," Andy said. "She was a normal person."

"Normally happy, or was she moody?"

"Happy," both men answered.

Robertson pushed off the hood of his car. "Who talked to her? Who went up to her room?"

Alvin shook his head. Andy answered, "Maybe only Emma."

"Do you know Emma went up, or are you just guessing?"

"I just think that maybe she would have."

"Were they confidantes?"

The men stared back, puzzled.

"Were Emma and Ruth close? Talk a lot?"

"Emma preferred Ruth to the rest of us," Andy replied.

"Enough that she might have talked to Ruth last night? Or maybe earlier, during the day? Or Saturday?"

Andy nodded. "Emma liked to sleep in Ruth's room. They were 'confidantes.'"

Robertson stuffed his hands into his pants pockets and toed the gravel, thinking. The Zook men stood in front of him, one short and round, the other tall and slender. They exchanged glances and waited for the sheriff to speak.

Robertson looked up to study the largest barn behind the house. Stan Armbruster's cruiser was still parked in front of it, at the far end of the driveway. To both men he said, "Do either of you know what my men are looking for in the bottoms below your broken dam?"

"Bags?" Alvin asked, tentative.

"Plastic wrapping," Robertson said. "They're trying to find all the wrappings that flushed out of your pond when you blew the dam this morning."

"Is that really important?" Andy asked.

"Yes. We'll be able to estimate how much cocaine your daughter brought home with her."

"What does it matter?" Alvin asked.

Robertson pulled his cell phone out of his pocket and said, "Because, Mr. Zook, later today I'm going to call a Sergeant Orton I know down near Sarasota. I need to be able to tell him how much cocaine someone was trying to send up here."

"But she dumped it all out," Alvin said. "So, she didn't want to bring it up here at all."

"I know," Robertson said. "The question is, who could have induced her even to try?"

While the men thought about that, Robertson punched Armbruster's number into his phone. When the corporal answered, he asked, "Stan, are you about done searching down there?"

"We need another half hour, Sheriff."

"How many wrappings so far?"

"Only four."

"Small enough to fit in one suitcase?"

"Probably."

"OK, thanks," Robertson said, and switched off. To the Amish men, he said, "If my Detective Lance comes back out here, gentlemen, I'd appreciate it if you'd answer all of her questions, as if I were asking them myself."

Alvin looked to Andy, and Andy nodded. Then Alvin said, "We will, Sheriff. But when she comes out, could you ask her not to wear the pants of a man?"

11

Monday, April 4
7:20 P.M.

IT WAS quiet at the jail when Robertson came in through the rear entrance. At the end of the hall, Ed Hollings had returned early to start his night shift at the radio consoles. He took a call and waved briefly to Robertson.

To his left, the sheriff heard the faint clacking of a keyboard and the whir of a printer. He stepped into the duty room and found Ricky Niell typing at a small desk at the back of the room. Ricky stood to retrieve a document from the printer beside the desk and said, "I'm just finishing my report."

Threading his way past long tables, Robertson crossed the room and asked, "How's Ellie?"

"She's better," Ricky said, stacking the pages of his report. "Wasn't so great this morning."

"You'll let me know how she is?"

"Sure. Or she will."

"OK. And you talked with Missy?"

"She doesn't have much yet, Sheriff. She's made a preliminary assessment of the body, and there was cocaine residue on Ruth Zook's hands, sleeves, and apron. Also on the knife that was in her pocket, plus inside one of her suitcases. But Missy hadn't started on a full autopsy when I left."

"You tested the horse and buggy," Robertson said. "Was the residue just what we'd expect if Ruth had handled the reins and harness?"

"Yes. That and the seat. The bit and bridle, too. But nothing else."

"Did Stan finish up at the pond?"

"Yes, and his report is appended here. They found a total of four wrappings. He says they searched a good mile and a half, along both sides of the creek. He came back muddy and tired, but he's sure he found everything that was there."

"Four bricks of cocaine," Robertson said, "and Ruth Zook just poured it all out in her pond."

*   *   *

Missy and the sheriff lived in Millersburg in a large Victorian home on the Wooster Road, north of the courthouse square. The house sat on a west-facing hill, with a commanding view of the old neighborhood.

When Missy came into the kitchen by the back door, the sheriff was cooking sautéed chicken in a deep skillet, with a pan of water heating on the stove for pasta. Despite the cool spring temperatures, Missy was still dressed in her green autopsy scrubs. She hooked her jacket on a wall peg beside the back door and said, "I need a shower."

The sheriff said, "Twenty minutes," and Missy climbed the steps to the second floor.

At dinner, Robertson gave Missy details about his conversation with the Zook men, and about Stan Armbruster's search for plastic packaging in the bottoms below the Zook's pond.

Dressed in house slippers and a long burgundy robe, Missy ate and listened. As they cleared the dishes, she told her husband what she had learned at the morgue and concluded by saying, "She hadn't eaten, Bruce. Maybe for three or four days."

Opening the dishwasher, the sheriff asked, "Small woman, right? Maybe she never ate much."

"It was more than that," Missy said. "I don't think she had

eaten a decent meal in days. And she had a rash on her hands and wrists."

"But she was bruised and cut, right? The horse pounded her. I mean apart from the fact that she was shot. So, are you sure about the rash?"

"She had a rash, Bruce. And one gunshot wound to the forehead. On top of all that, she was bruised, cut, and broken—three fractured limbs and several broken ribs—so yes, she was bruised and cut. But, she also had a mild rash on her hands."

"Would you be able to tell if she had been harmed before she came up on the bus? Or physically coerced in some way?"

"Not yet," Missy said. "Maybe I'll have an answer for you tomorrow. I'll be with her all day."

*   *   *

After he had finished loading the dishwasher and cleaning up the kitchen, Robertson joined Missy in her first-floor study. Bookshelves lined three walls, and an antique writing desk sat in front of a window that looked out over a wide front porch of gray boards, edged by an ornate, cast-iron railing under yellow porch lights. Missy looked up from a letter she was writing and said, "There's another thing, Bruce. I took a liver temperature reading when I got out to the glen. The way I figure the time of death, she can't have been killed more than a few minutes before Mervin Byler says he found her."

Standing in the doorway, the sheriff said, "OK, we'll have to talk with Byler again. But it's the why and the how, Missy. That's what I'm not seeing."

"Why would she transport drugs?" Missy asked.

"And how could anyone have convinced her even to try?"

12

Tuesday, April 5
6:45 A.M.

WHEN THE sheriff arrived early the next morning at the jail, there were flurries dusting the courthouse square, stirring soft whiteness into the air around the granite Civil War monument. Robertson checked in with his night dispatcher, Ed Hollings, and then, in the duty room at the other end of the hall, he filled his coffee carafe with water. In his office, he put up a full pot of brew, settled behind his desk while the coffeemaker chattered, and searched the list of contacts on his computer for the phone number of Sergeant Ray Lee Orton in the Bradenton Beach Police Department north of Sarasota. As he was punching the number into his cell phone, Hollings came in briefly and said, "I'll be staying over a few hours, Sheriff. Ellie called in sick this morning."

Robertson punched out of his call and followed Hollings out to the front counter. "Did she say what was wrong?"

Hollings sat at the radio consoles and started to answer, but a call rang in, and he held up an index finger and answered the call. It was a brief report from a motorist who had witnessed a fender bender in the parking lot of the Walmart. Hollings dispatched a unit and turned back to Robertson. "She said stomach flu, Sheriff."

Robertson gave a distracted scowl, turned around, and stepped back down to his desk, punching in the number again for the Bradenton Beach Police Department. Before he could put the call through, Pat Lance knocked at his door and entered. Again Robertson switched off his call.

Lance was dressed in the same navy blue pantsuit she had worn to the Zook farm the day before. Her blouse was a butter yellow color, open at the neck. She sat in a chair at the front of Robertson's old cherry desk and asked, "Learn anything useful after I left?"

Robertson sat back in his battered swivel chair and tented his fingers in front of a broad smile. "Lance," he said, "they don't like women in pants."

"Are you kidding?" Lance blurted.

"Not at all. They asked me to tell you not to wear 'the pants of a man' when you go out there."

Lance popped out of her chair. "You're kidding!"

"Not at all."

"What did you tell them?"

"Nothing," Robertson said, smiling to cover an urge to laugh. "Is that going to be a problem for you?"

"What am I supposed to wear?" Lance asked indignantly. "A long Amish dress?"

"Yes, I think they'd prefer that, Lance. Again, is that going to be a problem for you?"

This time Robertson couldn't hold back. He laughed, took his fingers down, and smiled openly at his detective.

Lance sat down and asked with an awkward calm, "How long have you been planning to ambush me with that one, Sheriff?"

"Oh, since they told me," Robertson said, and stood behind his desk. He came around to his coffeemaker and asked, "Black, right, Lance?"

She nodded, and Robertson poured coffee into two white mugs. He carried the mugs to his desk, handed one to Lance, sat behind his desk again, and chuckled. "It worked fine, Lance. By the time you left, they were ready to talk."

Not finding anything particularly humorous in the exchange, Lance set her mug on the corner of Robertson's desktop. "They're fossils," she muttered. "Misogynistic fossils."

Robertson chuckled again. "Somebody called me that same thing last year, Lance. Do you women sit around a campfire and agree on these phrases, like 'misogynistic fossils'?"

Lance started a reply, saw the sheriff's broad smile, and gave up with, "Oh, forget it."

Picking up his phone again, Robertson said, "I put my report on the system last night. The only thing I learned at the Zooks' is that somebody in Sarasota has a drug conduit running up here. I was just going to call Ray Lee Orton."

"Who?" Lance asked, still distracted by the issue of attire.

"Cop in Bradenton Beach. Gonna ask him who the lead people are down there, in drug enforcement."

Lance looked up and nodded, keeping to her seat as she sipped coffee.

Ed Hollings came back down the hall. Pausing only briefly in the sheriff's door, he said, "Amish girl to see you, Sheriff," and returned to his consoles out front.

Robertson pushed down on his intercom button and said, "Can you ask what she wants?" but Hollings appeared again at his door with a young Amish woman and said, "She said it can't wait."

Lance stood up and ushered the visitor into Robertson's office. The sheriff stood behind his desk and said, "What can we do for you?"

The Amish woman looked nervously at Lance and then turned, unsure of herself, to Robertson.

The sheriff came out to the side of his desk with his coffee mug and said, "This is Detective Pat Lance, and I am Sheriff Robertson. How can we help you?"

Lance held a straight chair out for her at the front of Robertson's desk, and the young woman sat down on it. In her early twenties, she was stocky, bordering on overweight. Her face was round and pale, with a complexion as flawless as refined flour.

Her brown eyes were large and set wide over a thin nose and small mouth that seemed to curve perpetually down at the corners. Her hands rested nervously in her lap, fingers knitted together and struggling with tension.

Her long dress was made of a winter-heavy dark plum fabric, and her white apron was spread across her shoulders, over her bodice, and down to the hem of her dress. Folded over her arm was a black winter shawl. Her black bonnet covered all of her hair, and it was tied close to her cheeks for modesty. She wore black hose, soft black walking shoes, and round, wire-rimmed spectacles, gold in color.

Briefly she glanced again at Lance and then looked back to the sheriff. She studied the backs of her hands, nervously spreading her fingers over her knees. "Is it safe to talk here?" she asked, and knitted her fingers again in her lap. "Do I need a lawyer? I'm not sure how this works, but I heard this was a problem last year for the Burkholder boy." Her eyes remained fixed anxiously on her hands.

Robertson stepped back behind his desk and sat down. "Why would you need a lawyer?"

Without looking up from her hands, she said, "Because I think I broke the law."

Lance sat down beside her, and Robertson asked, "Can you tell us why you think that?"

"I don't need a lawyer, first?"

Lance said, "You don't have to tell us anything, unless you want to. Maybe you could start by telling us your name."

"I am Fannie Helmuth," she said, looking over to Lance, straight ahead to Robertson, and back to her hands. "Was a girl killed yesterday?"

Robertson leaned forward to rest his forearms on his desktop. "Yes, a girl was killed down near Farmerstown."

"She was shot?"

"Yes," Robertson said. "Ruth Zook. Do you know her?"

"No. I mean, I know who she is. Who she was. Did they find drugs at her house?"

"We think she poured drugs out into her farm pond," Lance answered.

"Is that why all the fish were killed?"

"Yes," Lance said. "We think so."

"Was it all in an old leather suitcase?"

"We think so," Robertson said, eyeing Lance. "We think she brought an extra suitcase home with her from Florida."

"From Pinecraft?"

Robertson stalled a moment and then stood up behind his desk. "Fannie, maybe you'd better tell us why you're here."

Fannie Helmuth tried to speak, but the words caught in her throat. Lance asked, "Do you want something to drink?"

Eyes still focused on the backs of her hands, Fannie asked, "Do you have Mountain Dew?"

Lance said, "They've got it across the street, at the BP."

Fannie didn't reply, so Lance said, "I'll go get you one," and left.

Sitting back down, Robertson said, "If you know something about why Ruth Zook was killed, I think you should tell me."

With a tragic smile, as sober as a brush with death, Fannie said, "I think I brought one of those suitcases home, too."

* * *

When Lance returned with a Mountain Dew, the sheriff had Fannie Helmuth waiting for a lawyer across the hall in Interview B. He took Lance over, went into the room with her, and said to Fannie, "Detective Lance is going to sit with you while I get a lawyer. You don't have to talk. Do you understand?"

"Is this the Mirad thing?"

"Miranda, yes," Robertson said. "I don't believe you can have done anything wrong, but you don't have to say a word. You aren't a suspect in any crime that we know about."

To Lance, Robertson said, "Linda Hart?"

Lance sat down beside Fannie, scooted her chair closer, gave Fannie the Mountain Dew, and said, "She'd be the best, Sheriff. Under the circumstances, Hart would be the best."

* * *

Linda Hart, tall and austere with cropped black hair, wearing a chocolate brown skirt suit, sat with Fannie for the better part of an hour. When the two crossed back to Robertson's office, Lance and Robertson were seated across from one another at the sheriff's big desk, and Captain Newell was standing at a west-facing window, polishing his thick black glasses. Robertson introduced the captain and asked Fannie to take a seat next to Lance, at the front of his desk. As if adversaries, Hart and Newell positioned themselves at opposite corners of the desk.

Hart started by saying, "Sheriff, so far as I can tell, Fannie hasn't broken any laws."

"We need to know about the suitcase," Robertson said evenly.

"For all she knew," Hart said, "the suitcase contained old clothes. She never looked inside."

"If that's all it was," Robertson said to Hart, "then she hasn't broken any laws, and we're not interested in pursuing anything criminal. We just want to know how someone like Ruth Zook could have been induced to bring a second suitcase home from Florida." To Fannie, Robertson added, "There's no harm in telling us that."

Hart turned to Fannie. "You can tell them about Jodie."

"And the suitcase?" Fannie asked.

"Only *why* you thought you had to transport it for them, Fannie. You aren't admitting that you actually did it."

Robertson complained, "She's already told us that much, Hart."

"Not with her attorney present," Hart said. "If you prefer, we won't tell you anything."

"OK," Robertson sighed.

Hart nodded a "go ahead" to Fannie.

"I had to do it," Fannie said. "They were going to kill Jodie."

Robertson pulled a pad out of his center desk drawer and took a pen out of his shirt pocket. "Jodie?" he asked.

Nearly inaudibly, Fannie spoke with her gaze fixed on the

front edge of Robertson's desk. "Jodie Tapp," she said. "She is a waitress at Miller's Amish Restaurant and Clock Shoppe. I work there as a waitress, too. To help with expenses when I'm in Florida. She's just a little Mennonite girl, and those men know where she lives."

Eyes fixed on his pad, Robertson wrote notes and asked, "Address of the restaurant?"

"I don't know the number," Fannie said, looking up to him. "It's four blocks north of Bahia Vista, on Beneva, right on the northern edge of Pinecraft."

"How long have you known Jodie?" Robertson asked.

"Three years. She's been at Miller's longer than anyone else. She kinda looks after us snowbirds."

"Where does she live?"

"She has a little trailer in Cortez. Just over the bridge from Bradenton Beach. I've only been there once. She doesn't have hardly anything at all, except what's in that trailer. And they'll kill her if she talks to anyone about this."

Robertson held his gaze on his pad. "Who, Fannie? Who threatened to kill Jodie?"

Fannie looked up to Hart, and Hart said, "You can tell them about the boat, Fannie."

"I only met them once," Fannie said, anxious with her memories, fingers clenching and releasing in her lap, eyes ranging from Hart to Robertson and back. "When we went out on their boat for a sunset."

"What were their names?" Robertson asked.

"Jim and John."

"Last names?"

"I don't know."

"Name of the boat?"

"I don't remember. It was white, and it had fishing poles sticking out of tubes on the top. Really, I don't remember the boat very well."

Agitated, Fannie stood abruptly. Quickly back in her seat, she muttered, "I'm so stupid. Now she's after *me*."

"Who is?" Robertson asked.

Fannie stared blankly at Robertson for a long moment, focusing inward, as if she were pondering a decision. Eventually, she sighed and said, "The angry woman I gave the suitcase to. If I had been smart, I'd have come home without that suitcase. Or I'd have tossed it in a lake."

Trying to sound reassuring, Robertson said, "Ruth did something like that, Fannie. I think you're safe, now, because you didn't."

"I'm not safe at all," Fannie groaned. "She said if I talked to anyone about the suitcase, she'd come back. She said she knows where I live, and I believe her."

"Detective Lance is going to ask you a lot of questions about this angry woman, Fannie," Robertson said. "We need to know all about her. Everything you can remember."

"OK. I'll try."

"It's going to take quite a long time to go over it."

"I can stay, Sheriff, but I don't know how much I'll remember."

"And this all started with a sunset boat ride in Florida?" Robertson asked.

Fannie nodded and held a kerchief to her eyes. "We thought we were just going out for a sunset. That's when they beat Jodie and said they'd kill her if I didn't carry a suitcase home for them."

13

Tuesday, April 5
8:20 A.M.

WHILE DETECTIVE Lance questioned Fannie in Interview B, Robertson called Ricky Niell into his office. Bobby Newell poured coffee into a Styrofoam cup at the credenza and sat down next to Niell at the front of Robertson's desk.

The sheriff leaned back in his swivel rocker and asked, "Have you listened to any of what Lance is asking Fannie Helmuth?"

Ricky nodded, sipped coffee, and said, "I've listened on the other side of the mirror. She's not making any of it up."

"No," Robertson agreed. "We need to know if something like this happened to Ruth Zook."

"I can find out if she worked at the Miller's place in Sarasota," Ricky said. "I'll ask her father, maybe her mother."

"Yes," Robertson said. "But Ruth wrote home to Emma, and Alvin Zook thinks Emma still has the letters. So ask if you can read them, Ricky. Maybe bring them here."

"Anything else?" Ricky asked.

"Yes, go see Mervin Byler again," Robertson said. "Missy thinks he might have seen something. Or that maybe he heard something, because he found the body so soon after Ruth was shot."

As Ricky was leaving, Cal Troyer angled through Robertson's

door. Dressed in jeans and a blue corduroy work shirt, Cal greeted Robertson and Newell and said, "You're not going to believe what's going on out at the Zooks'."

Robertson held up a hand. "First, Cal, do you know a Fannie Helmuth?"

"No. Should I?"

"Probably not."

"Does she know why Ruth Zook was killed?" Cal asked, sitting down next to the captain.

Keeping to his seat, Robertson said, "I think she does, Cal. At least she's given us an approach to take. It ties in with the drugs."

"That's what I came here about," Cal said. "You're not going to believe it."

Newell stood and moved to the door, saying, "Sheriff, I'll follow up with Fannie Helmuth."

Newell left, and Robertson came out from behind his desk. Walking to the windows overlooking the Civil War monument, he said, "Let me guess. The EPA is throwing its weight around?"

Cal joined the sheriff at the window. Together they looked out at half an inch of new snow on the courthouse lawn. "How'd you know about the EPA?" Cal asked.

"This morning, they faxed us a copy of their initial complaint against the Zooks. They consider the farm to have suffered a toxic spill. An *intentional* toxic release, to be precise."

"It's a disaster," Cal said. "They're quarantining the milk cows. They've roped off the bottoms, below the pond. Their scientists are crawling all over the place. Won't let the Zooks go back into their own house."

"There'll be fines, Cal. Cleanup expenses."

"Zooks can't afford that, Bruce. It'll wipe them out. If they can't put water back in their pond, they'll lose the herd. If they have to pay any fines, they'll lose their farm."

"There's nothing I can do about it."

"There has to be."

"It's both state and federal, Cal. They're going to bring a

trailer with a lab. Test the soil, water. The Zooks will have to clean it all up."

"This is a disaster. It's an unmitigated disaster."

Robertson shrugged. "I don't like it, Cal, but there's nothing I can do."

"I want you to figure a way out of this, Sheriff. You need to fix this."

"Cal . . ." Robertson started.

Troyer turned from the window to glower at Robertson. "You need to fix this, Bruce. There has got to be a way."

"I'll go out later today," Robertson said. "I'll see about it."

"Good."

"No promises."

"Of course."

"We've got our hands full, Cal. Fannie Helmuth has just opened this up to an outfit in Florida. I'll need to send someone down there."

"Mike and Caroline Branden are already there," Cal said. "They're at a policeman's cottage on Longboat Key."

"Didn't know that," Robertson said. "Last I heard, they were both at Duke."

"They're taking a vacation," Cal said. "So you might not need to send anyone from here."

"You don't know about Fannie Helmuth," Robertson said. "Her story changes everything about Ruth Zook's murder."

"Right now, I'm focused on helping the Zooks."

"I know," Robertson said, returning to his desk chair. "You know anything about Miller's Restaurant and Clock Shoppe, in Pinecraft?"

"No. Why?"

"We need to know if Ruth Zook worked there as a waitress."

"I can ask the Zooks," Cal said, turning for the door.

"I've already sent Ricky to do that. I might need you to help us talk with Emma Wengerd. We want to read the letters that Ruth Zook sent up to her."

"She's fragile right now, Bruce."

"We'd just make copies, Cal. Then give them right back to her. I've got Ricky going out to ask her, but if she's reluctant to trust us, maybe you could help Ricky convince her."

* * *

Once Cal had left, Robertson crossed the hall to the observation room where Ricky and the captain were watching through one-way glass as Pat Lance questioned Fannie Helmuth in Interview B.

Robertson turned up the volume on the intercom and stood in front of the glass to listen for a while. Then he pulled Newell off to the side and whispered, "Anything more about this Jodie Tapp?"

"They went back over that before you came in," Newell said. "I think she's more worried about Jodie than she is about herself."

"OK, Bobby, Jodie lives in a trailer park in Cortez. That's right across the bridge from the Bradenton Beach Police Department. I'm gonna ask Ray Lee Orton who the players are down there. On both sides of the drug war. If Amish girls are getting trapped in the crossfire, I'll want to send someone down."

"This the sergeant that Ricky worked with last year?"

"Yes, and Jodie Tapp works at one of the restaurants in Pine-craft. So, maybe there's a connection between Fannie Helmuth and Ruth Zook."

"It's worth a try," Newell acknowledged.

"OK, Lance or Niell? Who do we send?"

"Niell knows the layout down there," the captain said. "And maybe Mike Branden will help."

* * *

Robertson called the number for the Bradenton Beach Police Department and asked for Sergeant Orton. The dispatcher put his phone down to place a radio call to Orton and then picked back up to say to Robertson, "It'll be a few minutes, Sheriff. We've got a capsized boat out in Longboat Pass."

"Can you give me his cell number?" Robertson asked, and the dispatcher read out the digits.

Robertson switched off and redialed, and the sergeant answered with a curt "Orton."

"Bruce Robertson, Holmes County. Got a minute, Sergeant?"

Orton said a few muffled words to a colleague, and Robertson waited. Then Orton came back on the call. "We're about done here, Sheriff. What do you need?"

"We've got a murdered Amish girl up here, Ray Lee. And another girl is involved. I think they both knew a Mennonite waitress from Cortez who works at Miller's Restaurant in Pinecraft. A Jodie Tapp."

"I know Jodie," Orton said back over the call, sounding distracted.

"Why?" Robertson asked. "I mean why do you know her?"

"She's a windsurfer, Sheriff. And I'm a kite surfer. We all know each other at the beaches. It's a community."

"She's Mennonite—right, Orton? So, here's the deal. We've got a drug outfit preying on young Amish girls up here in Ohio, and your surfer friend down there is probably in danger, too."

"Right, yes," Orton mumbled.

"You working on something, Ray Lee?"

"No, yes—sorry. We're fishing a capsized boat out of the water at Longboat Pass, and I'm not sure what it means."

"I don't follow," Robertson said. "I'm worried about a murdered Amish girl up here, and another Amish girl who's in danger here. Also your Mennonite friend in Cortez. I think a drug ring is sending junk up from Florida."

"This boat might be part of that," Orton said. "We've been trying to take down a drug conduit here, running cocaine into the beaches on stolen boats from the Keys. And I think we just found one of the boats, capsized off Coquina Beach. This might be our first really good lead."

"OK, Ray Lee, who's leading the investigation down there?" Robertson asked. "Who are your drug enforcement people?"

Orton held a beat and said, sounding distracted again, "I can send you a file attached to an e-mail."

"Can you do that today, Sergeant? Like right now?"

"What? OK. I'll send it when I get back to the station."

After a pause, Orton said, "Jodie is a nice girl, Sheriff. A little withdrawn, but still a nice girl. If she were to be hurt, well, it'd be a personal problem for me. I like her."

"Are you two in a relationship?"

"No, I just like her. She's just a young girl, really, but older, if you know what I mean. No bigger than a middle-schooler, but scrappy out on the surf. I like the way she tears it up out there. So, if she's in danger, I need to know it."

"We've got one of those nice girls too, Orton. Up here in Ohio. She's dead. So, yes, Jodie Tapp is in danger, and I'm gonna send Ricky Niell down there, if you can set up the introductions for him."

* * *

Robertson waved Lance out of Interview B, and Lance asked Fannie to wait while she spoke with the sheriff.

In the hall, Robertson told Lance about Orton's hunt for a Florida drug outfit using stolen boats and added, "But don't tell Fannie that's she's mixed up with an organized drug ring. Not yet, because it'll rattle her more than she already is. Wait until you have gotten everything she can remember. Even then, maybe she doesn't need to know any particulars."

"She likes Jodie, Sheriff. It'd hit her hard if she were harmed."

"I can't help that," Robertson said. "Truth is, I'm not sure about anyone, now. Ruth Zook, Fannie Helmuth, even Mervin Byler. Not sure about any of them, at all. So, do what you can to keep Fannie here, Lance, and ask her every question you can think of. Buy her lunch if you have to, but keep her here."

Lance thought and said, "She's scared, Sheriff. If I offered to stay with her here, I'm sure she'd agree. She doesn't want to go home."

"Then you're on the Fannie Helmuth project, Lance. Protecting and interviewing her. Find out everything she knows about this woman who threatened her. Get a sketch of her if you can. And find out everything Fannie knows about Jodie Tapp."

"More than what she's told us?"

"Everything, Lance. Pinecraft and the restaurant. Maybe that boat she was on. Get it all as fast as you can, because there are just too many weird connections here to suit me. And I'm guessing this woman who threatened her up here is the key to all of this."

"If you're right about that," Lance said, "she's looking for Fannie and Jodie, both."

"If I'm right, Lance, she's on the phone right now to Sarasota."

14

REALIZING THAT she risked changing Fannie's understanding of everything she had been through in Florida, Pat Lance went back into Interview B and sat down next to her. One more pass at this, Lance thought, before Fannie learns the truth about how big a scheme she's mixed up in. About how much danger there really is, now, for Jodie Tapp.

Lance flipped pages in her notebook, found Fannie's account of the beating, and decided to probe harder for details about the sunset boat ride with Jim and John.

"Fannie," she said, "do you remember where you went to see the sunset? Was it out to the ocean, or did you stay on the bay?"

Fannie closed her eyes and remembered. "We went out through a channel and under a bridge, and they said we were on the Gulf of Mexico." Remembering a detail, Fannie opened her eyes and said, "There was a sailboat in front of us, and the bridge had to lift up."

"You didn't mention that before," Lance said.

"I didn't remember the sailboat until just now."

"Was it a drawbridge, then?"

"Yes. To let the sailboat go through, it had to lift apart in the middle."

"And their names were Jim and John?"

"That's what Jodie told me."

"Do you remember if they actually called each other Jim and John, or do you just remember that Jodie introduced them that way?"

Fannie closed her eyes again. "When we got on the boat, Jodie introduced me to them." She opened her eyes and added, "Jim was the skinny one. John was heavier."

"Where did you get on the boat?"

"At the far end of the big white bridge. There's a little lot beside the water there, where Jodie parked her car."

"Is this the big Sarasota bridge? The arching one you described?"

"Yes. It runs up very high, from right downtown. When you drive over the arch of it, you can see all around Sarasota Bay."

"How did Jodie know to meet the boat there?"

"I guess she arranged it like that. She said she knew people who would take us out to see the sunset. Jim and John. That's all we were supposed to do. Take a boat ride to see the sunset."

"How long did it take them to get through the channel and out to the Gulf?"

"Maybe twenty minutes, but I wasn't watching a clock."

"Were there other boats that evening? I mean besides the sailboat."

"Oh, there were dozens. Maybe more. Going out through the channel."

"Then they brought you back to the park? The one where Jodie had parked?"

"Yes," Fannie said, growing agitated again. "It was dark by then. There were some streetlights at the little park to the right. I could see them when they stopped the boat. And the city was all lit up at the left end of the bridge."

"That was after the sunset?"

"Yes," she moaned, handkerchief up to her eyes again. "They didn't take us over to the shore right away. And that's when they beat Jodie up so bad."

"After they brought you back through the channel?"

"Yes, but I don't remember getting back to the car." To Linda Hart, Fannie said, "Why can't I remember getting off the boat?"

"Did they hurt you, Fannie?" Hart asked.

"No. They just hurt Jodie!" Fannie cried, standing abruptly to pace a long circuit around the table. "They stopped the boat in the dark and turned off the lights. I remember seeing the bridge all lit up at night. And the orange lights at that little park, over at the far end of the bridge. That's when they dragged Jodie into the cabin and beat her."

"Did you actually see them hit her?" Lance asked, standing too.

"No, but I heard it. Oh, I heard it! And I wanted so bad to jump in the water and hide."

"But you didn't?"

"I can't swim."

"Did they just bring her out on deck and threaten you?"

"Yes! Oh. She was bruised. Had a bloody lip. She was crying, and they said they'd kill her if I didn't do what they asked!"

Lance embraced Fannie and then guided her back into a chair beside her lawyer. "Fannie, did they tell you right then what they wanted you to do?"

Interjecting, Hart said to Lance, "I want it reiterated, here, Detective, that Ms. Helmuth has agreed to speak only because the sheriff has stipulated that there will be no charges brought stemming from Fannie's involvement in any of this, either in Florida or in Ohio, or along the bus route between the two. That includes any criminal enterprise associated with the transportation of a suitcase given to her by Jodie Tapp, or arising from Fannie's associations with, or interactions with, either Jim or John and their associates, or with the woman to whom Fannie delivered Jodie Tapp's suitcase, or any of her associates."

Lance sighed. "You already have all that in writing, Linda."

Hart smiled. "I know you're taping these sessions, Pat. I like having it on the recordings."

Turning to Fannie again, Lance asked, "Did they tell you what they wanted you to do?"

"No, Jodie did that later," Fannie said, drying her eyes again. "Later that night."

"When, exactly?"

"In the parking lot. At that little park beside the water."

"So, you do remember getting off the boat?" Lance asked.

"Not really. I just remember that Jodie said they had let us go, and if I didn't bring an extra suitcase home on the bus, they'd find Jodie and kill her."

"Are you sure it was Jodie who told you that?"

"Yes. In the parking lot. She took a towel out of her trunk and knelt beside the water to wash the blood from her face."

"How did you get home?"

"Jodie drove me."

"Did you see Jodie the next day?"

"I didn't go to work. But the day after that, she came to the little cottage where I was staying. She looked terrible and had to wear sunglasses. There were bruises and cuts on her face. That's when she gave me the suitcase."

"Did you see John and Jim again?"

"No."

"Did you see Jodie after that?"

"No. I got on the bus that afternoon."

"Did you ever look inside the suitcase?"

"I was too scared, and Jodie said I shouldn't look."

"Where'd you keep the suitcase once you got home?"

"Under my bed."

"Do you know what happened to Jodie?"

"No," Fannie said, eyes spilling tears again. "I should have done something, but I was just too scared. Who's going to help her now?"

"That's the sheriff's job, Fannie," Hart said. "He's sending Detective Niell down to Pinecraft."

Lance finished writing and closed her notebook. To stop the recording that had been running, she flipped a switch mounted under the table. She pulled a tissue out of a box for Fannie and asked, "Can you stay, Fannie? We should take a break, but can you stay here today?"

Fannie nodded and said, "I can't go home, because that angry woman knows where I live. But I need to use the bathroom."

"No problem," Lance said, and rose. "You can stay with me today, and we'll sort this all out. I need you to tell me everything you can remember about the woman who met you for that suitcase."

Fannie nodded and said, "OK, but I'm hungry."

Lance smiled. "Then let's get something to eat. An early lunch at the hotel. We can walk there."

Hart stood too, and said, "You can tell them about Florida and Ohio, Fannie. You can tell them about the woman and the suitcase. They know you never looked inside the suitcase, and you have immunity from prosecution."

Seeming not to appreciate the importance of what her attorney had said, Fannie nodded to Hart and said to Lance, "I need to water my horse, too. I have a pail in my buggy."

* * *

Pat Lance helped Fannie fill her pail at a spigot under the exterior steps of the courthouse. Fannie carried the water around to the east side where her buggy was hitched to the rail, and Lance followed her to the buggy and back. Then the two stepped back into the jail next door.

In Robertson's office, while Fannie waited in the hall, Lance gave a summary of her interview and said, "We're going to the hotel, to get an early lunch."

"I saw that you were taping the session," Robertson said. "Can you post the file?"

"Sure. I went at it three different ways, but she doesn't remember anything useful about 'Jim and John.' I don't think she knows any more than she told me. They stopped the boat, turned out all the lights, pulled Jodie into the cabin, and beat her up. Then they turned them both loose at the parking lot of that little waterside park at the end of the bridge. Fannie never saw them after that."

"Did Jodie come in to work the next day?" Robertson asked.

"Fannie doesn't know. She didn't go to work herself."

"How'd she get the suitcase?"

"The day after that, Jodie brought it to her. Then Fannie came home on the bus. That same day. The second day after the sunset."

"So Jodie Tapp was afraid of them, too."

"I'm sure she is," Lance said. "Now that Ruth's been killed, it seems like she has good reason to be."

"The problem is," Robertson said, "she probably doesn't know yet that Ruth Zook has been killed."

15

Tuesday, April 5
11:40 A.M.

IN SUNLIGHT so bright that he was wearing shades, the sheriff
pushed out of his Crown Vic on the Zook driveway and sur-
veyed the orchestrated chaos of a determined federal invasion.
Inclined toward animosity for federal law enforcement agents,
Robertson made a quick count of strangers on the property and
concluded that the Zooks had captured the intense scrutiny of at
least a dozen feds, more if a significant number were hidden
from view inside the house. Amplifying the sheriff's ire, parked
in front of him on the driveway were two panel vans, one let-
tered EPA TOXIC WASTE ANALYSIS and the other, EPA HAZARDOUS
MATERIALS INVESTIGATIONS.

On the front porch, Alvin and Andy Zook stood in front of
three federal agents in green Windbreakers and green ball caps,
each sporting a prominent embroidered EPA logo. The Zooks
were dressed in plain Amish attire, and in their expressions and
body language, they were silently broadcasting the kind of mis-
ery that Robertson surmised could arise only from long hours of
immoderate federal interrogation.

Two more EPA agents in green Windbreakers pushed out
through the screen door on the front porch, each carrying an
evidence box sealed with EPA tape. Around the back corner of

the house, another agent appeared, carrying a similar box forward to the vans. And on the hill behind the largest barn, Robertson saw a black SUV pulling a wheeled gasoline generator over the crest, heading into the marshland below the Zooks' broken dam.

Robertson went up the porch steps purposefully, muttering dogged invectives against the federal intrusion. He pulled one of the EPA agents over to the corner of the porch and growled out in a stage whisper, "What do you think you're doing here?"

The agent took a business card from his jacket pocket, handed it to Robertson, and said, "This is a federal investigation. Who are you?"

Robertson took the time to study the business card, emblazoned with the EPA insignia, before he answered. ROBERT ANDREW WELLINGS, it proclaimed, along with a phone number and an e-mail address, printed above the EPA Web site URL.

"Wellings," Robertson said, "what do you think you're doing here?"

"And you are?" Wellings asked with the assurance of authority ringing in his tone. "And why are you interfering with a federal investigation?"

Robertson drew his wallet out of his hip pocket and displayed his badge card, saying, "Sheriff Bruce Robertson. This is my county. So, why didn't I get a heads-up on this?"

"We sent you a fax this morning," Wellings chimed.

"That's nothing more than a perfunctory notice. I mean why didn't I get the real word? That you've launched the invasion of a private household, as if you've discovered some *mega waste dump*?"

"This is a routine investigation, Sheriff, and . . ."

"This is an industrial-scale response to a minor spill, Wellings."

The agent squared up to Robertson's nose and poured out heat. "This is a crime scene, now, Sheriff. We're federal, and we have *all the authority* we need."

Wanting to berate a bureaucrat for his arrogance, Robertson

considered an impertinent reply, thought better of it, eased back a step, and said only, "You don't have any idea who it is that you're investigating, Wellings. These are Amish folk. They are no more involved in drugs than you are involved in *routine* investigations. You're gonna push too hard, here, and shut down any chance I had of learning how this all got started."

Undeterred, Wellings said, "This is federal, now, Sheriff. You've been notified. Please stay out of it."

Forcing himself into an unsatisfying calm, the sheriff said, "If you push too hard, Wellings, we'll lose a chance to roll up the creeps in Sarasota who are responsible for this. And we'll lose our chance to find out who killed the Zook girl. So, while you're testing soil samples in some D.C. laboratory, we'll be letting a murderer go free because of your lack of restraint."

"We brought our own laboratory, Sheriff. In a trailer. And we know about Amish people. So, we brought our own electric generator."

"You're missing my point, Wellings."

"I don't think I am."

"These aren't drug runners, Wellings."

"At the very least, Sheriff, there'll be assessments of environmental damage, cleanup expenses, and fines. Also, there may be criminal charges. State and federal. So, my duties here are clear. Assess the damage to our environment, and advise the agency in Washington on laws that have been broken."

"And the murder of an Amish girl?" Robertson asked.

"That's not in my wheelhouse, Sheriff."

Robertson gave an impertinent smile. "You parked a mobile lab in the bottoms, Wellings?"

"And a generator."

"Then good luck with that," the sheriff said. He stepped down from the porch, eyeing gray skies to the west.

*　*　*

Standing beside his sedan, Robertson called Pat Lance's cell phone. When she answered, he asked, "Pat, are you still with Fannie?"

"Yes, we're at the hotel. I thought we'd go back to the jail after lunch, to talk some more."

"OK, listen. The EPA is out here at the Zooks'. They think they've got a major spill to investigate."

"Don't they?" Lance asked.

"That's not the point. We've got a murder investigation to run, and maybe we have a chance to shut down a pipeline for drugs coming up from Florida."

"I've been thinking about that," Lance said. "Fannie's in the bathroom, so I can talk. But if something like this happened both to Fannie Helmuth and to Ruth Zook, then maybe other girls have been coerced like they were."

"I know," Robertson said. "Plus, figure the bus company angle."

"How's that?"

"They've got bus companies running from Florida up to Indiana and Pennsylvania, too."

16

RICKY NIELL pulled into the driveway at the Byler farm on Township 166 and waved to John and Mahlon, who were on the front lawn working intently to hitch a white pony to a cart. Dressed in identical conservative outfits of muted denim, with black cloth vests and short-waist denim jackets, the two lads wrangled a bit into the mouth of their steed. Once finished, they ran the reins back to the pony cart they had hitched to the harness, stepped back to admire their accomplishment, and then came bashfully over to Ricky's black-and-white cruiser.

Ricky got out, punched the lock button on his key fob, and said, "Nice pony, boys."

Standing side by side at the edge of the driveway, the boys smiled back at Niell without speaking.

Ricky knew well not to expect much talk from the lads, but he tried another question. "Yesterday, when your grandpa sent you after that girl's horse and buggy, did you have to go far to chase it down?"

The older of the boys shook his head, but did not otherwise reply.

"Where did you find it?" Ricky asked. "I saw you go over the saddle between those two hills, but I didn't see you coming back."

Mahlon looked to John to provide an answer, and John said, "It was just the next farm over. Down in the valley, beside Troyer's shed."

Ricky waited to hear if there would be more, but clearly there wouldn't be. He looked around for others and said, "Is your grandpa here? I need to speak with him."

Both lads pointed toward the little Daadihaus beyond the curve in the driveway. Niell thanked them, got no reply, and walked up the drive to Mervin's little house. He climbed the worn wooden steps to the front porch and knocked on the door, urgently aware of the sheriff's haste, but knowing too that a good interview with Byler was going to take some time. Some Amish kind of time.

When Mervin answered the knock, he was holding an open box of Coblentz chocolates. He pushed out through the screen door and let it slap back against the jamb. Offering the box to Niell, he said, "I eat more of this than I should."

Ricky took a piece out of the center of the box and popped it whole into his mouth. "Coconut," he said, and sat in one of the rockers on the porch. Mervin sat beside him and took another of the chocolates from his box. He set the box on the gray porch boards between the two rockers, bit into the candy, and said, "Take more. I buy too much as it is."

"Is it always Coblentz chocolates that you buy?" Ricky asked. "Or are you more adventurous?"

Mervin smiled. "It's not the chocolates. It's the widow Stutzman."

"So, if she made baskets?"

"Then I'd have more baskets than I do right now. The problem is, I don't have much of a sweet tooth. Chips are better. And I favor Mug root beer. I'd really be in high clover if she made one of those."

"You said that's where you were headed, when you found the body. To Coblentz, in Walnut Creek."

"Yes, but I never got there. Found the body and called 911."

"That's what I need to talk with you about. Finding her body."

"If I never see something like that again, it will be too soon."

"But did you see anything that you've remembered since we talked yesterday?"

"I don't think so. What I saw was enough. Plenty enough."

"You didn't see a vehicle?"

"No."

"Maybe you remember hearing something."

"No."

A shout came from one of the lads out front. A harmony of laughter followed. Directly, the boys shot around the corner of the house in their pony cart, John holding a buggy whip lightly against the rump of the pony. Mahlon slapped the reins and drove the pony around the bend in the driveway. A thin pole fixed to the back of the cart waved over their heads, with a triangle of orange fabric flying at the end. Mahlon slapped the reins again, and the pony darted along the wide drive behind the house. They made the circuit around to the front and soon reappeared at the side where Ricky and Mervin could see them again. Faster now, the boys drove forward, rounded the bend balanced on one wheel, and shot around to the back, heading toward the barns beyond.

Niell and Byler watched them disappear behind the woodshop, and Mervin said, "I used to do that, when I was a lad."

Smiling, Ricky asked, "Have you always lived here?"

"No. I grew up over near Charm. But Leona and I built the big house, here, when we first bought the land. Now it's Daniel's, but our sons built us this cottage. So I guess that's fair. The old step aside to make way for the young. Anyways, I used to have a pony, too. When I was just a lad."

"When did you put that little phone booth in, out by the road?"

"I'm not sure who put that there," Byler answered circumspectly.

"It had to have been after you moved here," Ricky said.

"I can't watch the whole family, Detective. Not all the time."

"Maybe one of your sons installed the phone."

"Oh, it could be. Maybe, I suppose. I'm really not sure about it."

"Does your bishop approve of phones?"

Byler gave a wry smile. "I think he's making a study of the matter. Hasn't really decided, yet."

"What would you have done yesterday, if a phone weren't handy?"

"Oh, there are plenty of phone booths around. I'd have found one."

"Do you expect that your bishop will ever make a ruling about phones?"

"Not if he's clever," Mervin said.

"He'll stretch it out?"

Byler ate another chocolate with obvious satisfaction. "He's going to decide about the phones one at a time. Might not get to ours for a while."

"Clever man," Ricky said.

"He's the bishop. He's supposed to be clever."

Standing, Ricky said, "Thanks for the chocolate, Mervin. But are you sure you didn't hear anything yesterday morning? Maybe before you left for Walnut Creek?"

Byler stood with his box. "Like a gunshot?"

Ricky nodded.

"If I did, I don't remember it. Or I didn't understand what it was. There's a lot of noise on a farm in the mornings."

From the barns at the back, John and Mahlon ran their pony cart up to the rear of the house, hopped down laughing, and hitched the reins to a cast-iron post beside the back door. Still laughing, they scurried up the steps into the house.

Mervin watched them run into the house and said, "That's what Ruth Zook should have been doing yesterday morning, Detective. Having good fun with a white pony."

"I think she was a little too old for that," Ricky remarked.

Byler shook his head. "We're never too old to have fun with a pony."

17

IN A high-backed wooden booth at the restaurant in the Hotel Millersburg, less than a block west of the courthouse square, Pat Lance poured another cup of coffee for Fannie and said, "We should think about going back soon. The sheriff will probably want to talk with you again."

"But are you sure it's really that big an organization? Did Sergeant Orton say they were sure? That it's a big drug ring?"

"Yes, Fannie," Lance said. "They've been stealing boats for a couple of months. It's bigger than you knew."

With tears puddling over in her eyes, Fannie drew a hankie out of her little purse and dried her cheeks. "Why would they hurt her now? I gave them their stupid suitcase."

Lance let a moment pass and said, "Maybe the sheriff can tell us more."

"I think I should just run away. I think Jodie should run away."

Lance smiled. "Maybe you could hold off on that idea for a while."

Fannie smiled, too, grateful for the friendship.

Lance asked, "Can we talk with the sheriff again?"

Eyes dried, Fannie said, "I need to use the bathroom first."

Lance waited in the narrow lobby of the old hotel, standing beside the oak staircase to the second-floor rooms, then she escorted Fannie through the heavy walnut door to the sidewalk. They crossed Clay Street to the flagpole in front of the Civil War monument, and Fannie sat on one of the wrought-iron benches to tighten a shoelace.

Crossing over the lawn in front of the tan sandstone courthouse, Fannie remarked, "Sun is bright today," and Lance asked, "Do you miss Florida? The sun and beaches?"

"Not on days like this," Fannie said as they climbed the steps to the front entrance of the jail. "But I know northern Ohio weather. We get bright days like this only because some storm is brewing out west, and then we'll pay for it."

Behind the reception counter, Ellie sat at her desk in front of a wall of radio equipment. She looked pale to Lance, and the detective asked, "Still not feeling well?"

"Just in the mornings," Ellie said, smiling. "But don't tell Bruce."

"He's here?" Lance asked, returning Ellie's smile.

"He's still out at the Zooks'."

"OK," Lance said. "We'll just talk a little and wait for him. Interview B, when he gets here."

In the interview room across from the sheriff's office, Fannie dropped onto a chair at the end of the table and said, "Long day. I couldn't sleep last night."

Lance sat at the corner beside her. "When did you learn about Ruth Zook?"

"Yesterday afternoon. On the gossip mill. A neighbor lady drove by the Zooks' when deputies were carrying her suitcases out of the house. She said there were deputies searching the bottoms along 557, too. Below the pond, and around through the woods down there in the marshes."

"You knew by then that she had been shot?"

Fannie nodded wearily. "We got calls from the Byler phone. My brother has a cell phone. His wife told me Ruth Zook had been shot dead. Then the neighbor came over to say that she had seen the deputies at Zooks'."

"Did you meet them with your own suitcase at the same little turnoff where Ruth was found?"

"No. I did that closer to home."

"Did anyone tell you where to take it?"

"No. I picked the spot."

"How did you tell them about it?"

"I didn't. Jodie showed me a Holmes County map, and I marked it for her."

"Jodie told them? And she had a map down in Florida?"

"Yes. That was the same day she brought me the suitcase. Before I got on the bus."

"Then she must have told Jim or John."

"I'm not really sure about that. But she's the only person I told. I marked it for them, on Jodie's map."

Reaching under the interview table, Lance flipped on the switch for the room's recorder. "OK, tell me where it was. Where you met to hand over the suitcase."

"I met her on a hilltop just south of Charm."

"Can you describe her?"

Fannie closed her eyes to remember. "Short. Black hair, not so long. Kinda brownish skin. Stocky and strong. Eyes close together on a pudgy face. Got out of a little Buick sedan. It was old and gray and beat to pieces. And she had a silver gun."

"Did she threaten you?"

"No, but she let me see her gun. It was sticking out of her purse."

"Do you remember her license plate?"

Fannie opened her eyes. "No, I'm sorry."

"It's OK. Where did you meet her?"

"Up on the hills south of Charm. Right where 156 cuts into 19. There's a little gravel berm there, on the high ground. That's where I waited with the suitcase."

"Why'd you pick that spot?"

"It's isolated, remote, so no one would see us. I thought if I did a good job, nobody would hurt Jodie. Who's going to help her, now that Ruth Zook is dead?"

"The sheriff will send someone down to Pinecraft, Fannie. And Ruth wrote some letters home to Emma Wengerd. Maybe she told Emma something that'll help them in Florida."

Restlessly, Fannie pushed up from her chair and paced the length of the room once and back. Sitting down next to Lance, she asked nervously, "What now?"

"I want you to stay with me. Maybe sleep at my place for a while."

"Oh, I couldn't do that," Fannie said. "I'd be in the way."

"Really, Fannie, I think you should plan to stay at my place for a while."

"But why?"

"Maybe we're wrong," Lance said. "But if these drug runners are dangerous for you right now, you should stay with me."

"They'll come after me, now that I've talked?"

"Maybe."

"But why?" Fannie asked, crying again. "I don't really know anything."

"But you know too much. And you might remember something about Jim or John. Or about their boat."

"Or about the woman I gave the suitcase to?"

"Yes, and about her car."

"But I don't remember anything more," Fannie said, kerchief pressed again to her eyes.

"They don't know that, Fannie. Really, they have no idea what you've told us. Or what you'll remember. And if they've killed Ruth, then we've got to consider that they might try to kill you."

Crying softly with her hankie to her nose, Fannie asked, "Did I do the wrong thing? In coming here?"

"No," Lance said. "If you hadn't come here, you'd be home, where they could find you easily. You wouldn't know it, but they may be trying to find you right now."

Eyes shifting about, Fannie got up again and paced. "But I

wrote letters home, too. To my brother and his wife. So, what if these people know that? What if they think my brother knows something?"

"Maybe I'm just being too cautious," Lance offered.

"You don't really believe that, do you?"

"No. Not really. That's why I want you to stay with me for a while."

18

Tuesday, April 5
1:00 P.M.

CAL SEARCHED for Emma Wengerd in each of the three Zook barns, but he didn't find her. On a patch of barnyard gravel outside the massive doors of the largest barn, he turned in the sun and studied the back of the big house and the outbuildings, trying to guess where Emma might be. Typical of most Amish homesteads, the Zook farm offered many fine places to hide.

Beside the house, on a low knoll, there was a metal door that Cal knew covered a staircase leading into an underground fruit cellar. It'd be dark inside, Cal thought, but Emma might use a candle. He would check, but it had been a cold spring, and the fruit cellar still likely held the chill of a long winter. Other places were better to search first.

Next to the fruit cellar, set into the foundation stones of the house, he saw the exterior entrance to the house's basement, low-angled doors hinging up and over to the left and the right. There was another good place to check for Emma, but it would also be a cold place for her to sit.

Alvin Zook's little Daadihaus sat on a concrete pad adjacent to the Zooks' back door, and it was connected to the back porch by a breezeway with a grape arbor cover. Emma might be fond of spending time with her adopted grandfather, but he was inside the big house with the others, and Cal doubted Emma would be in his house alone.

A carpenter's shop beside the Daadihaus occupied a shed with a red metal roof. On the near side of the woodshop, there was an angled exhaust pipe with a mound of wet sawdust lying on the ground underneath its wide aluminum vent. Between the house and the driveway, the Zooks had a swing set, a sandbox, and a green-padded trampoline. A sand-carpeted volleyball court sat on the opposite side of the driveway. Other than the three barns, which Cal had already searched, the only remaining structure above ground was a wood-framed garage attached to the side of the largest barn behind him.

Cal entered the garage through tall doors that had been swung out and propped permanently open. The doors lay back flat against either side of the entrance, held in place by unfinished four-by-four poles set fast, with each of their ends anchored in the dirt and the other ends nailed to the top of the wood of the hinged doors. The rusty metal roof of the garage was high enough to make room underneath for the Zook family buggies, but nothing taller.

To let his eyes adjust, Cal stopped several paces inside the dim interior of the garage. There was a kerosene lantern hanging from one of the uprights supporting the roof, and he considered lighting it. But he heard soft crying from a back corner and decided he could best start his conversation with Emma without the intrusion of the lantern's light. He called out, "Emma?" and walked toward the sound of her crying.

In one far corner, there was a long buggy with two seats and a large cargo bay at the back. He found Emma sitting there alone, on the covered rear cargo deck, with her legs hanging over the side. In light so dim that his eyes still hadn't adjusted, he saw only the vaguest outline of Emma's oval face, framed by her bonnet and shawl.

Standing a few feet back from her, Cal said, "I've been looking for you," and he saw Emma's head move side to side in a slow-motion rejection that told him silently what he had hoped he wouldn't find.

Slowly he approached her, saying, "Have you been crying?" but she pushed back from her edge seat, scooted farther into the buggy's cargo bay, and disappeared completely from Cal's view.

Thin blades of light shined through slits between the rough-hewn slats of the garage walls, but it wasn't enough light for him to see even the outline of her inside the flat-black buggy. Cal knew she was still there only because the buggy hadn't rocked on its strapped metal springs as much as it would have if she had climbed down through a side door.

"Emma," Cal said to the darkness. "It's OK if you've been crying."

Emma said nothing, so Cal turned around and sat back against the rear ledge of the buggy, facing away from her. With neither of the two speaking, a long moment passed as Cal's vision began to adjust to the darkness. With his silent reserve, Cal hoped again to earn her trust. As Emma settled in behind him, he felt the lightweight buggy rock on its springs. He wanted to speak, but he knew he shouldn't. So he chose the response of wordlessness, and his eyes began to pick out the details of the buggy parked in the corner beside Emma's.

Ten minutes passed, maybe more, by Cal's estimation, and he sat as still and as quietly as he could manage. Then with the faintest of whispers—as if the breath of her song shouldn't stir even the flame of a single candle—Emma began to recite the words of a martyr hymn Cal recognized from the Amish *Ausbund* hymnal. With little audible sound and no discernible movement, Emma's whispering seemed to Cal to be the voice of goose down sprinkled on a breeze, recognizable as an Amish martyr hymn only because of its slow cadence of heartache and loss. He listened through the hymn, and still he didn't speak. When the whisper of another hymn came to his ears, he listened with his eyes closed in the dark.

When Emma was finished with the second hymn, the buggy shifted on its springs, and Emma whispered behind Cal's ear, "Those were Ruth's favorite hymns. She sang them to me in her bedroom, Sunday night."

Without turning to her, Cal said, "Tears are prayers, Emma."

Pulling back, Emma said, "I'm not crying. And I don't pray anymore."

Cal stood and turned to face Emma in the dark. "It's OK," he said. "You're supposed to be sad."

"I'm not crying," Emma said again. "I won't ever cry again."

"OK," Cal said, "but come talk with me for a little while."

"I don't want to see you," Emma whispered.

"Then here in the dark is a good place for us to talk," Cal said. "You don't have to look at me."

He turned around to sit again on the back ledge of the cargo bay, and again the buggy shifted under him as Emma moved closer. "Sit here on the end," he said. "We can sit in the dark and talk."

Close to his ear, as if she were on her hands and knees behind him, Emma whispered, "Does anyone know where I'm at?"

"No," Cal said, "just me."

"I don't want them to know that I come here."

"They don't know, Emma. And I won't tell them."

"They're not my real family."

"I know."

"I haven't seen Ruth's body. So I don't really know that she's gone."

Cal waited a beat, then said, "You'll see her at the funeral."

"I won't look at her. I can't."

"That's OK," Cal said. "No one says you have to."

"The Zook kids say I do."

"Not if you don't want to."

Emma came forward and sat next to Cal, with her legs hanging over the back ledge.

Without turning to the side to face her, Cal said, "Emma, we want to find out who killed Ruth."

"Why?"

"It's important."

"Not to me."

"You're stronger than you realize."

"I don't cry anymore."

"I know. And you don't have to. Not right away. But when you do, I think it will help you."

"I don't need any help."

"OK, but instead, maybe you could help us."

Hesitating, Emma asked, "How?"

"The sheriff wants to read the letters that Ruth wrote home to you."

"They're private."

"I know, but if we can read them, it will help."

"They are all I have left of her. I couldn't give them to anyone."

"You can carry them, Emma. I'll drive. And we can tell the sheriff that all he is allowed to do is make copies."

"Does that ruin them? The copy part?"

"No. They lay them flat, and only the light touches them. They're like photographs."

"We are not permitted to make any graven images. No photographs."

"I know, but these aren't people. They're only objects. We won't be taking any photographs of people."

"Will I get them back?"

"Of course. You can stand beside the copy machine. You don't have to let anyone take them away from you."

"Some of them might be smeary. Someone might have cried on them, but nobody knows that."

"God sees all our tears, Emma."

"I don't cry anymore."

"I know."

"I missed her so much. I couldn't wait for her to come home from Florida. Then when she did, she was so sad."

"You said that she cried. The night that she came home."

"Both nights," Emma corrected. "Saturday and Sunday. But she wouldn't tell me why. I slept in her bed, and she sat up in her rocker."

"I thought she came home on Friday night."

"Yes, but I was already asleep. I sat with her Saturday and

Sunday, but when I woke up Monday morning, she was gone, so I should have stayed up with her Sunday night, too. I should have sat with her all night."

"How could you have known?"

"I was supposed to know. I should have gone with her Monday morning. But I fell asleep while she was singing those hymns. She must have cried all night. She wouldn't let me tell anyone about it. I'm the only one who knew that."

After a long pause, Cal said, "This is a good place to talk."

"It's secret," Emma said. "No one else can know."

Turning in the dim light to face her, Cal said, "I won't tell anyone about it, but can we talk like this again?"

"I don't know."

"Maybe it would be OK if I look for you here? Maybe another time?"

"I don't know. Maybe."

"OK for now." Cal smiled. "How about if we take those letters to the sheriff?"

"In your car?"

"Yes, but it's a battered old carpenter's truck."

"I've never ridden in one."

"In a truck?"

"Anything at all," Emma said, shaking her head. "All I've ever ridden in is buggies."

19

AFTER AN interview with the sheriff, Fannie rode with Pat Lance south and east around the curves and over the rises in the little hill-country burg of Charm, a curious mix of houses, businesses, and restaurants stretched out along the slopes overlooking blacktopped 557. At Township 369, Fannie directed Lance northward, and they crested the hills behind the sleepy town. A right on Township 371 took them to the Helmuth farm on the north side of the road, with the main house set back nearly a hundred yards. Lance slowed to turn into the drive, but Fannie cried out, "It's her!"

Lance straightened her wheels immediately and looked down the drive as she rolled her cruiser slowly past the turn-in to the farm. She caught the briefest glimpse of people gathered on the front porch and of a car on the drive.

Driving east for another two hundred yards, Lance turned around in the drive of the next farm. She came back slowly to have a look up Fannie's drive, and as they approached, Fannie crouched beneath the level of her window, wrung her hands and whispered, "That's the lady! That's her car. That's Jonas on the porch."

In front of Fannie's house, an old gray Buick sedan was

parked with its front end pointed out toward the road. There's no front plate, Lance thought, and continued along TR 371.

"That's my family talking to her," Fannie whispered, still crouched low in her seat. "That's my brother Jonas and his wife. Now she knows my whole family lives there. We've got to go back."

"We can't, Fannie," Lance said. "She's looking for you."

Lance keyed her radio mic and called in to the jail. "Ellie, we've got a problem."

A scratching of static preceded Ellie's response. "Go ahead."

Lance reported, "I'm on TR 371, a quarter mile east of TR 369. We just passed Fannie's farm. Send two units, Ellie. They've gotten a visit from the woman who met Fannie for her suitcase. She's there right now, Ellie, and she's a suspect in the murder of Ruth Zook. I couldn't stop to help."

"OK, what's your twenty?"

Lance gave her the farm number and said, "But we can't stay out here. Put the sheriff on. We need to guard Fannie."

"Have you got a cell signal?" Ellie asked.

Lance stopped, pulled her phone off her belt, checked the display, and said on the radio, "It looks like it's a good connection."

"I'll have him call you," Ellie said, and switched off.

Lance continued on to the intersection with TR 369. There she turned north toward Ohio 39. Robertson phoned her, and she answered as she drove faster over rolling countryside.

"Fannie's still with you?" the sheriff asked.

"Yes. We couldn't stop to help."

"But are you sure it's the right woman, Lance?"

Lance asked Fannie, and Fannie nodded, "And she had the same car."

"Yes," Lance said into her phone. "I've got confirmation of the woman and the sedan. A gray Buick."

"Did you get a plate number?"

"No front plate, Sheriff."

"Then bring Fannie here, Lance. To the jail."

"Ten minutes," Lance said. "Are we going to keep this quiet?"

"We're not gonna broadcast it," Robertson responded. "But they need to know that they can't get to her."

Lance switched off and drove faster over the blacktop. The road rose and fell, twisted and turned, and traversed a pastoral countryside with large farms, wooden fences, and tall red barns. The peacefulness belied the worry in Fannie's eyes.

Focused forward, Fannie asked, "Why don't you care if she knows where I'm at?"

"The jail is the safest place to guard you, Fannie. She'll know that she can't get to you anymore. If we keep you at the jail, she'll know it's useless for her to try."

"They can't get in the jail?"

"We'll guard you, Fannie. No one will be able to get to you."

"Really, Detective Lance, I think it'd be better if I hide in the country, you know, with people I know."

"The jail is better," Lance said, focusing on the road.

"Jails make me nervous," Fannie muttered, but Lance gave no reply.

"Will I have to sleep and eat there?"

"For a few days, Fannie, yes. At least until we've got them—her and all her people—in custody."

"Should I call my brother? It's really his house that she's at."

Lance drove past the boxy white Troyer Ridge schoolhouse at TR 368 and handed her phone to Fannie. Fannie keyed in a number and waited. When she was connected, she said directly, "That English woman's not safe, Jonas. She's trying to find me."

When she handed the phone back to Lance, Fannie said, "They've already figured that out, Detective. She slapped Jonas's wife on the face."

* * *

At the Helmuth farm on TR 371, Ricky Niell followed Stan Armbruster's cruiser down the long potted driveway with their light bars set to flash and strobe, sirens switched off. They pulled to a stop in front of the Helmuths' porch and scrambled out of their cars. A woman in Amish attire held the front door open for them, and they ran up the porch steps, Armbruster keying his shoulder mic to say, "We're here, Sheriff. No Buick, though."

At Ellie's radio console, Robertson bent over to push the switch on the microphone stand and answered, "Secure the location, Stan. I'll have more people there in five minutes, maybe less."

Inside, Ricky pulled the four adults aside and asked, "Has she left?"

A younger man stepped forward and answered, "Yes. Just before you got here. She hit my wife."

Beside him, a middle-aged woman in Amish-plain dress stood holding a wet hand cloth to her cheek. Niell asked to see her cheek, and she took the washcloth down to reveal a red welt under her right eye.

"It looks like she backhanded you, Mrs. Helmuth," Ricky said, and the woman nodded silently, a fatalistic resignation to violence showing in her expression. She put the cold cloth back over her cheek and stepped behind her husband.

Turning back to Jonas, Ricky asked, "Did you notice her license plate number?"

"No," Jonas said. "We didn't pay any attention to her car."

Armbruster keyed his mic again and said, "Ellie, post a unit on 557 north of Charm. South, too, as soon as possible. We're looking for a gray Buick sedan, woman driving. But wait, Ellie."

To the men, he asked, "What was her hair color?"

"Black," Jonas said, "and short."

"Short black hair, Ellie," Armbruster said into his mic. "We just missed her."

Ricky asked, "Do you have a basement?"

The oldest man, a grandfather, Ricky judged, answered with a nod and said, "The stairs are off the kitchen."

"Then take the children down there, and don't open the door unless it's a deputy knocking."

The two women ushered the kids toward the kitchen at back. Eyes cast to the floor, Jonas said, "We have no locks on our doors."

Ricky nodded, not surprised, and said, "Take the back door, Stan." Armbruster followed the family along a narrow hall toward the back of the house and into the kitchen.

Once they had descended the steps and Armbruster was in the kitchen, Ricky called out, "OK?" and Armbruster shouted back, "Got it."

"Please go downstairs with the others," Ricky said to Jonas and the older man. "Block the basement door with something heavy."

Grandfather Helmuth complied without speaking, but Jonas stood his place, reproachfully passing judgment on his circumstance. Passing judgment, Ricky assumed, on all English harmfulness.

"Please, Jonas, go with the others," Ricky said, and Jonas turned wordlessly for the kitchen stairs.

At the front door, Ricky shouted back, "I'm on the front door, Stan, and you're on the back."

Armbruster shouted back, "There's no gray Buick, Ricky," and Ricky thumbed Robertson's speed-dial number on his cell phone, with his pistol out in his right hand.

Again, Armbruster shouted from the back kitchen. "No cars behind the house, Ricky," and while his call to the jail rang through, Niell shouted, "Stay put, Stan. Nobody gets past you."

"Done," Armbruster said, not bothering to shout anymore.

"And don't let anyone up from the basement just yet," Ricky answered.

*   *   *

Pacing indignantly behind his desk, Robertson complained to Captain Newell, "I can't spare the people, Bobby. This woman's out driving on my roads, and if we don't find her in the next five minutes, she'll be long gone, and there's nothing I can do about it. And we can't really guard all the Helmuths out there. Our resources have got to go toward protecting Fannie."

"At least leave a deputy there," Newell argued, "with a black-and-white parked in the driveway."

Still pacing, Robertson punched up Ricky's cell number.

When Niell answered, Robertson asked, "How many do you have, now, Ricky? To guard them, I mean."

"Three units, Sheriff. Four deputies."

"OK, leave one unit there for Armbruster. Park it on the drive where it'll be conspicuous. Then get everyone else back here."

"What if she comes back looking for Fannie?" Ricky asked.

"If she sees that cruiser parked on the drive, she won't come anywhere near the place."

"I should stay, Sheriff," Ricky offered.

"No, Ricky. Stan can handle things there, until I get more people called in for an extra shift. Otherwise, I'm putting out everyone we've got, patrolling for this Buick."

"What do you want me to do?"

"Come back to the jail, Ricky. I need you to go down to Florida."

20

Tuesday, April 5
5:15 P.M.

SHERIFF ROBERTSON was pacing again behind his cherry
desk, frustrated by the tangled knot of his problems.

Ruth Zook in the morgue.

Fannie Helmuth in protective custody.

EPA on his turf.

Jodie Tapp, most at risk. Most exposed.

Ricky Niell to Florida.

The woman in the gray Buick.

Bobby Newell was sitting up in a straight-backed chair in
front of the desk, hoping to calm the sheriff. He watched Robertson's frustration mount and decided on a series of gentle questions. First he asked, "Is Cal Troyer still going to try to get those
Ruth Zook letters for us?"

After a distracted pause, Robertson said, "Yes," and dropped
heavily onto his swivel rocker. "But I've got something in mind
that Cal isn't going to like very much."

"Something concerning the letters?"

"Yes."

"And is Ricky coming back from the Helmuths', but he also
talked again with Mervin Byler about finding the Zook body?"

"Yes to both questions," Robertson muttered, struggling for
a happier equilibrium.

"And Pat Lance is bringing Fannie Helmuth here, from her brother's farm out near Charm?"

"Yes again," Robertson said. Still frustrated, he popped out of his chair. "I need to call Mike Branden. Tell him Ricky's coming down there."

Newell stood and retreated to a west-facing window. Robertson advanced from behind his desk, stepped to the coffee credenza, and asked the captain, "Decaf?"

"No thanks," Newell said, and let a moment pass before asking, "Is there anything other than Fannie that connects this woman to the Zook murder?"

Abandoning his pot of coffee, Robertson returned to stand behind his desk and said, "I had lunch with Missy. She was only halfway finished with her autopsy of Ruth Zook's body. She says there's nothing there that we can use. Ruth died of a gunshot wound to the forehead. So far, there's nothing else in the autopsy that can help us. And there wasn't anything on the exterior of her body."

"You'd expect something to have been left there," Newell said. "Fibers, prints, residues."

"Well, there was cocaine on her hands and her knife. But Missy says the horse obliterated everything else that might have been usable. She also says it'd be unlikely that there was anything there, anyway. Zook just met someone in that clearing, and they shot her. End of story."

"We still have the tire track moldings that Pat and Ricky made," Newell said as Robertson sat again.

"A Humvee," Robertson said, elbows forward on his desk. "Has to be about a thousand of those in Ohio."

Ricky Niell had appeared at the sheriff's open door. "Stan found some more tracks," Ricky said, casting a glanced at Newell. "Before I left the Helmuths' place. They said the woman pulled her car in and backed around. Stan found her tire tracks where she ran off the gravel. We made impressions."

"We can use that," Captain Newell said, returning to the front of the sheriff's big desk.

"That's good, Ricky," Robertson agreed. "If it really was an older Buick, then maybe those are aftermarket tires. Not originals. So, we can trace that purchase."

"I saw Rachel Ramsayer in the squad room," Ricky led.

Robertson nodded and seemed to regain some focus. "She's installing new desktop systems."

"She could help develop a search strategy," Ricky said. "We've got access to all the databases."

"That'd be good," Robertson said. "And you can get a better description of this Buick woman from Fannie Helmuth."

"We also should send a sketch artist out to the Helmuth farm," Newell said.

"Has Lance made it back here with Fannie Helmuth?" Robertson asked Ricky.

"They're in the squad room, too," Ricky said and sat in front of the desk.

Newell sat beside him, tenting his fingertips in front of his lips to say, "They probably don't have electricity at the Helmuth farm."

"They don't," Ricky said. "Just kerosene lamps."

"OK," Newell said. "We'll just go old school out there. Send a sketch artist with a pad, pencil, and eraser."

"Rachel's good at this sort of thing," Robertson said to Ricky. "I mean here at the jail, with facial recognition software. We could get a second description here from Fannie."

"I'll set it up," Ricky said, rising to leave.

"Wait," Robertson said, motioning for Ricky to reclaim his seat. "I want to call Ray Lee Orton while you're still here."

"Is this the Florida trip?" Ricky asked. "Because I'll need help beyond what Orton can give me."

"Mike Branden is already down there," Robertson said. "I'll call him first."

While Niell and the captain listened, the sheriff punched in Mike Branden's cell phone number, but got the professor's voice mail.

Rolling his eyes, Robertson waited for the message announcement to finish. To Ricky and the captain, he said, "They're probably out on the beach."

Ricky started, "You can just push . . . ," but Robertson cut him off with an outward palm. "OK, Mike!" he said into the phone. "Bruce. We need your help, if you can pull yourself back to the real world for five minutes. Fun, sun,—I know, all of that. But call me, OK?"

As Robertson set his phone on his desk, Newell quipped, "Cute, Bruce. You're so good at sweet talk."

"Give me a break!" Robertson barked. "It's just Mike."

"This Jodie Tapp," Ricky said. "I'll have to interview her and all of her friends down there. And all of her coworkers."

The sheriff agreed and asked, "Did you talk with Emma Wengerd?"

"Tried to. She ran off when I tried to see her."

"You scared her off?" Robertson shot.

"She ran off," Niell bristled. "They said she doesn't like to talk to people. Said it'd be useless to try to find her."

"Then it's up to Cal," Robertson said. "Maybe he'll do better."

"What'd you want me to do, Sheriff? Chase her down?"

"No, sorry. She's a strange girl is all. I just wanted the letters."

"She's adopted, right?" Newell interjected.

"Yes," the sheriff said. "But I don't like it that a young kid can stall us out like this."

Calmly, Ricky said, "Cal will get the letters, if anybody can."

"OK, what'd you get from Mervin Byler?" Robertson asked.

"He doesn't remember anything more," Ricky said. "He just found Zook and phoned us."

While the three men were still seated, Cal Troyer appeared at Robertson's door. The sheriff waved him in.

Stepping forward to Robertson's desk, Cal said, "I've got Emma Wengerd out front. I told her she could watch while we made copies of her letters. Then she wants them back."

"That's going to be a bit of a problem," Robertson said. "I want them tested for cocaine residue."

"I told her she could keep those letters," Cal said. "Do you really have to take them from her?"

Evenly, Robertson said, "They're evidence, Cal. We need to test them."

"I'd still like her to be able to keep her letters."

Robertson started, "I don't know . . ." but Newell interrupted. "We don't have to harm the letters, Sheriff. Missy can run a damp swab over the paper. It might smear a little ink, but that's about all."

Cal nodded a degree of satisfaction. "But Emma has to stay with her letters. She won't understand if we have to take her letters away from her."

Robertson rolled his eyes. "If you want to babysit her in Missy's labs, Cal, go right ahead. But Missy's gonna test the paper. And the envelopes. That's just how it is."

Cal circled around behind Niell and the captain to stand by a window, saying, "Ruth Zook didn't handle any cocaine until she got home with that suitcase, Bruce. There won't be any residue on her letters."

"That's just what everyone is saying, Cal," Robertson argued. "But it's just one theory of this whole sorry mess. We have the letters, and I want them tested."

"You're fishing, Bruce," Cal complained.

"I don't think so," Robertson said. "We've only gotten one version of this. It's supposition and conjecture, nothing more. I just want to test another theory—that Ruth Zook knew what she was doing."

"Well, it's a bad theory," Cal said, moving toward the door. "I think you should reconsider. You're going to put Emma Wengerd through more heartache with this, and it's just a bad theory."

With his knuckles planted on his desk, Robertson said, "Look, Cal. I'm sending Ricky down to Florida. I've got a call in to Mike Branden. We're guarding Fannie Helmuth because some woman in a Buick is searching for her, and I've got guards out at the Helmuth farm. Then the EPA is crawling all over the bottoms, assessing damages 'to our environment' because they want to issue fines. Fines to an Amish family, for crying out loud! They've got a daughter to bury, and the EPA is pulling everything of hers out of their house. We've got Jodie Tapp to worry about down in Florida. Humvees and Black Talons, too. So, if I have to test a few pieces of paper to put my mind at ease, then that's just how it's got to be."

* * *

After leaving the sheriff's office, Ricky stepped down to Ellie's front counter. Ellie came out from her consoles and embraced him, saying, "You have to go to Florida?"

"Yes," Ricky said, pulling her close. "But Mike Branden is already down there, and he can help."

"The last time you two were down there, he had to fish you out of Sarasota Bay."

"I know," Ricky said, releasing her. "But if we can't find this Buick woman here in Ohio, we'll have to figure this all out down in Florida. It's the right move. Bruce is just being thorough."

"I don't like it, Ricky."

"It's what I'd do, Ellie. If I were sheriff."

"And what, Ricky? You'll be back before I know it?"

"Something like that. I'll call each night, but will you be OK in the mornings?"

"Yes, but don't tell Bruce anything. I'm not yet ready to deal with him."

* * *

In the squad room at the other end of the first-floor hallway, Rachel Ramsayer was finishing her late-afternoon installation of a new desktop system for the deputies. As Ricky crossed the room to her, she pushed off her chair and said, "A woman in a gray Buick? That's all I've got to work with?"

Ricky pulled a chair out for her and sat down at a long roster table. She climbed up onto the chair beside him, and he said, "We have more now. Stan found her tire tracks at the Helmuths' farm."

"So, that gives us a tread pattern for the Buick," Rachel said.

"Yes," Ricky said, "and it's an old car. So there's a good chance that they're not the original tires."

"Aftermarket treads," Rachel said. "That'd be good. Easier to identify and trace. Or at least there won't be as many matches as there would be with originals. Originals would all be the same tire."

"Also," Ricky said, "Fannie Helmuth can give us a description for the facial recognition software."

"Even better."

"And we're sending a sketch artist to the Helmuth farm. They'll give us a description, too."

"Also, I've been thinking," Rachel said. "There ought to be some connection between this Buick woman and the owner of that Humvee. She's likely involved with whoever killed Ruth Zook."

"Maybe we'll get lucky," Ricky said. "Maybe this woman owns both an old Buick and a Humvee."

Scooting off her chair, Rachel said, "Pat Lance told me to tell you that Fannie's in the captain's office."

"Where's Lance?"

"She went to get Fannie some supper. We asked her what she wanted, and she piped right up, 'McDonald's!'"

*   *   *

Ricky walked into Captain Newell's office on the second floor of the jail. Fannie Helmuth wasn't there. He used Newell's desk phone to call Ellie first, and then Rachel, and neither one of them had seen Fannie.

Lance stepped into the office carrying bags of take-out food, and Ricky asked, "Where's Fannie?"

"I left her here," Lance said, and dropped the food on the captain's desk.

"Check the women's bathrooms," Ricky said, and Lance left to do that.

Next, Ricky called the sheriff's desk. "Sheriff, we're looking for Fannie Helmuth."

"Well, she's not here, Detective," Robertson said.

Lance came back shaking her head.

Ricky thought, and then said into the phone, "Sheriff, let's lock it down right now. Search the building."

"Done," Robertson said.

A determined forty-minute search of the jail, the courthouse, and the square did not produce Fannie Helmuth.

Outside the sheriff's west-facing windows, a sudden, heavy pelting of rain began an insistent thudding against the glass.

21

CHIEF DEPUTY Dan Wilsher paced in front of Ellie's counter at the front entrance of the jail. He had been giving her radio calls to make, placing checkpoints on the major roads leading out of Millersburg. They set cruisers first on Route 39, eastbound at Walnut Creek and westbound at Nashville, and on Route 62, northeastbound at Wilmot and southwestbound at Killbuck. While Ellie dispatched units on her radio, Wilsher pulled off his gray suit coat, threw it across the countertop, and called the Wayne County sheriff to the north, to ask for cooperation on Route 83 northbound, at Moreland, and on US 250 between Wooster and Mount Eaton.

Wilsher finished his call, switched off, pulled his tie loose at the neck, and asked Ellie, "What else? We've got every unit out looking, but what are we forgetting?"

Ellie kept her seat at her consoles and thought. "What about 83 south?"

"Millersburg PD is covering us there," Wilsher said.

Subdued, Ellie said, "We don't know that they actually came for her, Dan. It would have been foolish for them to have tried."

Wilsher had no reply, so Ellie added, "Ricky says her buggy is still parked on the other side of the courthouse."

As Ellie answered a dispatching call, a deputy in uniform pushed in through a wall of rain at the front door, lumbered out of his slicker, and shook it out over a floor tray under wall pegs to the left of the door. He took off his foul weather hat, drained water from the brim, and said to Wilsher, "She's not out on the streets, Chief. We've been up and down every street and alley for ten blocks all around, and she's just not out there."

Wilsher nodded. "I'd be surprised if she just walked out of here on her own."

"If she did," the deputy said, "she can't have gotten very far in this weather. So unless she's already inside somewhere, we should have found her."

"Did you check at the hotel?" Wilsher asked.

"First thing."

"OK, Dave," Wilsher said, "you dry out a little and then ride with Baker for a couple of hours. Check the lesser roads and gravel lanes between here and Charm. She lives with her brother out on TR 371. Also, try to figure out what we can do for her buggy horse."

As the deputy headed for the squad room at the back, Wilsher eyed Ellie ruefully and said, "This is a train wreck."

"You've boxed them in, Dan. Both this Buick woman and Fannie."

"Woman's long gone," Wilsher argued.

"Well then, Fannie, anyway."

"Fannie knows all the small roads. If she's still alive, she's run off on her own, or someone took her out of here. Either way, we're not going to find her."

* * *

Wilsher knocked on the sheriff's door, entered, and nodded to Captain Newell, who was seated again in front of Robertson's desk. To Robertson, Wilsher said, "Checkpoints are up and running, Bruce. I had to use Millersburg PD to put a unit on 83 south. And Wooster is helping to the north. But there's no Amish girl fitting Fannie's description, and no gray Buicks or Humvees out in this mess. I think we've lost the edge, here."

Lightning flashed at the windows, thunder clapped and rumbled to the west, and the rain pelted harder against the glass. Robertson waved Wilsher into a seat in front of his desk.

Newell said, "We've rechecked the jail and all of the courthouse. She's just not here, and Lance feels terrible. We never figured she'd walk away on her own."

"She must have, Bobby," Robertson said, drumming his thumbs on the top of his desk to dump anxiety. "I just can't believe anyone got to her inside the jail."

"Did she have a cell phone?" Wilsher asked.

"Lance says no," Newell said. "Fannie had to use Lance's phone to call her brother earlier today."

Robertson asked Newell, "Could she have made a call using the phone in your office?"

Newell frowned, said, "I'll check," and pushed up from his chair to leave.

Robertson stood, too, and called after the captain, "Check with Niell and Ramsayer in the squad room. They're tracking Buick owners with Goodrich aftermarket tires."

When Robertson had sat back down at his desk, Wilsher asked, "Do we still have Stan Armbruster out at the Helmuth farm?"

Absently, Robertson answered, "Yes."

His intercom chirped, and Ellie said, "Nancy Blain's here, Sheriff."

Wilsher arched an eyebrow. Blain was a photographer for the *Holmes Gazette*.

Robertson spoke into his intercom. "Send her in, Ellie," then said to Wilsher, "I asked Marty Holcombe if we could use her as a sketch artist again."

Blain, a short and slender woman with black hair in a pageboy cut, came into Robertson's office wearing black jeans, work boots, and a waist-length, light-blue Marmot rain shell with a hood. She pulled the wet hood off her head and said, "Marty says you need a sketch or two." To Wilsher she added, "Hi, Dan. Bad night out for your people."

Wilsher stood to offer his chair, and Blain laughed and said, "I'll just stand, OK?"

Wilsher sat back down with a mix of chauvinistic unease and embarrassment, and Blain smiled and said, "Thanks, but I'm not going to be here that long."

"OK," Robertson said. "I've got the Helmuth farm marked on this map." He handed Blain a folded Holmes County engineer's map and said, "Stan Armbruster is out there now. It's the older woman in a gray Buick who we're sketching."

"It's dark out there, Sheriff. I'll be working with kerosene lamps."

"Do the best you can," Robertson said, and Blain pulled her hood into place over her head and left.

Robertson came out from behind his desk and stood to gauge the storm outside his west windows. Behind the hard-pouring rain, gray gloom was pushing night forward like a curtain. Without turning from the windows, Robertson said to Wilsher, "Why would she just walk out of here?"

"We're not sure she did that."

"She didn't have a phone of her own, and there weren't ten people who knew we were keeping her here. Even if this Buick woman found out Fannie was here, she'd never have risked entry to try to get to her."

Wilsher shrugged. "What was Fannie gonna do here this evening, aside from sleeping at the jail?"

"Lance went to get her some supper, and Rachel was going to work with her on her computer, to render a sketch of the woman she gave her suitcase of drugs to. That's the same woman in the gray Buick she and Lance saw at her brother's farm this afternoon."

After a pause, Wilsher asked, "What do you need me to do?"

"Manage your patrol captains, Dan. Everybody puts in overtime on this one, and double the shifts."

Wilsher rose and said, "By the way, I think you should reposition Armbruster."

"Oh?"

"Instead of right at the house, I'd have him park his cruiser at the end of the long drive, so he could watch the front road better."

"Sensible," Robertson said, distracted.

"Anything else?" Wilsher asked at the door.

Robertson turned from the window and ran a palm over the bristles of his hair. "No, Dan. I'm gonna call Chester, to see if he can take me this late, so I'll be down at his shop for a half hour or so."

"You'll be on your cell?"

"Of course. And Dan. If we haven't found Fannie by the morning, pull everybody in. Rachel will have to solve this with her database searches, or Ricky will have to solve this down in Florida."

Wilsher shook his head unhappily and left.

At his intercom, Robertson said, "Call Stan, Ellie, and tell him Nancy Blain is coming out to get sketches of that woman. Also, tell him to park his cruiser at the front end of the Helmuths' drive, out by the road."

Then he phoned Chester's barbershop.

* * *

Bobby Newell found Rachel working at a computer in the duty room, and he asked her, "Do you have everything you need?"

Rachel fanned through several photos of the tire tread moldings that Armbruster had made at the Helmuth farm, and said, "It's an older Buick fitted with Goodrich 215s, so that's all I need, at least to start with."

"You know that's the right tread pattern?"

"Definitely," Rachel smiled, tapping the screen. "I just made the match, and now I'm running a cross search for Goodrich 215s and older gray Buicks, covering all of northern Ohio."

"What about Humvees?" Newell asked.

"Once I get a list of the Buicks, I'll cross-check registrations for those, to see if anyone owns both."

"And that'll do it?"

"Can't be sure."

Two deputies came in through the jail's back entrance. Dripping water from their slickers, they stood in the hall at the door to the duty room. One reported to Newell, "Nothing yet, Captain."

"OK," Newell said. "You two get some coffee and try to dry out a little. But get back out there in about twenty. It's gonna be a long night."

*   *   *

In a dark pounding rain that made the streetlights seem anemic, Robertson splashed three blocks on foot to Chester's shop and pushed in through the old glass-fronted door. The barber's pole over the sidewalk wasn't turning, but the inside bell over the door chimed, and soon Chester came forward from the stairwell at the back of his barbershop, switching on ceiling lights.

There were three barber's chairs along the left wall, but only Chester cut hair there anymore. His only customers were older men who didn't want styles, hairdos, or specials. Chester just did simple cuts with an ancient pair of electric clippers, and he always finished his work with scissors and a straight razor. He lived in an apartment over the shop, and if Chester cut only ten heads a week it didn't matter, because he owned the half-block, two-story building, and he derived a suitable retirement income from his renters.

Robertson pulled off his long black raincoat, draped it over one of the customers' chairs along the opposite wall, hung his rain hat on a wall hook, and sat back wearily in Chester's tall chair.

Chester didn't speak at first. He knew the fifties-style flattop the sheriff wanted, and he began by waxing up the sheriff's gray hair to take the level cut.

Eventually Robertson sighed and Chester asked, "Tough day at the jail, Sheriff?"

Robertson grunted. "I could use a smoke, Chester."

"I've got some, if you really want one."

"No," Robertson laughed. "Missy'd take me apart if she smelled tobacco on me."

"Suit yourself, but what's going on up at the jail?"

Robertson took his time and started with the discovery of Ruth Zook's body, the fish kill below the Zooks' broken dam, and the appearance and disappearance of Fannie Helmuth. He could discern no new revelation while giving his account, but as usual he found talking to Chester cathartic.

Characteristically, Chester listened without speaking. When he had the sheriff's hair finished, he laid the chair back and lathered Robertson's face for a shave.

Halfway through the shave, Robertson's cell phone rang, and he answered the call as he reclined in Chester's chair. He listened, barked a sarcastic "Great," asked a few quick questions, and switched off.

"More trouble?" Chester asked, and took a stroke with his razor through the white lather under the sheriff's chin.

Robertson closed his eyes and chuckled with a mix of ire and defeat. "That was Nancy Blain. I sent her out to the Helmuths' to get a sketch of the woman who is hunting for Fannie Helmuth."

"There was a problem?" Chester asked.

Robertson blew out a long, frustrated lungful. "The Helmuths told her that one of the Ten Commandments forbade their making any graven image."

"They wouldn't give you a sketch of the woman?"

"No. Sketches, photographs, statues, drawings, paintings of people—it's all the same to them, forbidden. Or so they told Blain."

"So you've got no way to identify the woman who's behind all of this," Chester said.

"Right," the sheriff said. He pushed out of Chester's chair, the barber's apron spilling clippings onto the floor, half the sheriff's face still lathered.

Chester put a hand on the big sheriff's shoulder, guided him back into the barber's chair, and said, "At least let me finish your shave."

As he reclined, Robertson complained, "There's nothing I can do. All my people are working this, and we're coming up with nothing. There's nothing I can do, and it's driving me nuts."

"More nuts than you usually are, Sheriff?" Chester laughed.

Mirthlessly, Robertson said, "Chester, you have no idea."

22

Tuesday, April 5
8:10 P.M.

WHEN THE sheriff stepped out of Chester's barbershop, it had stopped raining. The night air was cool and damp like a wet cloth on Robertson's shaved face, and the mist and fog lifting off the wet sidewalk seemed to penetrate his coat and hat like a cold bath.

Water coursed in the gutters, carrying sticks, leaves, and street debris down to the storm drains, which rattled with the surge of runoff into their grates. On the wet pavement, the streetlights and traffic signals cast an impressionistic splash of colors, which looked surreal to the plain-talking sheriff. As surreal, the sheriff thought, as an Amish girl's suitcase full of cocaine.

At the front counter of the jail, Ed Hollings was already working the consoles for the night shift, and Robertson asked, "Ellie's gone home?" as he came through the front door.

"She and Ricky, both," Hollings said. "They're packing a bag for him, for a ten a.m. flight."

Robertson went directly down the hall and climbed the rear stairs to the second floor, where his captains had their new offices. Dan Wilsher was in the chief's long corner office at the far end of the hall from Newell's south corner office, and when the sheriff appeared at the chief's door, Wilsher typed a few finishing strokes on his keyboard and said, "Patrols are running smoothly, Bruce. No luck."

"Double shifts?" Robertson asked, sitting in a corner chair.

"Yes, and everybody's been worked into the rotations. I sent Baker out to relieve Armbruster at the Helmuth farm, because Stan's been at this the longest today. I think Pat Lance needs to take some time, too. But everybody else is six on, and four off, and we're using empty cell beds to sleep at the jail."

"And nothing on Fannie Helmuth?"

"No. And no gray Buicks."

"If they took her out of here, Dan, they were past our checkpoints before we even knew she was gone."

"I know. But I think it's possible that she got rattled by the thought of staying here and figured a way to take off on her own."

"Then why didn't she take her horse and buggy?" Robertson asked.

Wilsher shrugged, unable to mask his pessimism, and Robertson frowned and left.

In the duty room on the first floor, Robertson walked up to the computer desk where Rachel and Pat Lance were working, and he asked Rachel, "This the database search?"

Rachel nodded. "It's almost finished. Two hits so far on older Buicks with Goodrich tires."

To Lance, Robertson said, "Can you let this run, Pat, and go get some rest?"

Lance answered, "I'd rather see it through, Sheriff. It won't be much longer."

Robertson looked to Rachel, and Rachel said, "Same here. As soon as we've finished with the Buicks, I'll set up a search to match Humvee registrations in the same cities. That's the search we can run overnight. I'll monitor it from home. Get a couple hours' sleep while it finishes."

Robertson turned to leave, but Lance stood and caught his sleeve. "I'm sorry about Fannie," she said. "I shouldn't have left her alone."

"Don't worry," Robertson said. "If she had made up her mind

to leave, she could have done it any time. No one even thought it was possible."

"Still . . ."

"Get some rest, Lance. I'm going home, and you should, too. If we don't find her tonight, we'll figure this out in the morning."

Sitting back down beside Rachel, Lance said, "In a bit, Sheriff. I'll stay a little longer."

In the hallway outside his office, Robertson met Bobby Newell, who said, "I just left a note on your desk."

"You traced the recent calls on your office phone?"

"Yes, and I think she made two calls. The first was to Jonas Helmuth, her brother. It lasted over eight minutes."

"That's time enough to formulate a plan," Robertson said. "They must have talked this over."

"Second call was less than a minute," Newell said. "To Howard 'Howie' Dent."

"Someone she knows?"

Newell nodded. "He lives about a mile from the Helmuth farm. He's not home, and his car isn't there. His parents don't know where he went."

"How old is he?"

"Twenty-five. Lives at home and works the family farm with his folks. They say he's known Fannie since they were kids. You know, friends growing up on neighboring farms. We're looking for his car."

"Have you tried those numbers again? Jonas and Howie?"

"Repeatedly. They're both switched off."

"Great, Bobby. Just great."

"But she was less than a minute on the phone with Howie Dent, Sheriff. That's only enough time to tell him something, or to ask for help."

Robertson thought and scratched absently at the short bristles above his ear. "She called him to come get her?"

"Probably, but that's just a guess. We haven't talked with him yet."

"Foolish," Robertson commented.

"Maybe she thinks he can get her away from here safely."

"Has Dan given this to his patrols?"

"I just told him. Ed is making the radio calls now."

Robertson toed the floorboards, frustrated. "Dent's car, the Buick, and a Humvee. You'd think we could find one of them, Bobby."

"I figure the Buick is long gone," Newell said. "Never coming back. Same with the Humvee. We may find them, but not around here. But the Dent car is still plausible. It's a 2007 VW bug. Yellow. That's the one we'll find first. We know the plates."

* * *

In the kitchen at the back of their Victorian home, Missy helped the sheriff out of his wet raincoat and hat, and while he pulled off his suit coat, she hung his wet overclothes in the alcove behind the door. Still cold and wet, the sheriff sat to strip off his Florsheims.

In house slippers, he followed his wife into the parlor and took a seat in front of the fireplace. Missy put in more wood, arranged the stack to burn hotter, and sat on the divan beside her husband.

Robertson stared for a long time at the enlivening flames, not offering any conversation. Missy sat quietly beside him. After a suitable spell, she turned to him and said, "I see you were down at Chester's."

"I needed to think."

"Did he offer you a cigarette to help you think?"

"Not really."

"Am I going to have to go back down there?"

"No, Missy. I don't smoke anymore. You know that."

"It doesn't hurt to check."

"Chester's OK."

"If you say so."

More quiet time passed, and the fire burned down. Missy got up to add more firewood, and she asked, "You want some supper?"

"Is there any chicken left from last night?"

"I ate that."

"Maybe a bowl of cereal."

"Maybe hot oatmeal, Bruce," Missy said, sitting beside him again.

"Did you finish your autopsy?"

"For the most part."

"Anything new?"

"Not on the autopsy, but I tested Emma Wengerd's letters from Ruth Zook."

"No cocaine, I'd bet."

"None. They were clean. Cal drove Emma home just before I closed up for the night."

"Do you have anything we can use to identify Ruth's killer?"

"A mangled bullet and a brass casing is all I have."

"Fibers, prints, residues, skin cells, hairs?"

"Nothing, Bruce. The murder scene was just too compromised."

"Wouldn't make for a good TV show, Missy."

"Real cases rarely do. But if you can find Fannie Helmuth, she'd be a good place to start—you know, unraveling who shot Ruth Zook."

"You heard she's missing?"

"Everybody in Millersburg has heard that one, Sheriff."

"If she's not already dead," the sheriff said, "then I hope she's a thousand miles away by now."

The sheriff's cell phone chimed, and he checked the display. "Linda Hart," he said to Missy. "This is gonna be good."

Answering the call, he said, "We're looking for her, Hart. We're looking everywhere."

Then he alternately listened and answered.

"No, Hart. We think she got a ride.

"Howie Dent.

"Neighbor kid. We're looking for his car.

"No. No, his phone's switched off.

"Look, Hart, we'll find her.

"OK. No. OK, I will."

And he switched off.

Missy said, "Let me guess. Linda isn't happy."

The sheriff drew a breath. "An understatement."

The front doorbell sounded, and the two rose together to answer it. On the front porch stood Andy Zook and his father, Alvin, each with his wet felt hat pulled down against the weather, black wool shawls draped over their shoulders.

Andy stepped forward but did not enter the house when the sheriff held the door for him. Missy pressed forward onto the porch and said, "Mr. Zook, I still cannot release her body to you. We talked about this at the morgue."

The sheriff stepped out beside Missy. A sudden patter of rain sounded on the porch roof over their heads as a blast of wind blew water out of the overhanging trees. Then more steady rain fell, and the gloom of the night pressed in around them as a cloying mist, the dreariness enhanced in the Amish men's faces by the pale yellow glow of the porch lights.

"You see, Doctor," Alvin said, "tomorrow is a proper day for a funeral. We've already dug the grave."

"I know, Mr. Zook, but I just can't release the body. Not yet, anyway. Really, I can't even tell you now when I might be able to."

Andy Zook took a step back to stand with his father. Alvin asked, "But Doctor, is she being properly stored? Will she be OK when we get her?"

"Yes, Mr. Zook. She's in a freezer room. And I'll fix her forehead, like we talked about. I have the clothes you brought for her, and we'll have her dressed for you."

Alvin turned his eyes down. "We'll bring plenty of ice, when you let us have her."

"I know, Mr. Zook. And I'm sorry. But there's more to her murder than just her death. There's another girl who's missing."

"Fannie Helmuth?" Andy asked.

"Yes, Mr. Zook," the sheriff answered. "Do you know anything about her?"

"No."

"How about you, Alvin?"

"No."

"If you hear something, will you tell us?"

In unison, both men answered, "Yes."

Then for a long half minute, they stood looking at Bruce and Missy, as if they hoped more could be said to assuage their grief. As if more ought to be said to honor Ruth.

Missy cleared her throat and said, "We are so sorry for your loss, Mr. Zook. I'll do my best to get her to you as soon as possible."

When it was clear to them that there was little point in further conversation, the Zook men turned, walked down the porch steps into the rain, got into their buggy, and tapped the horse forward from the curb.

The sheriff stood rigid and dejected on the porch to watch the buggy disappear into the night. "I hate this, Missy," he said. "I hate it like you wouldn't believe."

"I know," Missy said at his side.

"But it's Fannie, too. And Jodie Tapp. There's a drug ring operating in my county, and I can't even protect a witness."

Missy stood silently beside her husband and let him glower into the night rain until his expression softened and he brought his eyes to hers. Then she hugged him, and they turned for the door and went inside.

As they were closing the front door, they got a call on their home phone. The sheriff answered it on the desk phone in Missy's front study.

Pat Lance said, "Sheriff, Rachel's search is finished, and it's going to be just those two hits we had earlier."

"The Buicks?" Robertson asked.

"Gray Buicks in northern Ohio, older models, with Goodrich 215s. Two hits. One over in Marion and the other up in Barberton."

"Nearby," Robertson commented.

"I'm going to drive to Marion tonight," Lance started.

"Negative, Lance. Call their local police departments. Get them to do a check. In the meantime, you get some sleep. We'll have our answers in the morning."

"I can handle the trip, Sheriff."

"No, Lance. We're all tired. You, Ricky, and Stan have been at this all day, and I know Ricky and Stan are getting some rest. You need to take some downtime, too, or you're going to start making mistakes."

Lance hesitated and didn't speak.

"Also," Robertson said into the phone, "Rachel's search for area Humvees will be available in the morning."

"Maybe much sooner," Lance argued.

"I don't care, Lance. Get some sleep. That's an order. In the meantime, half my department is out on the roads at any given time. We'll likely have found Howie Dent's car before the others, and I'll need you rested when we chase after Fannie Helmuth, wherever he took her. Ricky's going down to Florida, and that leaves you as my only detective."

Silence came again from Lance.

"Go home, Pat," Robertson said. "Come back fresh in the morning."

23

Wednesday, April 6
7:30 A.M.

STAN ARMBRUSTER found Howie Dent's yellow VW bug the next morning, parked in a spot at the back of the lot for the Sugarcreek Family-Style Amish Restaurant, a quarter mile east of Sugarcreek's large tourist hotel on Route 39. The little car was backed in next to a row of Dumpsters.

Armbruster had been out checking parking lots at hotels and motels since daybreak, and when he decided to switch to checking restaurant parking lots, too, this was the second one he had searched. He parked his truck crosswise in front of the VW and got out to try the doors. They were locked.

Through the windows, Armbruster could see nothing inside beyond the usual for a farmer's vehicle: a battered umbrella on the backseat, a pair of muddy black rubber muck boots on the floor behind the driver's seat, coffee cups with brown-stained lids in the cup holders, a John Deere ball cap draped over the gearshift, and a fifty-pound bag of chicken feed wedged in behind the passenger's seat.

Inside the big restaurant, Armbruster took a circuit around the tables and booths, but Helmuth and Dent weren't there. At the front counter, he waited in line beside a revolving display of religious books and Amish romance novels, and asked, when it was his turn, if the cashier remembered the pair, explaining about the yellow VW parked at the back of the lot.

The young woman behind the counter was dressed in plain Mennonite attire, her hair in a bun that was rolled up under a white lace prayer covering. As she slotted money into her cash register, she answered without looking up at the corporal, "My shift started at five thirty. They might have parked here last night."

"But why would they leave their car?" Armbruster asked.

She turned to him, smiled knowingly, and said, "Could have walked up to the hotel. Maybe didn't want anyone to know they were there?"

"I checked there earlier," Armbruster said. "They're not registered."

The cashier shrugged and glanced anxiously at the line behind Armbruster. "Sometimes they leave their cars here when they take the bus."

She handed him a brochure for the Sugarcreek-Sarasota Bus Company and said, "Next," to the couple behind Armbruster.

Annoyed to have been dismissed, Armbruster considered badging the girl, but he was not in uniform, and he was more interested in the bus company than anything she might tell him, so he stepped away from the counter and stood beside the cheese cooler to read the brochure.

The Sugarcreek-Sarasota Bus Company ran buses between Sugarcreek and Sarasota, Saturdays and Sundays excepted. Two drivers made the trip down, spelling each other at intervals, and two more drivers brought the buses back to Sugarcreek the next day. A bus departed Sugarcreek from the back of the restaurant parking lot at 8:00 P.M. on Mondays, Tuesdays, Wednesdays, and Thursdays, while other buses made the reverse run from Sarasota to Sugarcreek on the same days. The buses each made five regular stops along their routes, one of which was a breakfast break of an hour and a half, at a restaurant in Charlotte. The last stop on the Florida runs was at 6:30 P.M. the next day, in Sarasota, at Miller's Amish Restaurant and Clock Shoppe on

Beneva. On the Ohio runs, the buses returned to Sugarcreek in the evenings on the next days, Tuesdays through Fridays. Ticket reservations were suggested by the brochure, and a phone number was provided. Otherwise, seats were available each day on a first-come, first-served basis. The address of the bus company was a PO box number in Millersburg.

While he called the bus company's reservations number, Armbruster left the restaurant to stand beside his truck. His call rang through to a recording, announcing that phones would be answered each weekday only between 1:00 and 4:30 P.M. Otherwise, customers could leave a message at the tone. Armbruster left a message: name, rank, badge number, phone number, urgent.

Then he double-checked the license plate on the VW and called Robertson's number at the jail.

*   *   *

Robertson had been in his office since seven that morning. He answered Armbruster's call, listened to the corporal's theory about the bus, and said, "That's good work, Stan. Run it down."

When he hung up the call, Robertson said to Detective Lance, "Stan thinks they took the bus to Florida," and he explained about the bus company brochure and the VW parked in the Sugarcreek lot.

"Do you want me to help with that?" Lance asked. She had been at the jail since 5:00 A.M.

"Stan can handle it," Robertson said. "Tell me again about the Humvees."

"The search was finished when I got here. There are over a thousand registered in northern Ohio. Eleven in Marion and Barberton. No one owns both a Buick and a Humvee."

"And the Buicks that Rachel did identify?"

"Only the Marion PD has gotten back to me. That one belongs to a widower in a wheelchair. Emphysema. He hasn't driven in months."

"And Barberton?"

"Nothing helpful yet. They've been to the address, but the

place is boarded up. Registration is to a Teresa Molina, fifty-one. Barberton PD is still running it down."

"They have all your numbers?"

"Home, work, and cell. And your numbers, too."

"When's the last time you talked with Barberton?"

"Ten minutes ago."

"OK, we'll wait for Barberton to call," Robertson said. "In the meantime, you can follow me out to the Helmuth farm. I want you to relieve Baker out front, but I also want you to talk to the Helmuths about those sketches we need. Try to convince them to help us identify this woman."

"Then it's a good thing I'm wearing a skirt suit," Lance said, "and not slacks."

"It's a skirt, Lance. What they'd prefer is a long dress."

"I shouldn't have to change."

"No," Robertson smiled. "Just be sure to talk to the women instead of the men. They might be more inclined to help, anyway."

"You'd think they could at least give us a good verbal description," Lance said.

"Go for that, Lance, if they really won't give us the sketch. A good description of her is more than we have now, anyway."

"I've got a driver's license photograph of Teresa Molina. We should show them that."

"We will, Lance. But after we get a description. If it's her, that'll make the ID more solid."

24

WITH RACHEL'S help at the jail, Armbruster was able to use a law enforcement reverse directory database to trace the name and address of the answering service that handled reservations for the Sugarcreek-Sarasota Bus Company, and armed with several phone numbers, he was able to contact the shift supervisor for the phone banks where bus reservation calls were answered. After some considerable time on the phone with the supervisor, he was able to talk his way past her objections to get another phone number—an accounting service used by the bus company.

When he called the accounting service, a woman answered, saying, "Holmes Payroll and Business Accounting, William J. Donaldson, CPA."

While Rachel listened in the squad room, Armbruster said, "Mr. Donaldson, please. Holmes County Sheriff's Department."

"I'm sorry, but he's not in yet. Can I take a message?"

"Yes, this is Corporal Stan Armbruster. It's important that I get some information about one of your clients."

"Your number, Corporal?"

Armbruster gave her his cell number and said, "Really, all I need is a name and an address for the owner of the Sugarcreek-Sarasota Bus Company."

"We just do their payrolls and taxes, Corporal. The company is owned by several investors from the Columbus area, and I couldn't possibly be responsible for giving out their names."

"Could you place a call to Mr. Donaldson?" Armbruster asked. "It's important."

"I'll give him your message. But I don't think he'll want to give you any information. Not without a warrant."

"Just a minute," Armbruster said, and muted the phone. To Rachel, he said, "They're a group of investors in Columbus. She doesn't want to give out the particulars."

Rachel thought. "OK, but they're investors, right? So maybe they don't run the day-to-day business."

Armbruster returned to his call. "Do the investors really operate and manage the company? On a day-to-day basis?"

"No, Corporal," the woman said, sounding exasperated. "The business is handled by a gentleman in Sugarcreek."

"Can you at least give me his name?"

"Everybody knows him out there. Mr. Earnest Troyer. He meets the buses when they return. Gases them up, and goes through them to clean them, before they turn around to go back."

"Can you give me his numbers?"

"Really, Corporal, he's in the book. Earnest Troyer, Sugarcreek. Spelled with an A. E-A-R-N-E-S-T Troyer."

Armbruster was thanking the lady when she switched off. He put his cell on speaker phone for Rachel, dialed the number she found for Troyer in the Sugarcreek phone book, and heard the click and tone of an answering machine that sounded old, as if it were sending and recording messages on a spool of worn magnetic tape.

Gruffly, Earnest Troyer said in his greeting, "I'm sleeping! Always am at this time of day. Everybody knows that, so call back after six. And NO! I can't get you free tickets to Florida."

* * *

Armbruster stopped home at the double-wide unit he rented from a farmer in a wooded valley east of Holmesville. He parked his truck in front of a fenced beagle run at the back of his trailer, and he fed and watered the rabbit dogs he raised for the farmer as part of his rental agreement.

Inside, he changed into his uniform, pinned on his badge, strapped on his duty belt, holstered his gun, and locked up. His black-and-white cruiser was parked in a shed behind the dog cages. As he rolled it down the drive, he buckled himself in.

In Sugarcreek, he found Earnest Troyer's home on a slope just north of the downtown district, sandwiched between a small neighborhood-bank parking lot and a white-sided prairie-style home on the other side. The sidewalk in front of Troyer's brown house was cracked and tilted by the wide trunk of a weathered maple tree on the curb lawn. All the trees in the neighborhood were catching a steady breeze in their canopies, coolness riding in with the clouds ahead of another storm.

On the front porch, Armbruster pulled the screen door open and proceeded to pound on the varnished hardwood of the front door. He switched to the doorbell for several rings, and then gave a final triple knock on the door.

From inside on the second floor, Armbruster heard a door slam shut, then a rumble of footfalls on wooden steps and cursing behind the front door. Earnest Troyer pulled the door open from the inside, shouting, "What!" His pillow-wrinkled face was red and his eyes were shadowed by sleep. He was dressed in long, blue-checked pajamas. He looked as weathered and rough as the old maple on his curb lawn. His face was deeply creased with his years, and his eyes were bleary bulges under unruly brows. Armbruster was reminded of an untended scarecrow, forgotten and left in place from a year gone by.

Armbruster displayed his badge and said, "I have questions, Mr. Troyer, about your buses."

"You couldn't just call?" Troyer growled, brows tilting in toward the center over his nose.

"I did," Armbruster said evenly. "Got your machine."

"What do you need? I'm trying to sleep." He rubbed his big hands over his hair, trying to lay it down.

"Did you sell bus tickets yesterday to an Amish woman and a farm lad? Fannie Helmuth and Howard Dent?"

"Can't be sure"—mobile eyebrows arching up—"we sell a lot of tickets on a cash basis."

"She's about twenty-two and a little stocky. He's about twenty-five. Tall. She'd have been dressed Amish, and he parked a yellow VW bug in the lot."

"They're not supposed to do that," Troyer said, his face a weary sag of wrinkles. "Not supposed to park in the lot on a long-term basis."

"But did they get on the bus?"

"Can't be sure."

"Why's that?"

"We don't really take any names," Troyer said, now bored and still tired. "Look, Deputy, cash gets you a ticket, whoever you are."

Armbruster thought, then asked, "Can we call one of your drivers? Ask if these two are on the bus?"

Seeming defeated by Armbruster's persistence, Troyer groaned consternation and held the door open to let Armbruster enter to a front living room with old furniture and worn carpet.

"Wait here," Troyer said, and he plodded into the kitchen at the back of the house. A drawer scratched open and there was a rustle of pencils and papers. When Troyer returned, he had a tattered scrap of paper with four phone numbers arranged in two pairs. He held it out for Armbruster and said, "You can call the second set of numbers, here. Those are the drivers making the run right now. They should be somewhere south of Charlotte."

Consulting Troyer's list, Armbruster entered all four numbers into his phone's address book. He thanked Troyer and stepped out onto the front porch. Before the screen door had closed on its piston, the heavy wooden door slammed shut behind him.

Coming down the steps, Armbruster keyed up the first number from the second set and stood on the front sidewalk to let it ring. More clouds had gathered overhead, and the morning light began to shade toward gray. A few sprinkles fell, and Armbruster carried his cell phone to the cruiser out by the curb. By the time he was seated behind the wheel, the rain had begun to patter on the windshield and hood.

After six rings, the call switched to a message center. Armbruster broke the connection and tried the second number. That one answered after two rings.

"Bruder," the man said abruptly. "Do for you?"

Armbruster introduced himself and explained that he needed to speak to either Fannie Helmuth or Howie Dent, passengers, he suspected, on the bus.

Bruder said, "I'll get them." After a pause, he returned. "Sorry, I guess they didn't get back on for Florida."

"They didn't make the trip?"

"Got on in Sugarcreek. Got off for breakfast in Charlotte, like everybody else. But it looks like they never got back on, and so I can't let you talk to them."

"OK," Armbruster said. "Where are you now?"

"Just crossed over the South Carolina border."

"Do people get on and off like that? I mean usually?"

"Most people want to go to Florida, Corporal. But we do make five stops along the way. And sometimes people make only part of the trip."

"Did Helmuth and Dent pay for the whole trip?"

"Let me check the receipts," Bruder said. There was another brief pause. "They booked for Sarasota. You have any idea why they'd get off in Charlotte?"

"I'm afraid I do," Armbruster said. "Have you got a phone number for that restaurant?"

Bruder gave it to him. Armbruster said, "Thanks," and switched off.

When he started his cruiser, a torrent of rain was blowing across his car. As he pulled away from the curb, it switched to a dense rattle of sleet. Rolling slowly down the curb lane, he tried Howie Dent's cell again, but got no ring. Then he punched in

Robertson's cell number and pressed his phone tighter against his ear, wondering if the sheriff would hear him over the clacking din of the sleet pinging his roof.

* * *

When he took the corporal's call, Sheriff Robertson had just wheeled into the Helmuths' drive under a steady, cold drizzle that seemed intent on drifting to flakes. Lance had preceded him down the lane, and Robertson had stopped to send Baker back to base. Robertson finished his call with Armbruster as he reached the house, and he pulled himself out of his Crown Vic under a red-and-black golf umbrella. Lance had already knocked on the front door, and as she stepped to a porch window to peer inside through the glass, Robertson mounted the steps to the porch, turned his umbrella upside down on the porch boards, and asked, "Nobody home?"

Lance shook her head, crossed to the window on the opposite side of the front door, peered in with her hands cupped to the glass, and said, "Baker would have told us if they went out past him."

Robertson pulled the screen door open and tried the knob. It turned, and the door opened when he pushed on it. He put his head inside and called out, "Sheriff, here. Hello?" but he got no answer.

He knocked loudly on the doorjamb, pushed the door all the way open, took one step inside, and called out again.

Inside the Helmuth house, it was as quiet as a library. None of the kerosene lamps on table stands in the living room or front parlor were lit. There was no heat in the house, and no light or noise came from the kitchen at the far end of the hall. He backed out onto the porch, pulled the front door shut, and asked Lance, "You wearing sturdy shoes?"

"Not really," she muttered, and descended the steps ahead of him to follow a concrete walkway around the side of the house. Robertson followed with his umbrella overhead.

At the back door, they knocked again. The screened back

porch and a mudroom leading into the kitchen were both dark. Robertson retreated onto a patch of driveway gravel between the house and the barn, and he studied the second-floor windows. No light came from any of them.

He called Lance down to the driveway, and the two crossed under his umbrella to a large, two-story barn whose doors stood open to the weather. The mud in front of the doors was thick, and it had been deeply rutted recently by wide and thick wagon wheels and thin buggy wheels, hoof prints, too, all tracing around the corner of the barn toward the fields at back. The morning rains had already begun to wash out the tracks.

Robertson handed his umbrella to Lance and waved her around the front corner of the barn. As carefully as she could, she stepped over to the grass beside the rutted path and disappeared from view as she turned the corner to parallel the wheel and hoof trail toward the back. The sheriff went into the dark barn.

Hanging on the first upright post to his left, there was a kerosene lantern, with a long-tipped butane lighter on a shelf next to it. He lifted the globe of the lantern, put fire to the wick, and replaced the globe. Orange and blue flame gave off a wave of black smoke, but once he had the wick adjusted properly, the light glowed pleasantly orange. He carried the lantern farther into the barn and saw Lance enter the barn through a door at the far end.

Robertson made a fast inspection of the several stalls inside the barn. No livestock was there. He met Lance at the back, and she said, "There ought to be tack in here—you know, harnesses, bridles, like that."

"What about the wheel tracks?" Robertson asked.

"They all overlie each other. There were several buggies and maybe two large wagons. They cross a field and head up over a rise behind the barn. It looks like they all just drove out of here last night."

Robertson frowned. "Keep the umbrella, Pat, and check all the outbuildings. I'm going to take a look inside."

* * *

The kitchen was dark, and the gray drizzle of the morning provided scant light for the sheriff's search of the house. He felt carefully above the stove plates, then felt the plates, too. They were cold. Underneath, the fire in the stove had long since burned out, leaving white and gray ash mounded in the bottom quarter of the firebox.

Next, the sheriff pulled kitchen drawers open. All empty. The cupboards he found empty, too. In a small pantry beside the basement stairs, the plain wood shelves were mostly bare. An odd half bag of flour and a few open boxes of pasta were all that remained.

In the hallway leading to the front, Shaker pegs hung empty, all the coats and shawls taken away. The cast-iron woodstove in the living room was as cold as the cooking stove in the kitchen.

Robertson climbed a plain wooden staircase to the second floor and found in all the bedrooms that the beds had been stripped of linens, blankets, and quilts. From the upstairs bathroom, toiletries, towels, and washcloths had all been taken away. He checked the bedrooms again, and the dressers were likewise empty, as if the family had packed everything into wagons and buggies and had driven away for good.

As Robertson came down the staircase, Lance came in through the kitchen door. "There's nobody here, Sheriff. About all that's left are the larger farm implements."

"Same in the house," Robertson said. "Fannie and her whole family are gone."

"You know something about Fannie?"

"I didn't tell you about Armbruster's call just now. He traced Fannie and Howie Dent. They took the bus to Sarasota last night, but got off and disappeared in Charlotte."

Lance considered that, looked around the cold kitchen, listened to the rain sounding on the roof overhead, and groaned, "We're never going to find them."

"Fannie?"

"Yes, but the woman in the gray Buick, too."

"Could be," Robertson said, "but neither is that woman going to find any of the Helmuths. They've all run off."

"You're assuming they left on their own," Lance said.

"What else?" Robertson said. "They were forced to leave?"

Lance replied only with an uncertain shrug of her shoulders.

25

Wednesday, April 6
11:10 A.M.

PAT LANCE was shivering as if she'd been caught out in a high mountain snowstorm in summer attire, so she drove home to Millersburg to change into warmer clothes and sturdier shoes.

Robertson tossed his folded umbrella into the Crown Vic and pulled himself in behind the wheel. Before he followed Lance down the long drive, he called Ellie on the radio and said, "Can you have Rachel call me, Ellie? I need to know if there's any hope we can connect Teresa Molina to an owner of a Humvee in or near Barberton."

Angling south, Robertson drove into Charm and turned east on 557, sandwiched between an Amish roofing crew in a van and a garbage truck whose driver seemed intent on passing everything in front of it. Angered by the speed of traffic on the country lane, Robertson pulsed several strobes on his taillights and rear window bar, and the garbage truck slowed immediately to widen the gap on Robertson's rear bumper. Irritated even more, the sheriff slowed to five miles an hour under the speed limit, and held that speed happily all the way to the Zook drive. When he turned into the drive, the truck found itself trapped behind a slow buggy on a curved section of road, and Robertson celebrated the frustration he saw in the truck driver's expression.

On the Zook drive, Robertson parked behind Cal Troyer's gray carpenter's truck. Farther up the drive, a black sedan with the EPA logo was parked beside the house, where two EPA officers stood under one umbrella, talking with a somber Andy Zook. The rain had lessened but hadn't entirely stopped, and Zook stood out in the weather, with his broad felt hat brim spilling a thin trail of water off its rear edge. The shoulders of his denim waistcoat were dark with the soaking they had already taken that morning.

In a rocker on the front porch, Cal Troyer sat with his legs stretched out and crossed at the ankles. He had on a winter parka over a work shirt and jeans. He got out of his rocker as Robertson climbed the steps, and he said, "Anything on Fannie Helmuth?"

Not surprised that the pastor would know about Fannie's disappearance, the sheriff smiled and said, "She's down in Charlotte, Cal, last we know. She's with Howie Dent, and they're running. Probably safer than staying here."

Cal nodded and smiled satisfaction. "You know about the rest of the Helmuths?"

"Gone, Cal. Bugged out."

Cal nodded again and smiled more broadly. "You going to try to find them?"

"And what?" Robertson asked. "Charge them with abandoning a residence?"

"They'll be back when this is all over. Neighbors have already taken the livestock in."

Robertson shook his head but smiled. "Cal, there aren't two families in a thousand who could pull up stakes overnight."

"Suppose not."

"Any idea where they'll go?"

"Probably New York. They have relatives up near Batavia. Moved there a year ago from Mount Hope. So maybe they'll head up there for a while."

"That's gotta be five hundred miles, Cal."

"They took food? Clothes and such?"

"Everything," Robertson said.

"And the house is closed up?"

"Closed, but not locked."

"Then they'll stay away as long as they need to, or they'll sell out to locals and start over in New York."

Robertson gave a bewildered shake of his head. "Seems extreme, Cal."

"Maybe."

"Any chance they were forced out? Or taken away?"

"Like what, by a drug gang?"

"Something like that. Or maybe they were warned?"

"I don't know," Cal said. "But they had their neighbor take the livestock. Milking cows, mostly. They just opened one fence up last night and put them over on the neighbor's pasture."

"How do you know that?" Robertson asked.

"Word gets around."

"Really, Cal, do you know for sure where they're headed?"

"North, I suspect," Cal said. "Back roads only."

"I could chase them down," the sheriff said.

"Why? Could you protect them?"

Robertson shook his head. "Not all of them. The best thing I can do is arrest this drug crew. But I need the Helmuths to provide a description. I need to find them, so that's a BOLO for all the sheriffs and the highway patrol."

"BOLO?"

"Be On the Lookout for. We used to call it an APB."

Cal didn't comment.

Robertson turned his gaze into the cold and gray drizzle washing over the valley and asked, "EPA's still down in the bottoms?"

"Yes," Cal said.

"Are we going to show them the topographical maps?" Robertson asked.

"I'm not. You?"

"Not today."

Cal sat back down in his rocker. "I'm waiting to talk with Emma Wengerd."

"She's not up yet?"

"Up, but not coming out of her room."

A curtain of sleet blew onto the porch, and Robertson moved in closer to the house. Cal scooted his rocker back away from the front edge and asked, "Missy can't release the body?"

"Not yet."

"That's a problem, Bruce."

"I know, but this is still an open murder investigation."

"But if Fannie and all the Helmuths are gone, you don't have any leads."

"I'm still connecting Humvee registrations to owners of old gray Buicks. And if I can find the Helmuths, they can still give us a description of the woman who's chasing after Fannie."

"They're not gonna do that, Bruce. They've left because they don't trust us."

"Law enforcement?"

"English, Bruce. They don't really trust any of us English."

"Then I've got no way to solve the Zook murder. Not if they won't cooperate."

"Isn't Ricky going down to Florida?"

"Left Akron/Canton at ten o'clock."

"Then maybe you don't need to chase after the Helmuths up here."

"I don't really have the assets to do that, Cal. Besides, the highway patrol will locate them soon enough. But if they don't want to give us sketches or a description, we're operating blind on the Zook murder."

"No leads on the Buick?"

"One, but it's weak."

"Still, maybe it'll pan out."

Robertson gruffed out a dissatisfied "Hmpff," then said, "Meantime, I'm going to have a talk with the EP-almighty-A."

"I'm still working with Emma," Cal said, and got out of his rocker. "I'll talk with her when she'll let me, but really, Bruce, she needs to get beyond Ruth's funeral. She needs Missy to release Ruth's body."

"I imagine that everybody out here needs that, Cal."

"Emma more than anyone," Cal said. "She's not a blood rel-
ative, but Emma seems to have lost more here. I'll stay here all
day if I have to."

"If you do, Cal, I'd advise you to move inside near a stove."

"Oh?"

"Weather report calls for more rain and sleet. Snow by late
afternoon."

*   *   *

The sheriff went back to his car and waited while Andy Zook
listened to the EPA officials. In his rearview mirror, Robertson
watched cars and trucks tearing by on 557, and his ire grew as
he gauged their speed. With a quick call to Ellie, he asked that a
cruiser be posted east of Charm to pull over offenders. Mentally,
Robertson made a note to apply for lower speed limits from the
state traffic commission.

Abruptly, Andy Zook broke off his conversation with the
EPA officers. From a distance, it had seemed to Robertson more
like an interrogation than anything else. Chastened but not subdued, Zook turned and walked around the back corner of his
house.

Robertson got out of his sedan and marched toward the
agents. Not stopping, he said as he passed, "Let's have a look,
boys," and waved the agents forward to the barn, then around
the side of it and up onto the high wall of the broken dam. Robertson stopped on top of the dam and waited for the two agents
to catch up to him. Inwardly he celebrated his small victory, that
they had followed him so readily.

"What?" Wellings called out as the agents scaled the muddy
wall of the dam under a shared umbrella.

Robertson waited for them to mount the crest. "You still intent on assessing fines here? And penalties?"

"We've got plenty of evidence, Sheriff," Wellings said. "But
we're still not done taking samples. The impacted area is vast."

"How long are you going to keep at this, Wellings?"

"There's poison spread all through that valley," the second

agent said. "Zooks are going to have to clean it all up. And fines? Yes. Penalties, I don't know. It depends on who did what."

"Ruth Zook did this," Robertson said, biting down on an urge to berate.

"But Alvin Zook admits to breaching the dam," Wellings argued.

Hiding his animosity, Robertson asked, "You got enough gasoline for that generator down there?"

Wellings took off his spectacles and dried them on the end of his tie. "Oh, we'll get some more gas down there, Sheriff. As soon as it's not so muddy."

26

Wednesday, April 6
1:25 P.M.

CAL WAS invited to have lunch with the Zooks in their kitchen, and he was happy to accept, as much for the meal as for the warmth of the kitchen stove. Hot food and bread was passed on platters and in deep bowls, and the family ate without much talking. Alvin finished first, cleared his plate, and said something in Dietsch that Cal understood to mean, "Going after my chores."

Andy got up, too, and then Irma rose to clear food and plates from the table. When nearly everyone had left, Irma handed Cal a plate of food and said, "Maybe Emma will eat something."

Cal popped a last piece of bread into his mouth, wiped his lips with a linen napkin, stood, and took the plate from Irma.

"Last bedroom on the left," she said. "She'll have the door closed."

Cal carried the plate up the steps, knocked on the last door, and opened it to look inside. Emma was lying back on her bed in her stocking feet, and when he appeared at the door, she sat up, put her legs over the side of the bed, and wiped her eyes with the flats of her fingers.

Cal carried the plate of food into her room, set it on a dresser, and pulled a straight chair up to her bedside.

"I'm not crying," Emma said sternly. "And I'm not hungry."

"I'll leave the plate in case you change your mind."

Emma shrugged indifference, and Cal sat silently beside her. Emma seemed determined to hold silence, and Cal was content at first to sit quietly with her, wondering how he'd start his conversation. Clearly she was intent on a show of bravery. Clearly, too, he thought, she had been crying.

Eventually he said, "I'm glad you got to keep your letters, Emma," hoping something positive from the day before would prove encouraging for her.

But instead of following his lead, Emma asked, "Why wouldn't she let me see Ruth?"

"Probably because she thought you wouldn't like to see her hurt that way."

Emma nodded as if grateful for the honesty. "Do bullets hurt?"

"I don't know," Cal said after a pause. "Really, I don't know."

"Is Ruth in heaven?"

"I believe so."

"Does it still hurt?"

"No, Emma. Heaven is not a place of hurting."

"Then I need to be there, with her."

"It's not time for you, yet," Cal said, emotion pushing a burn of tears under his eyelids. "You'll get there soon enough, like we all do."

"Will someone shoot me?"

"Really, Emma, I don't think so."

"Why did they shoot Ruth?"

"I don't know. The sheriff thinks they were mad because she dumped out their drugs."

"They tell us at school that drugs are bad."

"They are."

"Then why did Ruth have their drugs?"

"I don't know, Emma. But a detective has gone to Florida to try to find out."

"Does it mean Ruth was bad? That she was shot because she was bad?"

Unable at last to mask the sorrow that caught in his throat, Cal whispered, "No, Emma."

He was unnerved by Emma's capacity to juggle honesty as if it weren't a burden, and he struggled to know what next to say. "Ruth was not bad," he said at last. "The sheriff thinks she was trying to help a friend."

"But she carried drugs," Emma said.

Cal reached out for her hand, but Emma pulled it back into her lap and said, "I can't pray anymore."

Cal held his eyes on hers and prayed for guidance. He prayed for effectiveness with his words. "Emma," he said, "please don't be bitter. At least not with God."

As if he hadn't spoken, she continued, "And I don't cry."

"It's not a weakness, Emma."

"But it hurts too much. So I can't pray, and I can't cry."

"I saw your tears when I came in," Cal said, reaching again for her hand.

This time she let him take her hand, but her fingers were stiff and unyielding to his touch.

"You have tears for Ruth, Emma," Cal whispered. "And God knows your tears better than anyone."

Sternly, Emma said, "I think it's God who makes me cry."

"He doesn't, Emma, but he knows your tears. He knows all your tears, and he counts them as prayers."

Fiercely, Emma said, "My tears are angry."

"Those are still prayers."

"How would he know? He let Ruth die."

Cal took her hand in both of his and leaned forward. "God honors all our tears, Emma. He even knows the names of our tears. Every one of them. God names them all to honor our pain."

With a voice as frail and tragic as a plea for mercy, Emma asked, "How do you know?"

"Because I pray, Emma. And I have learned that, in our prayers, God tells us the names of our tears."

27

AFTER THE waitress had cleared his dishes, Robertson sat for a troubled half hour in the side-room sandwich café at Charm Amish Lumber and Hardware. He had worked his way nervously through a carafe of strong coffee, and then he had asked the waitress to switch him to decaf. She was an English girl from Millersburg, and she knew the mercurial sheriff well enough to let him sit unmolested as long as he wanted. The café wasn't busy this late after the lunch rush, and if the sheriff wanted to sit alone with his thoughts, she had plenty to do back in the kitchen.

Robertson stared blankly out at the showroom mix of storm doors, house siding, and hand tools, amused and also annoyed by the tourists who wandered in with their curiosity, obviously finding themselves inside an Amish hardware store for the first time in their lives, expecting to discover some exotic cultural nuance or perhaps a strange kitchen gadget to discuss back home, when they proudly told their neighbors and friends that they knew just where in Charm one could find the best local cheeses and hand chisels. Robertson shook his head at the irony of Amish culture, so doggedly withdrawn from greater America, but now so thoroughly overrun by tourists with cameras, who acted more like they were on safari than in a decent person's place of business.

But the sheriff's usual tendencies toward general disgruntlement about tourism weren't especially active this day. Instead, he brooded over a rising mountain of specific and immediate law enforcement worries, at the top of which sat Fannie Helmuth. A close second was her extended family, now rolling wagons and buggies over backcountry roads, carrying away everything that wasn't nailed down at the farm they had abandoned last night.

Then there were the bus drivers, Robertson thought. Need to get Ricky to interview them as soon as he gets to Sarasota. Maybe he'll get there in time to meet the bus. Robertson checked his watch. Should be there by now—at the airport in Tampa, anyway. Maybe driving south already. So, call Ricky.

And Howie Dent had to turn on his cell phone sometime. Call that number. Call it repeatedly.

Robertson stood and counted out bills for a tip. Then there was Rachel's search of the databases. A BOLO on the Helmuth caravan was needed. And figure an end run on the EPA. Something to help the Zooks out of the federal noose.

After a last sip of coffee, the sheriff crossed the showroom floor and pushed out through the glass doors into another cold and steady spring rain. Maybe the problem with the EPA would resolve itself, he thought, smiling, and ran through the rain to his Crown Vic parked in the second row of the lot.

Inside behind the wheel, the shoulders of his suit coat splattered with rain, he admired the weather for what it could accomplish for the Zooks. He switched on the engine, ran the fan up to max defrost, and called Ellie on his radio. She answered his call with a simple "Go ahead," as he turned on his wipers to see how much condensation his heater would have to conquer inside the car.

"Ellie," Robertson said. "Is the chief there? And Newell. Where's he at?" The inside of his windshield was heavily fogged, and he'd have to make his calls while he waited in the parking lot for it to clear.

"Chief Wilsher is in, but he's having a meeting with his patrol captains," Ellie said. "And you'll have to get Bobby on his cell."

"Thanks, out," Robertson said, and punched Newell's number on his speed dial.

"Newell," the captain answered, with a cash register sounding in the background.

"You at lunch?"

"Heading back now."

"Did you put out that BOLO on the Helmuth family?"

"Yes, of course."

"Anything?"

"Nothing yet."

"We need them to answer some questions, Bobby. Need to know why they left."

"Could have been threatened."

"I know, and Fannie, too. Why'd she leave on the bus?"

"Maybe just scared. You know, running instead of staying put."

"There has to be a way to track her down."

"Stan Armbruster has some ideas," Newell said. "He's making some calls. Also helping Rachel."

"Does she have anything for us?"

"Haven't checked in, Sheriff. Lunch."

"OK, I'm headed in," Robertson said. "Stan and Rachel in the duty room?"

"My office. The system's better there for database searches."

"OK, good. I'm gonna call Ricky before I get back. We need him to meet that bus in Sarasota this afternoon. He needs to interview the drivers about Fannie and Dent. Find out why they got off the bus in Charlotte."

Switching off, Robertson called Howie Dent's phone and got a recording, "Mailbox full." He punched out and muttered, "Has to turn it on sometime. Unless he can't."

*   *   *

Robertson put his head into Bobby Newell's office and saw that Rachel was working intently at the captain's desktop computer.

Armbruster was talking on his cell phone, standing with his shoulder planted in the corner of the room, his back turned to Rachel. The sheriff turned around and went down the hall toward Dan Wilsher's office.

On his phone, Armbruster said, "No, it'd have been just this morning. When the bus from Sugarcreek stopped for breakfast."

On the other end of the call, the restaurant manager in Charlotte complained, "You have any idea how many Amish people get off those buses? Everyday?"

"They'd have been noticeable," Armbruster said. "She was dressed Amish, but he's English. Might have been in jeans and a work shirt."

"Can't help you, Corporal. It's just not something I'd notice."

"How about your waitresses, then," Armbruster pressed. "Maybe one of them saw them."

"I've asked!" the man said sharply. "Nobody saw them in here!"

"Are there other places nearby? Other stores?"

"No, Corporal. Really, that's enough."

"No, listen. They had to go somewhere. They'd have been nervous, maybe. You know—careful."

A hesitation on the call.

"What?" Armbruster asked.

"There's a taxi stand," the manager said. "Cab company keeps a car there for when the buses come in."

"You think they caught a cab?"

"Don't know," the man said.

"Give me the number?" Armbruster asked, and he heard an irritated sigh as a drawer rattled open.

Curtly, the manager read out the number. Armbruster started to say thanks, but the call switched off before he had finished.

Turning around to Rachel, Armbruster said, "Maybe a lead here," and he stepped out into the hallway.

When he had the cab company on the line, he asked to talk

with the dispatcher. When he had the dispatcher on the line, he asked about a fare that was picked up at the restaurant that morning.

"I'll check," the woman said, and the call went to hold, Armbruster thinking it an improvement to have someone cooperative to talk with. He put his head back into the office, knocked on the jamb, and said to Rachel when she looked up from her search, "Really, I might have something here."

Rachel pushed away from the desk, climbed off her chair, and came out into the hall with Armbruster, the pair mismatched in height. Back on the phone, Armbruster asked, "When, exactly?"

Then Rachel heard him say, "OK, where?"

"Thanks," Armbruster said, and switched off. To Rachel he said, "Fannie and Howie took a cab as soon as their bus arrived at the restaurant in Charlotte for its breakfast stop. And the cabbie drove them downtown, to the Greyhound bus station."

A tone chimed on the captain's desktop computer, and Rachel and Armbruster went back in to study the search results. Rachel sat at the desk and put the data on the wall display beside her so that Armbruster could see from a seat in front of the desk. As she was scrolling through lines, Robertson came back to the office and stood beside Armbruster to watch.

Rachel read through the display quickly and then scrolled back to the top. She opened the second item and displayed the record of a traffic arrest in Barberton. A man in a red Humvee had been stopped for speeding nearly a year ago, and a gun had been found in the vehicle. The woman who had posted the cash bond for his bail was the registered owner of the gray Buick that Rachel had earlier uncovered with her first search. Teresa Molina, black hair and brown eyes, five feet six, 145 pounds, had used a driver's license from Florida. Her cousin, Dewey Molina, never showed for his court date. When a search of their Barberton residence turned up cocaine residue on a cutting table, with plastic bags, spatulas, and digital scales, the house had been boarded up, and an arrest warrant for both Molinas had been issued by Barberton PD. The warrant was still outstanding.

Robertson stared at the wall display with a snarl forming on his lips and the light of celebration in his eyes. "Got 'em," he said. "Teresa and Dewey Molina. What took so long?"

Rachel leaned back in her chair and smiled. "Just had to widen the search."

Robertson gave a bemused frown, and Rachel responded with a tone that reflected confident satisfaction. "Stan and I figured this drug crew must be mobile, Sheriff. I mean mobile like interstate and then some, mobile. So we had to expand our search to nationwide. Then we figured the connection between Teresa Molina and some Humvee owner might have been tenuous, so we had to search more than just vehicle registrations. Accidents, arrests, traffic tickets, convictions, incarcerations, DUIs, voter registrations, DHS records, everything. We've been running the searches—several simultaneously—since nine last night. And at the very least, we figured these vehicles might be registered in any state. Ohio and Florida for sure, but anywhere, really. Our first break was that Dewey Molina had two priors in Florida, driving a Humvee."

"How long have you known that?" Robertson asked, taking a seat next to Armbruster.

Rachel came around the corner of the desk and stood eye to eye with the seated sheriff. "We've had it since we first came in this morning."

"Why didn't you tell me?" Robertson asked, showing some irritation.

"We're telling you now," Rachel said confidently, and stepped back behind the captain's desk. "Wasn't any point in telling you sooner, because we needed the Barberton connection in order to be certain."

Robertson made no reply. Rachel held his gaze until he softened. Then she smiled and said, "Really, the search did the work for us after that. Teresa Molina posted Dewey's bail in Barberton. We have their plates."

"They could switch plates," Robertson argued.

"They could also paint their cars," Rachel said. "Point

is, they're on the run, but we know who they are, and maybe they don't know that yet. Maybe they haven't switched anything yet."

Robertson stood slowly to full height and seemed to stretch into mild relaxation. With a broad smile, he said, "That's really good work."

Rachel climbed onto the chair behind the desk, and said, "Stan has more."

Robertson returned to his seat, and Armbruster said, "Fannie and Howie took a cab at the breakfast stop. From the restaurant in Charlotte to the Greyhound station downtown."

"They're running," Robertson said.

"Right," Armbruster said. "And on a Greyhound bus, they could be going just about anywhere."

Robertson came forward on the edge of his chair. "I don't like it."

Rachel said, "If they're out there on a bus route somewhere, isn't that safer?"

"But out where?" Robertson said. "And if Stan could trace their movements that easily, why couldn't the Molinas do that, too?"

"But how would anyone know what bus they took?" Rachel argued. "And to what city? Plus, they could get off again almost anywhere, even if they bought tickets all the way to LA."

"You said it yourself," Robertson said, standing again. "This drug crew is interstate and mobile. For all we know, they followed Fannie's bus to Charlotte. Or had someone waiting there for the bus to arrive. Because I promise you, as soon as Teresa Molina shot Ruth Zook—or whoever shot her—she called her people in Florida. Called her people here in Ohio, too. And if she was looking for Fannie Helmuth that quickly, going to her house out in the open, like she didn't think anyone would suspect her, then that was Teresa Molina's trying to tie up a loose end before she knew we had talked to Fannie. Well, she knows now that Fannie came to see us. She's gonna tie up loose ends everywhere she can. And those buses run to Indiana and Pennsylvania, too.

How many loose ends do they need to worry about over in those states?"

"We know of only *two* Amish girls who carried drugs for them," Stan said, tentatively. He added, "We only know of the two. Could be others."

Robertson stood and said, "This may be bigger than we thought." Marching out of the room, he called back over his shoulder, "If you're right, I've sent Ricky into a hornet's nest, and he thinks he's just tracking down a single lead on the Ruth Zook murder."

* * *

In the stairwell headed down, Robertson passed Bobby Newell coming up. He stopped and gave the captain details about Stan and Rachel's search results, then said, "So, we know the names, vehicles, and plates on the Molinas."

"That's another BOLO," the captain nodded.

"And call Ricky," Robertson said, descending to the first-floor landing. "He thinks he's following a lead on the Zook murder, and it's quite possible that we've dropped him into a bigger mess."

"I think he still needs to interview those bus drivers," Newell said down the steps. "He'll have to go there first, if he's going to meet the bus when it pulls in."

At the bottom of the steps, Robertson turned back and said, "He needs to see Ray Lee Orton."

"I've already asked Mike Branden to do that," Newell said. "He's right there, just south of Bradenton Beach."

"Good, but call Mike back. Tell him where Ricky's gonna be."

"What're you going to do?" Newell asked.

"I want to call Ray Lee Orton. He needs to worry more about his friend Jodie Tapp."

Newell started back down the steps. "What about this Barberton connection?"

Robertson stopped with his hand on the door latch. Newell reached him at the bottom of the steps.

"What's Lance doing?" the sheriff asked.

"She's tracking the BOLO on the Helmuths. And now she'll do the Molinas, too. And she's talking with Barberton PD."

"We need to send her up to Barberton," Robertson said.

"OK," Newell said, turning back up the steps.

Robertson called after him, "And send Stan with her, Bobby. He seems to be getting the hang of this."

28

Wednesday, April 6
6:30 P.M.

"YOU'VE BEEN working on your tan," Ricky Niell said to Professor Branden. The two had been talking for half an hour. Branden had come over the Ringling Causeway into Sarasota with Caroline after he had talked with Ray Lee Orton in Bradenton Beach. Ricky had met him at Miller's restaurant after his drive down from Tampa, and he had quickly gotten Branden up to speed on the details of Zook, Helmuth, and the Molinas. They were standing at the edge of a gathering of Amish locals waiting for the bus from Sugarcreek, on the blacktopped parking lot behind Miller's restaurant. On the other side of the ornate, Swiss-style restaurant building, the professor's wife, Caroline, was holding a place in the dinner line at the front door.

"Still on sabbatical," Branden said, regarding his tan. "So we took some time to come down to enjoy Ray Lee's beach house. We get a lot of sun down here."

"Robertson said you'd be talking today with Ray Lee."

"Sheriff called you?"

"On my drive down from Tampa."

Branden studied the gathering Amish crowd, some on foot, some on adult-sized tricycles. "I wouldn't want to be dressed

Amish in this heat," he said. "And Robertson must be keeping a close tab, with all the calls he's been making."

"Robertson and Bobby Newell, both," Ricky said. "They're trying to find Fannie Helmuth—that's why we're to talk to these bus drivers—and they think Jodie Tapp needs protection."

"From the Molinas?" Branden said.

"Or from the Florida end of their crew. But for all we know, the Molinas are already back down here, too."

"Or they followed the bus to Charlotte?"

"Something like that," Ricky said, stepping off the blacktop to stand back on the grass, under the thin cover of a tall jacaranda tree. "Hot down here."

"Is this the Howie Dent who lives out by Charm? The fellow who took the bus with Helmuth?"

Ricky nodded. "He lives on the farm next to hers."

"I know him," Branden said. "He was a student of mine eight or nine years ago. Wrote his senior thesis for me, on political cartoons in newspapers during the Civil War."

Niell shaded his eyes and moved deeper under the branches. "I could have gone to Charlotte, to look for Fannie Helmuth. But Robertson thinks she's safer right now than Jodie Tapp. It's a toss-up, if you ask me."

"Seems like Robertson's grasping at straws," Branden said. "I'm not sure what you're going to accomplish down here that Ray Lee can't do himself."

"It was Robertson's call," Ricky said. "Fannie and Howie could be anywhere."

"But you don't actually know that one of the Molinas killed the Zook girl."

Ricky squinted at the bright sunlight and wished he'd bought a hat at the airport. The professor stood next to him in beach shorts, a plain T-shirt, and a broad-brimmed Tommy Bahama sun hat. His tan was deep—a ruddy bronze—and it made his gray beard seem almost white by contrast, the effect enhanced by dark sunglasses.

"All we know for sure," Ricky said, "is that the same woman

Fannie Helmuth gave her suitcase to is the registered owner of a gray Buick. And that Fannie saw her harassing her brother and his wife on the front porch of the family home. Plus, Teresa's cousin Dewey owns a Humvee, and we have the plates for both vehicles."

"And a boarded-up drug runner's house in Barberton."

Ricky nodded. "It's listed as Dewey Molina's address at the time of his traffic arrest. Pat Lance is going up to take a look tomorrow morning."

"And if one of the Molinas didn't kill Ruth Zook?"

"Then we really don't have anything," Ricky said. "But it all fits. The drug connection to the Molinas is solid in Ohio."

"Here's the bus," Branden said, turning Ricky around. "You're going to want to talk to Ray Lee about this drug running." They moved forward with the crowd as the bus pulled in and stopped at the far edge of the lot. "He's got someone scuttling stolen boats offshore."

The front door of the bus hissed open, and a uniformed driver stepped down. He turned and offered his hand to an older Amish woman, then held his post to help others off the bus. The second driver came down behind the third couple from the bus and stepped to the side to open the luggage bay doors along the bottom skirt of the bus. As passengers continued to exit, he took out packages, bags, and suitcases, lining them up beside the bus. While he worked, the first passengers retrieved their suitcases and bags, helped by friends or family from the waiting crowd.

Among the passengers, there were people of all ages—an infant boy in his mother's arms, older couples and single older women, teenagers traveling alone or with their families. They were all dressed Amish, the men in denim trousers, plain shirts of muted colors, and straw hats, the women in long, plain dresses.

Most flinched at first from the bright sunlight and heat, as they searched the crowd for relatives and friends. Some of the passengers helped the driver pull suitcases out of the bays, and then, once they had greeted one another on the parking lot, several stepped over to form lines in front of two portable toilets behind the bus. As locals paired up with their visitors, groups began to walk back down Beneva Road, toward the Pinecraft cottage community to the south.

Branden and Niell threaded a route through the thinning crowd. Niell produced his badge, showed it to the driver standing at the bus door, and asked, "Did you take a call south of Charlotte from Corporal Stan Armbruster?"

"My partner did," the driver said, pointing to the man who was still bent over beside the luggage bays. He was reaching in far to the back to remove the last suitcases from the bus.

"His name?" Ricky asked.

"Dick Bruder."

"Your name?"

"Dan Harrold. This about the Amish couple that got off in Charlotte?"

"Do you remember them?" Ricky asked.

"A largish Amish girl, with a tall fellow in jeans and a check-ered shirt. They didn't have any bags."

Bruder finished closing the bay doors and walked up, saying, "You two local cops?"

Branden laughed and held his arms out to his side. "Not dressed like this."

Ricky said, "Holmes County Sheriff's office."

Bruder nodded. "One of Robertson's boys."

Branden laughed again, and Ricky said, "You spoke with one of our *boys*, Corporal Stan Armbruster."

"I didn't mean any offense, Detective," Bruder said. "I talked with Armbruster, yes. But I told him everything I knew. Wasn't much."

"But how did they seem to you?" Ricky asked. "We think they were trying to disappear."

"They do something?" Bruder asked. "Because they seemed normal to me."

Ricky explained briefly about the murder of Ruth Zook and said, "So, I think that they think they can hide from these people.

They took a cab to the Greyhound bus station, and then who knows where."

"That's a long cab ride, all the way to downtown Charlotte," Bruder said.

Showing an edge of frustration, Ricky said, "Look, I need to know if you think they were scared."

"No."

"Anxious?"

"No."

"Watching over their shoulders?"

"No. Really, Detective, they just got off the bus with everyone else, but they didn't get back on."

"Did they go into the restaurant for breakfast?"

"Don't know," Bruder said, "because I wasn't counting heads."

"You did notice that they didn't get back on."

"Not at first," Bruder said. "We make announcements ten and five minutes before departure, and we pretty much assume everyone wants to get back on in time to head south again."

"How long until you noticed?"

"Not until Armbruster called me," Bruder said.

"Did they talk to anyone on the way down to Charlotte?"

"No, but they kinda huddled up. Whispered to each other."

"Did you make anything of that?"

"Not at the time. Most folks want some privacy on a crowded bus."

* * *

Crossing the vacant parking lot, Branden said to Ricky, "That didn't get us much."

"Nothing," Ricky said. "I don't think they were too scared."

"They were worried enough to change buses," Branden said. "Or smart."

As they rounded the front corner of the building, Ricky muttered, "Robertson has Ellie calling Dent's phone every hour."

"You've got the Molinas' descriptions, right?"

From the front of the dinner line, Caroline waved to them,

and, mouthing apologies, the two men worked forward to join her.

"We're next to go inside," Caroline said, and gave Ricky a long hug.

When she released him, Niell stepped back half a pace and said, "You've got the better tan."

Over a deep butternut tan, Caroline Branden was wearing a long, thin-strapped, peach-colored summer dress. Her light auburn hair was rolled up in a bun, without the prayer covering that would have marked her as Mennonite. Standing in the thin line of evening shade cast by the roof of the building, she had her sunglasses parked on top of her head. She pulled them up, put them on, and said, "You look better in a coat and tie than a man has a right to do, Ricky Niell, but we'll get you into a pair of shorts and a T-shirt soon enough. Until you get some suntan lotion, get in under here, out of the sun."

Niell eased in beside Caroline, and the professor said, "There's room inside now."

Caroline turned and stepped into the vestibule, and Ricky and the professor crowded in behind her. The line inched forward, and two more people pushed in behind them. In the cooler air behind the tinted glass doors, Caroline pulled her sunglasses up to the top of her head again and said, "I've been thinking about this interview, Ricky."

"Are we sure she's working today?" Branden asked.

"I checked," Caroline said. "But three of us might be too many of us."

Ricky said, "She needs to know about Ruth Zook. At the very least I should tell her about that."

"We can do that, Ricky. Mike and I can. We're just tourists. Less intimidating."

"There are a lot of questions," Ricky argued. "I'll have to talk to her eventually."

Branden said, "But if Caroline and I break it to her, we can ask her when she can talk. We can call you with a time and a place later this evening, and you can talk to her then."

"I don't know."

"You really need to talk to Ray Lee Orton, first," the professor said. "You can go do that, and we'll call you after dinner."

Ricky hesitated, thought. "What makes you think she'll talk with strangers?"

"I've got my wallet badge," Branden said. "It's as good as yours, and she'll trust that."

Caroline said, "We'll find out when her shift ends, Ricky. We'll have her talk with you then. But right now, she doesn't need all three of us pushing on her for answers."

The professor added, "She lives up near us, Ricky. We'll have her stop at the beach house on the way home. Ray Lee's going to want to see her, too. They know each other."

Checking his watch, Ricky said, "I'll need to get a room."

"You'll stay with us," Caroline said, scolding a bit. "Stay with us and talk to Jodie, once the shock has worn off."

"Ruth was her friend. So what if she wants to quit early?" Ricky asked. "I probably would, under the circumstances."

"Even better," Branden said. "We'll invite her to our cottage. Help her through this."

"And call you," Caroline said.

The dinner line moved forward toward the hostess's stand.

"OK," Ricky said. "I'll go talk to Ray Lee. But call me, one way or the other."

29

Wednesday, April 6
7:55 P.M.

THE PROFESSOR asked to be seated at one of Jodie Tapp's tables, and this caused the hostess some mild consternation. She seated two other couples while the Brandens waited at the side of her podium, and then reluctantly she led them past a dozen large round tables to a corner café-style table near the kitchen doors, asking perfunctorily, "This OK?"

Caroline said, "Yes," and took a seat facing the swinging doors to the kitchen. The professor sat beside her, facing a corner window that looked out to the back parking lot and the restaurant's metal Dumpsters. When a petite Mennonite girl with well-tanned face and hands came to their table, the two ordered sweet tea, and Caroline asked, "Are you Jodie Tapp?"

Hurried, the girl nodded and walked away with her pad and pen. Behind the drink counter, she poured iced sweet tea from a large plastic pitcher and set the glasses on a small round tray. Then she pushed through the kitchen doors, leaving the drinks on the serving counter.

When Tapp returned, she was carrying a tray of food over her head. She delivered it to a server's folding stand at one of the center tables, and another waitress served the plates from the tray while Jodie retrieved the two glasses of tea for the Brandens.

As she set them on the table, Caroline asked again if she was Jodie Tapp, and Jodie took note this time, saying, "Do I know you?"

"No," the professor said, "but we're from Holmes County."

Jodie brightened and stood a little straighter, eyes shifting back and forth between the Brandens expectantly.

Caroline said, "I'm afraid we have some bad news, Jodie. Can you sit?"

Jodie looked over her shoulder and said, "I shouldn't. Do you want to order?"

"Jodie," the professor said. "It's not good news. About Ruth Zook."

Jodie hesitated, then cautiously drew a vacant chair from the adjoining table. She sat down and asked, "Is she OK?" seeming to Caroline to be resigned, as if she were inclined toward the negative or forewarned of something tragic.

Branden leaned across the small table toward Jodie and said, "She's been killed, Jodie."

Jodie threw a hand over her mouth, stiffened, and stifled a cry. Eyes wide, she asked immediately, "Was it an accident? On the highway?"

"No, Jodie," Caroline said. "She was murdered."

Hand still covering her mouth, Jodie began a muted wail, as if she wanted to cry out but had managed only to direct a scream inward where she alone could hear it. Caroline reached for her hand.

Choking down her cry, Jodie popped up on her feet and swayed out of balance. She grabbed for the edge of the little table, and it toppled over, spilling glasses of iced tea across the floor. Jodie landed on her butt, legs out straight, one arm planted behind her, the other still covering her mouth.

From across the room, a manager lady in Mennonite garb came immediately toward the Brandens, who both had knelt to help Jodie to her feet. They righted her chair and got her seated, and as they were pulling the table up onto its legs, the manager reached them, solicitously inquiring if the Brandens were hurt. Caroline assured the woman that they were not, and without inquiring about Jodie, the manager turned for the corner closet and came back with a mop. As she drew the mop through the spill, she said to Jodie, "Get two more teas." To the Brandens, she said, "This is on the house."

"Really, it's no problem," the professor said.

He would have said more, but Caroline advanced on the manager and insisted, "Jodie has had some bad news. Maybe you could give us a moment, here."

The manager seemed startled. Caroline held a determined stare, with polite antagonism showing openly in her gaze. The manager read her rebuke and retreated.

The Brandens positioned their chairs to flank Jodie, and Caroline said, "We heard you were friends, Jodie. Tell us about Ruth."

Jodie had to struggle to bring her mind into focus on Caroline's words. She didn't answer.

Intending encouragement, the professor said, "They tell us you were friends with Fannie Helmuth, Jodie. Were you also friends with Ruth?"

Alarm showed in Jodie's expression, but she said nothing. Realizing he didn't actually know it to be true, Branden said, "We think Fannie is fine, Jodie. And we have a friend who wants to ask you some questions."

Jodie said nothing.

"Our friend is a Holmes County detective," Caroline said. "He wants to ask you some questions about Fannie. And maybe Ruth, too, if you knew her."

Jodie nodded, but slumped on her chair. She seemed to pull inward, becoming as small as a frightened child, as wounded as a broken wing. Slowly she began to turn her head from side to side. Her eyes closed and opened again to stare denial into vacant space. "It has to be a mistake," she said. "No, really, you're wrong."

"It's not a mistake," Caroline said. "She was murdered. Shot."

"But she was just here," Jodie said, searching Caroline's eyes for agreement.

Branden spoke, and Jodie turned slowly toward him. "Jodie," he said, "she brought drugs up to Ohio on the bus."

After a long pause, as if her thoughts were forming themselves inside a confusing dream, Jodie asked, "How?"

"In an extra suitcase," Branden said. "It was cocaine. We don't think Ruth knew what it was until she opened it the next morning."

Jodie stared incredulously at the professor. He added, "She dumped the drugs out in the farm pond behind her house, and then when she met someone in a secluded glade the next morning, they shot her."

It took Jodie a full minute to ask her next question. "Who would kill an Amish girl?" As she asked it, her fingers rubbed her cheek, as if remembering a wound.

"That's what Detective Niell wants to talk with you about," Branden said. "How did Ruth get the suitcase?"

Caroline added, "And was it anything like the one you gave to Fannie Helmuth?"

Jodie's fingers came to rest beneath her eye, and she looked back and forth between the two Brandens as if confused. "Is Fannie OK?" she asked. "Did they hurt Fannie, too?"

"Who would hurt her, Jodie?" Branden asked. "Who do you mean?"

Jodie looked even more puzzled and seemed to recoil from her thoughts. She stood, eyes wide open, then sat back down, shutting her eyes. She pulled her fingers away from her cheek, slowly opened her eyes, tugged nervously at her long dress at the knees, and then resumed rubbing mechanically at her cheek.

The manager came back and asked for someone to explain to her what was wrong.

Jodie looked up at her vacantly and said, "I need to go home."

The manager lady started to protest, but Caroline said, "Jodie has gotten some really bad news about Ruth Zook."

"Just what kind of bad news?" the lady asked.

"She's dead," the professor said, and watched the manager for a reaction.

Jodie moaned in her seat, and the manager said, "You're kidding!"

"No," Branden said, "and if you don't mind, we're going to take Jodie home early."

Directly, the manager said, "She can't leave her truck parked here. I need the spot for customers."

Caroline stood and advanced. "She's gonna come with us, now."

"Where?" the lady demanded.

"To our beach house on Longboat Key, not that it's any of your business."

"Well, one of you is going to have to drive her truck."

Jodie stood and tried to mollify the manager. "I can follow them," she said. "Or I'll just go home."

"You follow us, Jodie," Caroline said. "We'll make you some dinner on the grill, and we can talk."

"OK," Jodie said distantly.

Caroline took her arm and began guiding Jodie between the tables toward the front door. "Better yet, you ride with me," she said. "Mike can drive your truck."

Hanging back, the professor pressed a crumpled ten-dollar bill into the manager's hand and said, "We'll pay for our tea."

30

WHEN RICKY Niell pulled up to the butterscotch building of the Bradenton Beach police station, beside the long and low Cortez drawbridge spanning the waters of northern Sarasota Bay, Ray Lee Orton was climbing down an aluminum ladder he had propped against the side of a forty-foot cabin cruiser. The all-white boat was awash in lights from two tall floods that Orton had set up behind the stern, and the fiberglass hull of the boat rested on the padded supports of a salvage trailer that had been used to haul it out of the channel waters of Longboat Pass. A ragged hole in the starboard hull, well below the waterline, showed the damage where someone had placed a charge inside a lower hold of the boat to scuttle the craft.

Niell stopped his rental car at the edge of the light, on the parking lot of white sand and crushed shells, and as he got out and walked up to the ladder, he called up to Orton, "This the boat you told Robertson about? Stolen boats and drug running?"

Orton stepped down the ladder and stuck out his hand with a smile. "Yes. Hi, Ricky. Good thing you called first. I was headed home."

Orton was out of uniform, dressed in cutoff jeans, a flowered tropical shirt in peach and turquoise hues, and white loafers. He had the muscular legs and narrow waist of a bicycle cop, and he was strong in his arms and broad through his shoulders from what Ricky remembered was Orton's passion, kite surfing along the windy stretches of beach on the barrier islands west of Sarasota Bay.

Niell shook hands with the sergeant and said, "I flew down this morning. I've been over in Pinecraft since I drove down from Tampa, interviewing bus drivers."

"Robertson asked me to send the Brandens to meet you," Orton said.

"They did. And they stayed to talk to Jodie Tapp. To tell her about Ruth Zook's being shot."

"Good," Orton said. He drew a handkerchief out of his hip pocket and rubbed at the tips of his fingers on his right hand. Then he nipped a splinter with his teeth, spat it out to the side, and rubbed on the wound again with his handkerchief. "Splinters," he said. "I've been poking around in bullet holes."

Orton put his handkerchief away and rapped his knuckles against the hull of the tall boat. "We're dealing with a bad outfit, here," he said. "The owners of this boat have been missing for about two weeks, now. Can't really be sure about the time, because they were boating casually between Key West and Marathon. Their float plan didn't put them back to Fort Myers right away, and their kids didn't report them missing for a couple of days after they were supposed to have gotten back."

Niell paced the length of the boat to inspect its hull, and then he returned to the hole. "Why would anyone sink it?" he asked Orton, lightly fingering the frayed fiberglass strands along the edge of the breach.

Orton pulled his ladder down and folded it on the ground. "They use them only once, Ricky. They hijack the boats in the Keys, make the run up the coast, offload on one of the remote beaches at night, and then scuttle the boats out in deeper water. We find debris floating in on the tides, and twice we've been able to find and dive on the wrecks. Mostly, nobody ever sees the boats again."

"This the first one that didn't sink?" Ricky asked.

"We think so."

"Why do you have it here?"

"As opposed to what?"

"Well, there's the Coast Guard, customs, other agencies that would want it."

"Customs is coming for it tomorrow morning," Orton said. "The Coast Guard has already been through it."

"You've gone through it, too?"

"I was taking a second look," Orton said. He pulled his ladder up again, propped it against the side of the boat, and led Niell up to the aft deck.

The stern lounge consisted of padded wraparound seating along the back of the boat, with a deck table bolted between that and two padded swivel chairs. A sliding glass door gave access to a small salon inside, and outside passage was available along either side of the salon to the bow. Ricky could see through the glass that inside the salon a companionway led belowdecks and a short run of steps led up to the wheel deck. The exterior brass work and stainless trim shined brightly in the light from Orton's flood lamps, but the teak decking planks under Niell's feet were dull gray and smooth from wear. Standing on the stern deck, Niell could see no evidence of a gunfight.

He asked Orton, "Bullet holes?" and Orton said, "It's all inside. All I've got is nine-millimeter holes. The Coast Guard extracted all the lead for ballistics, not that it'll do them any good without a weapon to match it to. But there are bullet holes sprayed around inside the salon, all down the companionway, and into the galley. Same thing up on the bridge."

Niell crossed into the salon, climbed to the upper wheel deck, and examined an irregular line of bullet holes crossing through the instrument dash, the side panels, and the back of the wheel chair. Orton led him down into the quarters below, and Niell saw more bullet holes splintering through the galley and into the stateroom door.

Back out on the stern deck, Niell asked, "You think they just killed the owners?"

"Boarded, killed them, and put the bodies overboard. We'll never find them."

"It looks like all their personal gear is still on board."

"Whatever didn't wash out when they scuttled her," Orton confirmed. "All these drug runners want is the transportation. They don't bother with the gear, equipment, anything. They just jack the boats, use them once, and blow holes in the hulls when they're done."

Niell stepped over the gunwale and started down the ladder, with Orton following. They folded the ladder again, carried it to the side of the police station, propped it against the building, switched off the floodlights, and went inside the lower entrance, through the booking station with its single cell, into Orton's ground-floor conference room. Niell took a seat at the long table there, and Orton produced a file folder, saying, "Photos taken underwater."

While Orton ran out two glasses of water at a corner sink, Niell opened the folder and started laying out pictures, most of them five-by-sevens, in sequence according to numbers on the backs of the prints. One set of photos showed a smaller cabin cruiser lying on a sandy ocean bottom, its ruined hull exposed like a crater, edges blown out around a jagged hole. The second sequence of prints showed a similar fate for a sport-fishing cruiser, its bow blown out, as well as its hull at the keel line, as if two separate charges had been used inside the larger boat.

Niell stacked the photos loosely, returned them to the folder, and said, "Looks like they'll take any type of boat."

Orton sat across the table from Niell and straightened the photos in the folder. "This is a bad crew, Ricky. We think they fly in junk from South America, hijack boats in the Keys, run up the coast—even in daylight, they'd look just like pleasure boaters—and then offload and scuttle at night."

"Do they really just kill the owners outright?" Ricky asked.

Orton nodded grimly. "But until Robertson called and told us about your Ruth Zook and Fannie Helmuth, we didn't know where the drugs ended up. As it is, sending suitcases north on Amish buses might be just one of the routes they use."

"Did Robertson tell you the latest about Fannie Helmuth?" Ricky asked.

"Said she ran."

"Well, took a bus to Charlotte, anyway," Ricky said.

Orton stood and led Ricky up the rear staircase to his office on the top floor. From a metal filing cabinet beside his desk, Orton pulled a case folder of handwritten notes. He directed Ricky to a chair and sat behind his desk. From his notes, he read a summary of what Robertson had told him on the phone, and asked, "That about cover it?"

"Except that we think Fannie Helmuth got on a Greyhound bus in downtown Charlotte."

Orton shook his head and closed his folder. "She thinks she can run from these people?"

"She's with a friend. Howie Dent, about her age. Lives on a neighboring farm."

Orton leaned forward and planted his elbows on his desktop. "Robertson says he thinks this organization will close the Ohio route and 'clean up loose ends.'"

"Right. They may also fix problems down here. But we don't think they know yet that we have their identities. Rachel is especially good with computers, and she got their descriptions pretty fast."

"Rachel called earlier this afternoon," Orton said.

"Where does it stand, then?" Ricky asked.

"Customs wants the boat, and I think they're going to salvage the two wrecks we were able to locate."

"DEA?"

"Rachel called them, too, with the information about the Molinas. They're searching known addresses. Combing through criminal and civil records. It helps that they know now who we're looking for."

"Coast Guard?"

"They'll get involved again if we get a lead."

"What do you plan to do now?"

Orton shrugged his shoulders. "I don't really have any jurisdiction off the beaches. None outside of Bradenton Beach."

"How about Jodie Tapp?"

"I think she needs to be in protective custody."

"Can you do that?"

"If she'll cooperate."

"The Brandens have asked her to come out to your beach house," Ricky said. "They called from the restaurant while I was driving up here."

"They told her about Ruth?"

Niell nodded.

Orton stood behind his desk. "If I know Jodie, she'll take this hard."

"She did," Niell said. "She left work early, to follow the Brandens up to your place."

*   *   *

Niell followed Orton's Jeep across the drawbridge over Longboat Pass after sunset. A half mile farther south, Orton pulled into a sandy rectangular parking lot in front of a set of three narrow houses positioned lengthwise on a patch of sand that fronted dunes and the beach beyond. The leftmost house was sided with weathered boards, and in front of that house, a single rental sedan was parked with its nose pointed out toward the road. Once the two men had switched off their headlights, the lot fell into complete darkness, as did all the approaches to the beach. Orton threaded a path in the dark to the far side of the beach house and spoke back over his shoulder, "We keep all the lights out this time of year, because the turtles want to come in to lay their eggs."

Niell followed the sergeant down the length of the house, wondering how anyone not familiar with the property would find their way in the blackout.

At the back of the long house, Orton knocked on the glass of a patio door, and Professor Branden pulled long slat drapes open, flooding the patio with light. Orton slid the glass door open and led Niell inside. Then the professor closed the heavy drapes.

Caroline rose from a low sofa and laid her book on a glass-topped coffee table, as Niell looked around at the decor of ocean paintings, shell collections in glass jars, and rope-and-anchor furniture. He took a seat in a wicker chair and asked, "How would anyone know we're at the beach?"

Orton laughed. "Sorry. It was my mother's house. She liked it this way when she came down from Chicago. I just haven't done anything with the place."

Caroline crossed behind the breakfast bar and pulled a pitcher of tea out of the refrigerator. The professor lined up four tumblers, and once Caroline had filled them, he carried two at a time out into the living room. As they took seats, Orton asked, "Jodie still here?" and Caroline said, "She's resting in a front bedroom."

Ricky's phone rang with Robertson's tone, and he stood and asked, "Can I take this on the patio?"

Standing, the professor said, "I'll get the drapes. We have to leave the lights out."

Niell went out into the night and answered the call. From the other side of the dunes, he heard the rush of surf coming ashore. A stiff onshore breeze was lifting a mist of salt and sand off the dunes, so Ricky turned his back to talk to the sheriff. "Niell," he answered. "We've got Jodie Tapp here, and she's safe."

"Where's that?" Robertson asked. "And what about the bus drivers?"

"We're at Ray Lee Orton's beach house, with the Brandens. Jodie's sleeping right now. I came north to see Ray Lee after interviewing the bus drivers, and now we're at Ray Lee's."

"Anything on the Molinas?" Robertson asked.

"Not that Ray Lee knows."

Letting impatience sound in his voice, Robertson asked, "What'd you talk about?"

"We went through the boat that they found capsized. Scuttled, really. Hole blown out in the hull."

"Does Ray Lee think they've got any chance of catching these pirates?"

"He thinks Rachel's information is going to help the DEA. They're the ones running it down, now."

"They know about our BOLO?"

"Rachel will have given them everything," Ricky said.

"I don't like playing second fiddle, Niell."

"I know, Sheriff. I thought I'd contact the DEA tomorrow morning."

"You planning on sleeping, Niell?"

"Thought I would."

"Kidding," Robertson said. "Really, I'm just kidding."

In the background, Niell heard Missy Taggert say something curt to the sheriff, and muffled, he heard the sheriff say, "I'm not being bossy."

Niell waited through the exchange and asked, "You get anything on the Helmuth caravan, Sheriff?"

"They're already down south of Zanesville," Robertson said.

"Then they went south, not north?"

Robertson harrumphed into the phone. "Highway Patrol found them camped beside the road at about eight o'clock. Said the Helmuths told them they had left home voluntarily. Said they didn't want to stay in Holmes County anymore. Called it a lawless frontier."

"So they just picked up overnight and moved?"

"That's what they say, Ricky. They're not coming back. They gave a general description of the woman who came to look for Fannie, but that's all we got from them."

Ricky shook his head in the dark but didn't speak. The sheriff asked, "You still there?"

"Yes, sorry. I was thinking. The Molinas can easily have changed their plates."

"Right."

"And the boat Fannie says she was on with Jim and John—that can easily have been another stolen boat."

"I know, Niell."

"So, if the DEA can't tie the Molinas to an outfit down here, and if Fannie Helmuth can't ID a boat for us—or even if she could and it was stolen and then scuttled like these others—then we've got nothing."

"We've got Tapp, Niell," Robertson barked. "That's half of why I sent you down there."

"She's scared, Sheriff. And I don't blame her. What if she's like Fannie? Just wants to get away from this."

"I don't know," Robertson said, frustrated and sounding it. "If I can't find Fannie and convince her to come back, then Jodie Tapp is our only lead. You need to find out what she knows."

"She's sleeping, Sheriff."

"Then wake her up! Look, Niell, she's all we've got right now."

"I know. I know. I'm just sick of thinking about young Amish women putting it on the line for a job we should be able to do without them."

"They're in the mix, Niell. We didn't do that. And we need Tapp to tell us what she knows. If my BOLO on Fannie gives us nothing, then Tapp is all we've got."

Wearily, Niell turned back for the sliding door and said, "I'll wake her up."

"I want to know about that boat, Niell," Robertson said. "Even if it was stolen."

"Right," Niell said, and switched off.

He knocked on the glass, and Branden let him in. Caroline was at the counter pouring more tea. To Niell she said, "How's Bruce? No improvement, I'll wager."

Niell smiled, shook his head. "He wants us to talk to Jodie tonight."

"She's sleeping," Caroline said. "I don't want to wake her up."

Ray Lee stood in front of the sofa and finished a last swallow of tea, saying, "I didn't see her car. She ride with you?"

"No," Branden said as he closed the drapes. "She parked beside us."

Orton came forward around the glass coffee table. "Her car's not out there."

Caroline turned and started down a long hallway in the center of the house, the men following. She pushed open the last bedroom door, switched on the lights, and led the men inside. Although the covers had been disturbed, the bed was empty.

At the window, Orton said, "The latch isn't locked." He lifted the sash, and night air flooded in from the front parking lot. The screen was lying outside on the ground.

31

BRANDEN AND Niell rode in the back of Orton's Jeep. They raced over the bridge and past the long and deserted parking lots at Coquina Beach, ran through dark and sleepy Bradenton Beach, skidded to make the turn at the intersection in front of the Cortez Bridge, and slowed on the other side of the long bridge to make a sharp right turn down off the bridge approach into Cortez. Orton passed one little trailer-park lane and then a second. He turned left at the third lane, with only his headlamps to light the way. When he pulled up in front of the narrow end of a single-wide aluminum trailer, the parking spot was empty. Orton popped out of his Jeep and marched down a thin strip of concrete walkway to a side door on the trailer. While Niell and the professor extracted themselves from the backseat of the Jeep, Orton rapped on the screen door and called out, "Jodie, it's Ray Lee."

Then he tried the knob, and the door pushed open. As he entered the dark trailer, he called back over his shoulder, "She always leaves it open."

Niell and Branden came up the sidewalk. A light switched on inside, and Orton waved them in. "She always leaves it open," he said again. He was standing beside a slender black lacquer floor lamp in the front living room. All the rest of the trailer was dark inside.

Orton stepped past a hammered-copper cube-shaped coffee table and switched on a floor lamp at the other end of a gray leather sofa, and Niell and Branden got their first good look at the rest of the room—decorated in sleek tones of black, gray, platinum blue, yellow, and white.

"She's a decorator?" Niell asked.

"A good one," Branden offered.

"Jodie's a bit of a puzzle," Orton said. "Mennonite and modern."

"It looks as if she watches a lot of HGTV," Niell said. He lifted a stack of decorating magazines from the coffee cube and started reading covers. "A lot of HGTV," he said again.

Orton turned to cross through a kitchen-and-table nook, and he stepped into a back hallway. A light came on in the first of two bedrooms, and he called the men back.

In the first bedroom, the hand of a dedicated modernist was evident again, the theme being black and crystal, with silver accents and plum drapes. On a carefully made bedspread with a light rose and bamboo silhouette pattern, two old leather-strapped suitcases, nicked and scratched from hard use, were laid out beside each other, one opened and empty, the second closed and strapped. Orton undid the straps, pulled up the lid, and found it empty, too. Both old suitcases were lined with blue satin and lace.

Branden said, "Those are the only vaguely Mennonite things in the whole place."

"Like I said," Orton mumbled, but didn't finish his remark.

"I'm not comfortable being in here like this," Ricky said.

Distracted, Orton said, "She's a good friend."

"Still," Ricky said, "we shouldn't be inside."

Orton turned and left the bedroom frowning. "She's running," he said. "She's scared, and she's running."

Niell followed Orton to the front door of the trailer. Branden turned out the bedroom light and came back into the living area.

"If she was thinking about packing both of those suitcases, then she had it in mind to stay away for quite a long while."

"I'm getting tired of losing witnesses," Ricky said.

"You'll need to call Bruce," Branden said.

"Maybe in the morning," Ricky said. "Maybe she'll just turn up at work tomorrow."

"This isn't right," Orton muttered. He pulled out his phone and opened the door. "Need to call some people."

Branden switched off one of the lamps and followed Orton. Ricky turned off the other light and came out through the door behind Branden. Orton was propped back against the side of his Jeep, talking on his phone.

"Look, Danny, everybody needs to know," Orton was saying. He listened with an impatient expression and said, "OK, but DEA especially." Then he pocketed his phone.

Standing at the front of the dark trailer, Orton said, "She's not safe like this, on her own."

"Two empty suitcases," Ricky said. "That means she's still here."

"Or, they've got her already," Orton said. "She was going to pack, but they've got her now."

"Who's Danny?" Branden asked.

"Night dispatcher over at the station," Orton said. "He's going to make some calls."

"You have any idea where to look?" Ricky asked. "Know where she'd go, now?"

"The beach," Orton said. "Work, the beach, that's all she does."

"Then I don't see that there's anything we can do tonight," Ricky said. "Maybe she'll go in to work tomorrow."

After a pause, Branden said, "Caroline and I can go over first thing in the morning. But, Ricky, there's one thing you still should do tonight."

Niell groaned. "That's not a call I want to make."

* * *

Robertson hung up with Niell and threw his phone against the back cushion of the sofa. It bounced off the seat cushion and landed on the carpet next to Missy's feet. "Cute, Bruce," she said. "You really want to buy a new phone?"

Robertson retrieved his phone, stuffed it into his front bathrobe pocket, and flopped his full weight onto the sofa next to Missy.

"Bruce! Do you really think we need a new sofa?"

"Cut it out, Missy," Robertson shot. More coolly, he said, "It's just a phone."

"What's happened?" Missy asked. "That was Niell?"

"We've lost track of another witness."

"Jodie Tapp?"

Robertson nodded unhappily. "She ducked out of a window at the Brandens' place in Bradenton Beach."

"So she's running, too."

Robertson stood up and paced barefoot along the length of the parlor carpet. He came back to the sofa, more frustrated than before, and sat heavily back down. Missy gave him an eye, and asked, "Doesn't Ricky have any leads?"

The sheriff didn't answer. Missy turned a page in her novel and let her husband stew. She read a page in silence and then said, "It all tells you that you're right about Florida."

"How's that?"

"Two different girls are afraid of the same people. So, the Molinas really are connected to the people Jodie knows in Florida."

"We kinda knew that already, Missy."

"It's new information, that's all."

"Well, it's not very much. And the Molinas are all I've got, now. And I wouldn't have that if it weren't for Rachel."

"And Stan."

"Yes, and Stan."

"You've got Stan and Pat going up to Barberton tomorrow morning."

Robertson didn't respond.

"And you've got Ricky down in Sarasota."

Nothing from the sheriff.

"So, what more can you do, Bruce?"

"Nothing," the sheriff grumped. "Either I find one of these girls, or I'm sunk."

"Let the DEA chase people in Florida. Let the BOLO turn up the Molinas, wherever they are. And let your people do their jobs, in Barberton and in Florida."

Robertson threw up his hands. "There's nothing else I can do."

Inside his bathrobe pocket, his cell phone rang again. He stood and answered it gruffly, "What?"

He hesitated and said, "No, I'm sorry. I need to speak with you."

Missy stood and came to his side, and the sheriff listened and answered alternately.

"Fannie, I need you to come home.

"OK, but where?

"Why not?

"Fannie, listen. We've got people working on this in Florida.

"No, they're traveling down south of Lancaster—moving to Kentucky, they told the highway patrol—and they won't give us a sketch of her, either.

"Fannie, it's not safe out on the road.

"OK, but . . .

"No, Fannie. No. We don't know where she is.

"But you and Jodie are making the same mistake. If they catch up with either of you, they'll kill you. Just like Ruth.

"No, please, Fannie.

"That's not the smart play, here.

"What?

"OK, but where?

"Why not?

"Fannie, let me send someone to you.

"Pat Lance. You trust her, don't you?

"Just tell me where you are. I'll fly her out tomorrow.

"Fannie . . .

"Wait.

"No, I can help." Then the call went dead.

Again, the sheriff pitched his phone into the sofa. Missy said nothing.

"Won't tell me where she's gone," Robertson mumbled. "Just that she's headed someplace safe. With relatives."

"Are you going to try to track her down?" Missy asked.

"She could be anywhere," Robertson said. He picked his phone up from the couch and stuffed it back into his bathrobe pocket. "She thinks she'll be safe with relatives, and all her Holmes County family is out taking a wagon train through the countryside, as if nothing in the world could go wrong."

32

RICKY NIELL left the beach house early the next morning to meet Ray Lee Orton at the federal building in Bradenton, and the Brandens drove south past the tall, Spanish-tiled resort condominiums on Longboat Key. At New Pass, they joined the line of vehicles waiting for the drawbridge, and once the drawbridge had lowered into place, they crossed over to Lido Key, negotiated St. Armand's Circle, and went over the high arching span of the white bridge on the John Ringling Causeway into downtown Sarasota. Turning right at the busy intersection with Tamiami Trail, they skirted the long curve of the city harbor on the right. Once past the tall white-stone and mirrored-glass condominiums on the left, they turned east on Bahia Vista Boulevard, heading to Miller's Amish Restaurant and Clock Shoppe on Beneva, a few blocks north of Pinecraft village. The restaurant would open at nine thirty, and they hoped to speak with Jodie before that, if she showed up for work that morning.

When they reached the parking lot, there were eight cars and trucks parked at the back of the lot and one car in the front lot, with two older people sitting in the front seat with the windows down, waiting to be first in the breakfast line. The Brandens parked at the rear of the front lot, and another tourist's vehicle pulled in and parked near the front, causing the first couple to pop out and scurry up to the front door.

Caroline and the professor locked up, went around the back corner to the service entrance, and pushed through a screened door into a busy kitchen with a mix of Amish-dressed waitresses working at the sinks and long tables, and English-dressed cooks in hairnets working in front of hot stoves and ovens. A woman wearing a manager's badge walked up stirring a large bowl of bread pudding.

"We're not open yet," she said. "Can you go around to the front?"

She was probably in her fifties, Caroline thought, dressed matronly, as a Mennonite woman. She stirred the bread mix with a large wooden spoon and gave an air of disdainful authority, which Caroline decided to challenge.

"We're not customers," she said curtly.

The professor pulled out his wallet and stepped forward to hand the manager his badge card.

The lady read it and said, "Reserve deputy. You're not official?"

"As official as he needs to be," Caroline said, and took the card back. "We're looking for Jodie Tapp, and this is part of a DEA investigation." She glanced back at her husband, and he held to his place without challenging the assertion.

"Jodie didn't come in this morning," the lady said.

Caroline asked, "What is your name, please?"

The manager hesitated, and Caroline said, "Again, Jodie Tapp is missing. My husband is a reserve deputy attached to the investigation. So what's your name, and what can you tell us about Jodie Tapp?"

A sardonic smile broke out on the lady's face and she said, striking another disdainful pose, "Miriam Hostettler. And my guess is that Jodie Tapp isn't missing from anywhere."

"Is that your real name," Caroline asked, "or is that your stage name, for the tourists?"

"It's my real name," Hostettler asserted, turning back into the busy kitchen. She angled a path between cooks and waitresses, and the Brandens followed her. At a long stainless table against the far wall, Hostettler put her bowl down and led the Brandens out into the dining room. From a podium by the front door, she drew out a roster, read down the list, looked up, and said, "Well, Jodie's shift should have started at six. She helps in the kitchen before we open."

"Is she frequently late for work?" Caroline asked.

"No. No, she's not. I don't really like her, but at least she's always on time."

Mike Branden came forward and asked, "Why don't you like her?"

Hostettler picked up a gray tub of wrapped silverware and started setting tables. The Brandens followed her between the tables, and Caroline asked, "Is she not a good waitress?"

"She's fine," Hostettler said. "Just a phony, is all."

Hostettler was dressed in a long, aqua skirt and a high-necked white blouse. She wore an apron over her bodice and down the front of her skirt to her hemline, with modest black stockings and soft black walking shoes on her feet. Her Mennonite prayer cover consisted of a small round patch of lace tied over the bun of her hair. Her glasses were silver, wire-rimmed, and round. She wore no makeup.

Caroline studied her clothes and said, "Anybody can dress Mennonite, Mrs. Hostettler. Are you saying Jodie was just dressing the part, but really wasn't Mennonite?"

Hostettler paused beside a round table to face Caroline. "She's not much for church, is all I know. And I don't like the company she keeps."

"All we know about her is that she works here and that she likes to surf," the professor said. "She's a windsurfer."

"That's all I really know, too," Hostettler said. "But I've never seen her in church, and sometimes men come around."

"That's all?" Caroline challenged.

"They aren't nice men," Hostettler said, holding firm. "Jodie doesn't seem to have nice friends."

"You mean they're *surfers*?" Caroline asked. "You don't like surfers?"

Hostettler frowned through a long, thoughtful pause and eventually said, "There were some men with a fishing boat. And Jodie came in bruised. Like she'd been beaten."

"That's hardly a good reason to harbor ill-will toward Jodie," Caroline said.

Unapologetically, Hostettler said, "I just don't like to see that kind in my restaurant."

"What do the other waitresses think of her?" Branden asked.

"My regulars don't pay much attention to her. She takes to the snowbirds, mostly. They seem to like her a lot."

"Do you hire a lot of temps?" Branden asked. "Girls from up north?"

Hostettler nodded and resumed her work at the tables. Caroline reached into the tub to help lay out place settings.

As they worked, Hostettler said, "Plenty of girls come here for a vacation. If they have experience, we hire them part-time so they can earn a little down here, and maybe stay longer."

Branden asked, "Do you remember Fannie Helmuth?"

"Yes. She stayed almost two months last fall."

"How about Ruth Zook?" Branden pressed.

"Just left, maybe a week ago."

The Brandens exchanged a glance, but neither of them mentioned Ruth's murder.

"Did Jodie know them?" Caroline asked. "Both Fannie and Ruth?"

"She knows them all, Mrs. Branden. Takes them to the beaches."

A crashing of glass in the kitchen sent Hostettler rushing to the back, and Caroline said to her husband, "We need to tell her about Ruth."

Branden agreed, and they waited for Hostettler to return. When she did, they told her about Ruth's murder and Fannie's being missing. Hostettler dropped heavily onto a chair, saying, "This can't be true. Do you mean *our* Ruth Zook, from Ohio?"

"From Charm." Caroline nodded. She sat across the table from Hostettler. "Ruth took an extra suitcase home, and there were some drugs inside. It got her murdered."

"Drugs?"

"Cocaine," the professor said, still standing beside the table. Hostettler looked stricken, so he sat down, too.

"I don't understand," Hostettler said. "I don't much care for Jodie, but she's not the type to be mixed up with that sort of thing. Not in a million years."

"We think Ruth was coerced," Branden said. "We think she and Fannie were coerced."

"Fannie? I thought you said it was Ruth?"

"Fannie that we know of," Branden said, "but maybe Ruth, too. We're not sure how it all worked, but maybe both of them were involved."

Hostettler stared blankly at the backs of her hands. "Fannie and Jodie were good friends. I'm not sure about Ruth and Jodie."

"Mrs. Hostettler," Caroline said, "is it like Jodie that she wouldn't come to work?"

"Not without calling first. I have a policy on that. She's usually quite conscientious."

"So she *is* a good worker," Caroline said.

"Yes, I just don't like some of the company she keeps."

"You mean surfers?" Branden asked.

"Yes, I suppose so."

"Like Sergeant Ray Lee Orton?"

"Who?"

"A surfer, Mrs. Hostettler. He's also a sergeant with the Bradenton Beach Police Department. He likes kite surfing."

Hostettler looked puzzled.

Branden said, "You can't assume that all surfers are scoundrels."

"I don't," Hostettler said. "Just the ones that beat Jodie up."

Branden smiled. "Yes."

"Do you remember anything about those men?" Caroline asked.

Hostettler closed her eyes to remember. "Two younger men. Had a boat on a big trailer." She opened her eyes. "They were here only a couple of times, and I told them they couldn't bring that big boat into my parking lot. It took up too many spots for the customers. After Jodie got bruised up, they didn't come around anymore."

"When was that?" Caroline asked.

"It was back when Fannie was here. September? We get so many snowbirds. I can't remember them all."

Hostettler stood and smoothed out the front of her apron. "I need to tell the other girls about Ruth."

Caroline stood and held out her hand, saying, "Thank you for helping."

"Sure."

Branden stood, too, and asked, "If Jodie comes in, will you call us?"

Hostettler nodded, and Branden handed his card to her, saying, "My cell's on the back."

Hostettler took the card, slipped it into her apron pocket, started for the kitchen door, and then turned back. "Why are you asking about Jodie?"

Branden said, "We told her about Ruth last night. We thought she was resting at our cottage, but she ducked out a bedroom window."

"And then what?" Hostettler asked.

Caroline said, "All we know is that she hasn't gone home."

*   *   *

While Caroline was driving back over the bay bridge, Bruce Robertson called the professor's cell phone. Without preamble, he asked Branden, "Jodie Tapp?"

"Nothing yet," Branden said. "She didn't go in to work this morning."

"I got a call from Fannie Helmuth last night. On Howie Dent's phone."

"Oh?"

"She's not coming back. And Dent's phone is never on."

"I've got a feeling that Jodie's not coming back, either," Branden said.

"Anything from the DEA?"

"Ricky and Ray Lee are over there now," Branden said.

"I'll call them," Robertson said. "Where are you headed?"

"We'll check today at Tapp's trailer, once or twice," Branden said. "But if she doesn't show up at home, then Ray Lee says she'll be on a beach somewhere."

"Or on a Greyhound bus," Robertson complained.

"So, it comes down to what the DEA can do on the Molinas," Branden said.

"That, and Pat Lance."

"What does she have?"

"Don't know yet. She's up in Barberton with Stan Armbruster. Barberton PD is gonna show them through the boarded-up Molina house. At best, it's a long shot."

"Looking for what?"

"I don't know, Mike. Really, at this point, I don't know."

33

"THIS WAS once a nice house," Lance said to Armbruster. "It was somebody's home."

They were standing in a cold drizzle outside a small frame house. A tired concrete stoop hunkered in front of a boarded-up doorway. The porch shelter over the stoop had been pulled down and discarded. Tall weeds had overtaken the front lawn. Like a final insult to the house, rain pelted against the rotten plywood slab over the front door; the plywood had long ago started to crumble under the assault.

Where an entryway roof once had been fastened to the front of the house, there was now only a long ugly gash through the weathered siding above the door. The structural beams behind the exposed siding had taken a soaking over the months, and one had cracked and sagged into a weary angle. Flanking the door, twin dilapidated plywood slabs covered the two front-facing windows. The single dormer window on the second floor had not been boarded over, and there, broken glass and splintered framing showed the damage from the numerous stones and bricks that had been pitched at the side of the house.

Altogether, the front of the house looked like the weary face of a tattered B-movie monster—blank eye patches at the two windows, a ruined scab of wood for a nose, a long slash through the front siding for brows, and the cracked and bloodless lips of a concrete stoop.

"It's a Halloween nightmare," Armbruster remarked. "Somebody should take it down."

"Must have been somebody's home," Lance said again, sounding even more despondent.

The policeman who had met them returned from the back. He waved them down a weedy path between the side of the house and a chain-link fence along the property line, saying, "We can get in at the back."

In the rain, Lance and Armbruster followed the policeman to the rear door, where he put a key into a padlock and turned it. With the lock off, he pulled the flange apart and used a second key to unlock the dead bolt on the back door.

Inside a utility entrance at the back of the house, he said, "The power isn't on, but see what you can, as best as you can. The cutting table was in the front living room, and the one bedroom upstairs is where they slept."

Lance peered into the dark interior of the house and said, "Everything's boarded up. What were you going to do if we hadn't brought flashlights?"

The policeman shrugged. "My captain said to let you in. That's all I know."

Armbruster switched on his flashlight and said, "This could take a while."

To the policeman, Lance said, "You don't have to stay."

With a shrug, he handed Lance the two keys on a brass ring and said, "Captain Andersen gets the keys. You'll drop them off?"

Lance nodded, and the policeman left through the back door.

Armbruster led the way into a fifties-style kitchen with a green linoleum floor littered with fast-food wrappers and assorted trash. An old refrigerator stood in the corner near the chipped porcelain sink, mold and foul aromas spilling out around the edges of both. Flattened cardboard boxes had been stacked in a corner next to a curb-sized green plastic garbage bin with broken wheels on the bottom.

In a small dining room with a worn and scratched hardwood floor, there was only an old black rotary phone sitting on the floor in a corner. They lighted their way into the adjoining living room and saw that it had similarly been stripped of all its furnishings. Lance shined her light on one of the front windows and saw that the glass had been broken in before the opening had been boarded over with plywood. Rainwater was seeping in at the bottom edge and had started to ruin the wall, baseboards, and floor under the window. The wet patch had expanded over the weeks to reach the edge of a ratty area rug that showed only the vaguest residue of a reddish tint that once might have given some life and color to the drab room.

With his flashlight Armbruster found the stairs to the second floor, and he led Lance up. In a short hallway at the top of the stairs, there was a narrow table against the wall, and in its single drawer Armbruster found a scattering of take-out dinner menus and one pamphlet from a bank in Tampa, Florida. He pulled the pamphlet out with forceps, bagged it, and said, "Might be prints."

They briefly inspected the one bedroom at the front of the house where the dormer creased the roofline, then descended the stairs. Lance played her flashlight onto the floor and walked along the edges of the old rectangular rug. At each corner she lifted the rug to search underneath it, and when she let the corners down, they puffed up dust from the dirty floor.

Armbruster wandered back through the dining room into the old kitchen. Lance followed momentarily, and they stood in the middle of the room, shining their lights into open cabinets above a chipped, red-tiled countertop. They found nothing there. No dishes, no boxes of cereal, no bags of flour, no glasses, no plates or bowls—nothing on the shelves.

Lance said, "Captain Andersen said they pulled everything out when they boarded it up, but he also said the dealers didn't keep much here anyway. It was a roof over a cutting table, and that's all it meant to them."

Armbruster shined his light on the bank pamphlet from Tampa. "Captain Andersen didn't have the Florida connection."

"Or they just missed that," Lance said. "It'll mean nothing if there aren't any prints on it that we can match to someone."

Armbruster stepped toward the gray light at the back door and said, "Robertson isn't going to like it, that this is all we've got."

Lance followed him out and locked up. "He knew there was nothing here."

"Long shot," Armbruster said. "But at least we have something."

In her car with the heater and defroster running on maximum, Lance said, "Robertson gets two things, Stan. We can match prints on that pamphlet. Maybe."

"That's thin," Armbruster said, blowing warm breath onto the tips of his fingers.

"And he gets to check off the last thing we had to do here. He's done everything he can up here in Ohio. The rest is going to happen in Florida. He must have figured that all along."

"Florida, or wherever they find the Molinas," Armbruster said. "But that could be anywhere."

Lance pulled away from the curb, and rain fell harder against the windshield. She flipped her wipers faster and said, "I'm sick of dreary springs."

Over the labor of the fans, Armbruster said, "We've got prints from those plastic wrappers I found in the bottoms. But they don't match to anyone in the system."

"It's all straws, Stan," Lance said, sounding defeated. "We're grasping at nothing but straws, here."

"A bank in Tampa, though. That solidifies a connection to Florida."

Lance stopped at the police department to return the keys and then drove out to SR 21 South, to head toward Massillon. "All we can do is hand over our print collection to DEA," she said. "Two cents' worth. And we already knew there were connections to Florida anyway."

Heavier rain fell, and Lance switched her wipers to maximum speed. With the backs of her fingers, she wiped at condensation inside her windshield. "Baggers aren't runners, Stan. And runners aren't shippers, and dealers aren't bosses, and this is a big outfit. We'll never get them all."

"Trouble is," Armbruster said, "the ones we don't get? They'll just set up business somewhere else."

Muttering, Lance said, "I'm just sick of this rain."

"I'm sick of being ten steps behind," Armbruster said. "We've got nothing for Robertson."

"One lousy bank brochure, Stan."

"It's circumstantial," Armbruster admitted. "Even if Dewey Molina's personal prints are on it, it won't tie him to Zook's murder."

As they skirted downtown Massillon on the bypass, a dark cover of clouds settled low over the roads, and the streetlights switched on, their night sensors fooled by the darkness. Soon, rain was falling so heavily that cars on the bypass were pulling over to the side of the road to wait out the storm. A fine sleet mixed with the rain, and then hail started pinging off the roof of Lance's car. She pulled over, too, and turned on her hazard flashers.

Stopped on the berm, Lance complained over the din. "We have no leads on Dewey or Teresa Molina. We have no results from Robertson's BOLO on the Humvee or the Buick. We've got no contact with Fannie Helmuth or Jodie Tapp. There are no good leads on this outfit in Florida. There was no evidence on Ruth Zook's body or at the murder spot. Ricky says he's found nothing useful other than some spent rounds they pulled out of that boat in Bradenton Beach. And we can't get a decent description of Teresa Molina from the Helmuths."

"We do have a mug shot of Dewey," Armbruster said. "And license plates."

"Switched by now," Lance scoffed. "I'm sick of this rain. Sick of this case."

"The prints are going to match someone," Armbruster said.

"And that might be useful at a trial," Lance said. "But not useful at catching anyone. Not unless they're already in the system."

The downpour eased, and Lance started driving south again. She crossed over the US 30 interchange at the Walmart strip mall south of Massillon and turned onto SR 62, heading south and west through the countryside toward Millersburg.

"We need to call Bruce," Lance said. "Tell him we don't really have anything new here."

Armbruster pulled out his phone. "Maybe he's in a good mood."

He punched in Robertson's number, waited, and then said, "It's Armbruster."

Lance drove and listened.

"Nothing, really, Sheriff. Maybe a pamphlet we can lift some prints from.

"No. A bank in Tampa.

With a puzzled glance at Lance, Armbruster then said, "Yes, sure. It is another connection to Florida.

"OK, good. We're headed back now. And thanks. Yes, I will."

Then Armbruster switched off and sat quietly for a moment. Eventually, Lance asked, "What?"

"Sheriff says, 'Good work.' He really didn't think we'd find anything."

"You're kidding," Lance said, brightening somewhat.

"No. He's happy we got this much."

"But how did he sound?"

"Happy. I think. He's out at the Zook farm. Going to talk with the people from the EPA."

"And he sounded happy?" Lance asked.

"He sounded pleased." Armbruster chuckled. "The big sheriff sounded pleased with himself."

34

Thursday, April 7
9:45 A.M.

WHEN HE hung up on the call with Stan Armbruster, Bruce
Robertson was standing under his umbrella, on top of the broken dam behind the Zooks' tallest barn, watching rainwater
sluice out of the bottom of the pond and run down into the
lower terrain beyond. Like all the other low spots in the county,
the Zook bottoms were filling up fast. At least five watercourses
emptied into the lowlands beneath the sheriff's location, and
with a degree of satisfaction that he couldn't ever acknowledge
in public, Robertson watched the water rise steadily over the
tops of the wheels on the EPA's gasoline generator. Already
the water had reached the top steps leading into the EPA's forensics trailer, and knowing the topography well, Robertson esti-
mated that water would begin seeping in under the door within
the half hour. He smiled under cover of his umbrella. Old high-
water marks on all the trees in the bottoms should have been an
indication to the bothersome federal authorities that down in the
lowlands was not the best place to park a trailer filled with electronic equipment.

The sheriff was dressed for the weather—watertight hiking
boots, jeans, and a flannel shirt under a long, black, western-style

slicker that reached his ankles. A gun belt, he thought. All I need is a gun belt and a six-shooter.

With his phone still out, he tried Howie Dent's number on a whim, but it rang straight through to a corporate answering service. Robertson punched out.

As he slipped his cell phone into the shirt pocket under his slicker, the gasoline generator down in the bottoms began to sputter and cough. He pulled the collar of his rain slicker tighter around his neck and shook water off his umbrella.

He had called Agent Wellings, hadn't he? Earlier that very morning. Just after he had declared a flood warning for his entire county. Now Wellings would have to come the long way around from Millersburg, since the roads were posted where they were already impassable, at the lowest spots beside creeks and streams. And here he stood alone now, Robertson thought. No Wellings yet. Wouldn't arrive in time. Sad to see, really. Water rising.

Thinking about Ruth Zook, Fannie Helmuth, and Jodie Tapp, Robertson stood at his post under his umbrella for another ten minutes, waiting for Wellings and the rest of the EPA. When Wellings arrived, the man came racing up the muddy bank of the dam, the smooth soles of his new shoes slipping as he struggled. When he had climbed at last to Robertson's position, Wellings looked disbelievingly down at his testing site, all his equipment surrounded by a rising sea of dirty brown water, the wheels of both the generator and the trailer now completely submerged.

As Wellings caught his breath atop the dam, Robertson remarked, "Sorry I didn't notice sooner, Robert, but waters rise fast out here. It's a shame." Pleased by the earnest tone he had affected, the sheriff added, "I can't let you down there now. I've declared a flood warning. A flood emergency, officially. I'm surprised you got through on the roads."

Wellings started down the slope, but Robertson pulled him back. "You can't go down there, Wellings. I'm sure you noticed that most of the roads around here are closed, and I've declared a flood emergency."

"I can't just stand here," Wellings protested.

As he spoke, the generator coughed a last time and choked to a stop. "I can still save the equipment!" Wellings shouted. He turned back to wave two men up from an EPA panel truck that had arrived with him. The men ran forward in the rain, and Wellings said, "We'll have a pickup truck here in five minutes."

Robertson shook his head. "Can't let you go down there. Not until this subsides."

"You don't have the authority to stop us!" Wellings barked. "You can't expect me to stand by and let it all get flooded."

As solicitously as he could manage, Robertson asked, "The equipment in that trailer, Robert? Is it all up on tables?"

"Yes, but it all needs power. I've got to get that generator running again."

"If it stops raining," Robertson said, "maybe the water won't reach the equipment."

Wellings stared incredulously at the big sheriff. "You can't be serious. Water would ruin everything in that trailer. All my equipment and all our samples."

"Can't let anyone go down there, now, Robert. It's low ground to everything near here. At least five watersheds empty into these bottoms."

Speechlessly, Wellings stared through the rain at the trailer down below. The two men from the panel truck reached the top of the dam, their city shoes caked with mud. One said to Wellings, "We've got a pickup coming."

Wellings ignored him. "Look, Robertson, we'll take a boat. We can fix a line."

"And what?" Robertson asked. "Drag your trailer through a hundred yards of flooded swamp?"

Wellings had no answer.

Privately delighted at the Zooks' good fortune, Robertson gave an earnest frown and said, "Maybe the rain will stop."

Finding renewed vigor, Wellings shouted, "You can't stop us!"

Robertson looked back to the driveway beyond the barn and saw young Deputy Baker pulling his cruiser in beside the sheriff's

Crown Vic. He turned back to Wellings and said, "I'm posting a deputy here, Wellings. If you try to go down there, I'll have you arrested. For your own safety."

Wellings studied the sheriff's resolve, spun back toward his trailer in the bottoms, and flipped back around to nose up to Robertson. "If the equipment in that trailer gets ruined," he hissed, "I'll have your badge."

Smiling a threat, Robertson said, "The fine people of this county gave me my badge, Wellings, and if I thought you or any other federal creep could take it from me—well, I don't know, I guess I'd just have to let your superiors know that you parked a science lab in a swamp and then whined about the fact that it rains a lot here in April. How's that sound to you, Wellings? You came out here to ruin the lives of decent Amish folk, and you arrogantly sank a million dollars worth of what—gas chromatographs, mass spectrometers, computers, like that, Wellings—in a flood zone, during the rainy season?"

Wellings's gaze showed a mixture of puzzlement, spite, and anger. He started to say something and stopped. With aggression and defeat bunching together in his fists, he marched and slid down off the sodden dam, pulling his two men down the slope with him. The two men climbed into the panel truck, and Wellings got into his sedan. Both vehicles backed onto the lawn, leaving scars in the grass, and then they turned around and left.

As Deputy Baker reached the sheriff's position high up on the dam, Robertson said, "Sorry about the rain, Baker, but I want you posted right here, today. Let no one from the EPA go down into that flood."

"What about others?" Baker asked. "The same thing?"

Robertson laughed. "I expect that the other folks out here will know better than to try."

*　*　*

As he stepped carefully down the slope of the dam, Robertson got a call on his cell. He checked the number on his display, didn't recognize it, and answered with his official tone, "Robertson."

"Have you found my client?" Linda Hart asked. "She needs to be in protective custody."

"Look, Hart," Robertson said, "she's not willing to come back."

"Where is she, then?"

"We don't know."

"Trace her phone."

"She's using Howie Dent's phone," Robertson said, irritated. "He keeps it switched off."

"But have they called you?"

"Once. Last night."

"Didn't Rachel pull any data on that call?"

"Yes," Robertson sighed. "She did that this morning. They were somewhere near Memphis."

"Are you going to send someone?"

"And do what, Hart? Ask around about hitchhiking Amish girls, or farm boys who bought bus tickets?"

"You could try. Maybe the airports."

"They're not using credit cards, Hart. They have used his phone only once. And from Memphis, they could go anywhere."

"You're giving up, Robertson!"

"No, Hart, I'm not. When they ask for our help, I'll send everyone I've got. Until then, I need to let Ricky chase this drug gang in Florida. That's my best play."

"Call Howie's phone again."

"We're doing that every hour. Why don't you try calling yourself?"

Hart hesitated.

Robertson asked, "What?"

"I don't have his number."

"It won't do you any good, Hart. He doesn't answer."

"Give it to me anyway, OK?"

"I'll text it to you."

"Fine."

"Fine, then."

"Good-bye."

"Bye."

*   *   *

When Robertson reached the bottom of the dam, he lifted his umbrella to check his course, and he glanced down the long seventy yards of the Zook driveway to the far end out by the road. There he saw Emma Wengerd standing in the rain, without a coat.

Too cold and too wet, he thought, for a little girl to be standing out in just a plain dress. He walked faster along the driveway.

As he reached the back edge of the house, Emma took a single step forward toward the road. A car splashed by in the eastbound lane, close enough to Emma to spray water on her legs. The sheriff doubled his pace. Fifty yards.

Another car sped by, and again Emma took a step, now at the very end of the drive, her feet touching the blacktop of the road. A car hissed by in the westbound lane, and Robertson started jogging, calling out, "Hey there, Emma? Hey!" Forty yards.

Emma looked back at him briefly, turned to face straight ahead, and took another step out into the road. Louder, Robertson started shouting for the Zooks in the house. He glanced left down the road. No more traffic yet. Thirty yards.

Emma stepped forward again, and out of the corner of his right eye, Robertson saw Grandfather Zook splashing across the lawn toward his granddaughter. Twenty-five yards.

Running now, Robertson threw his umbrella aside and splashed forward as fast as his bulk would permit. A westbound delivery truck blew past Emma, the draft lifting the hem of her dress. Her prayer covering blew off and landed ten paces away on the wet pavement. Bolt straight and seeming as determined as a soldier, Emma stared straight ahead as the sheriff ran. Twenty yards.

To his left, on the crest of a hill some hundred yards up the road, a loaded timber hauler came forward in Emma's lane, and Robertson shouted again, running, stumbling, starting to lose wind, trying to shout again, but voiceless, both from alarm and from exertion. Fifteen yards.

A final determined step put Emma in the middle of the eastbound lane, and to her left, the trucker clamped down on every brake he had, air compressors screaming, gears grinding, tires skidding. Ten yards.

Relentlessly, it lurched toward her, unable to stop in time.

The desperate driver cranked his wheels left, held, and cranked back right. The truck broke left into the oncoming lane, but careened back immediately toward Emma.

Robertson churned his legs frantically up and down, racing forward, as awkward at full-tilt run as a wheel suddenly squared, and he thought he had surely lost her. Lost his chance. Failed. Still he ran. Five yards.

As the nose of the timber truck slipped past, inches from her head, Robertson threw an arm over Emma's shoulder and pivoted right with his last gasp of hope, to wrench her away from the pavement.

Alvin Zook ran up, and Emma and the sheriff fell together in the tall ditch grasses beside the road. The truck flashed past them, spraying water, foam, and road debris over them, hissing steam from its undercarriage as it shuddered to a stop some forty yards beyond.

The driver popped out of the cab and ran back toward Robertson.

The sheriff pushed up to his feet and then pulled Emma up from the ditch beneath him.

The driver was shouting, but Robertson didn't hear. Boots planted deep in the muck of the ditch, he held Emma tightly against his big, heaving chest and listened only to her weeping, as she cried time and time again, "I want to be with Ruth."

35

Thursday, April 7
11:10 A.M.

ROBERTSON'S FIRST call went to Cal Troyer. "She's inside now," he said, standing out on the Zooks' front porch. He had laid his rain slicker over the back of a porch chair, but even as cool as it was, the sheriff was still sweating under his flannel shirt. "Five-fifty-seven is closed north of Charm," he added. "You'll have to circle around through Farmerstown."

"Twenty minutes," Cal said. "I was headed to Walnut Creek for lunch."

"I'll stay until you get here," Robertson said. He clicked off as Andy Zook came out through the front door.

Robertson shook his head sadly and didn't speak. Zook returned his sympathetic wordlessness and nodded. Both men turned to face out toward the road where Emma had very nearly managed to kill herself.

As they stood there together, Irma Zook carried out two mugs of coffee and handed them to the men. "She's with her grandfather," she said, turning back into the house. "Alvin's the best one to talk with her now."

Andy held the screen door for his wife and then let it slap closed. "Been meaning to fix that," he said to Robertson, then asked, "Do you really think she was trying to kill herself?"

"Yes," Robertson said, eyes turned down. He took a sip of coffee. "I've got Cal Troyer coming out."

Andy pulled the screen door open and paused. "She has never really been willing to talk much. Since her family died."

"Cal said she had opened up to him a little bit," Robertson said, turning. He held the screen for Andy.

Zook offered a puzzled "Thanks" and went inside.

* * *

Robertson's second call went to Ricky Niell. "What have you got?" he asked. "I need some good news."

"The DEA hasn't turned up anything, yet, but they have the vehicle data and a description of Dewey Molina."

"I knew that!" Robertson shouted.

"Sorry."

Calmer, Robertson asked, "Really, Ricky, are we just dead in the water here?"

"Not yet. There are still two known locations to check here in Bradenton. The DEA wants to do that."

"They gonna let you ride along?"

"No."

"So, what are you going to do?"

"Orton and I are going to look for Jodie Tapp."

"You think the DEA has any chance on the Molinas?"

"Fifty-fifty."

Robertson blew a frustrated groan and held a thought. Ricky waited on the call. Shortly, Robertson asked, "You have any idea where to find this Tapp?"

"We're going out to check some parking lots on her favorite beaches."

"You're kidding!"

"That's all we've got, Sheriff. The Brandens will check for her at her trailer in Cortez."

"How many beaches have you got down there, Niell?"

"About a thousand."

"Thought so," Robertson said. "Look, I've got a girl up here who wants to die. Maybe it'd help if we could tell her who killed Ruth Zook."

"I don't know what more we can do, Sheriff."

"What about Tapp's friends? Or her known places?"

"Orton and I will be on that, Sheriff. All day long if we have to."

"What about finding the Molinas?"

"If they come down to Florida, the DEA will track them down. Your BOLO is nationwide, right?"

"Yes. How about tracing those stolen boats?"

"Customs, and the Coast Guard."

"That's all you've got, Niell?"

"It is for now."

"OK, then give it until tomorrow morning. If you don't have anything by then, the DEA will have to close this out for us."

"I'll call you if we get something," Niell said.

"You do that, Niell! Because I've got nothing but loose ends up here, and a little girl just tried to step in front of a truck!"

* * *

The sheriff's third call went to his wife. "Missy, when can you release Ruth Zook's body to her family?"

"I'd like to know more, Bruce," Missy said. "Has something happened?"

"Emma Wengerd tried to kill herself," Robertson said, weariness suffusing his tone. "Stepped out in front of a truck."

"Somebody stopped her?"

"I did. But it was close, Missy. Far too close. And it took me too long to realize what she intended."

"Then are you asking me as sheriff to release the body, or are you just frustrated?"

Robertson sighed. "I just think it'd help Emma if she could bury her stepsister. But maybe Cal is gonna have to fix this."

"Is he out there?"

"On his way."

"Is there going to be any more evidence?"

"No, Missy. Maybe. I don't know."

"Ricky's down in Florida, still?"

"Yes. The DEA is taking over the case."

"Are you still thinking it was one of the Molinas who killed Ruth?"

"Them, or one of their crew. That's where it all leads."

"But you can't do anything more up here?"

"Right."

"Then, under the circumstances, I don't have a good reason to hold the body any longer."

"Thanks, Missy."

"You'll tell the Zooks?"

"Yes, as soon as Cal gets here."

"OK, but tell them to bring plenty of ice. They're going to want to bury her as soon as they can manage."

* * *

Robertson's fourth call went to Mike Branden. The professor answered as Cal walked up the porch steps beside the sheriff. Robertson waved the pastor inside and said to Mike, "Anything on Jodie Tapp?"

"You just called, Bruce. It hasn't been that long."

"Sorry," Robertson said. "It's been as long as the ages, up here." He told the professor about Emma.

"Cal's coming out?"

"Already here."

"OK, Tapp, then," Branden said. "She's not at her trailer. She didn't show up for work. And we really don't have anyplace else to look."

"She knows where you're staying?"

"Yes."

"Then if you stayed put, maybe she'd show up to talk or something."

"Might."

"Can you do that, Mike? I don't have anything else to suggest."

*   *   *

In his Crown Vic, Robertson drove to the deserted Helmuth farm on the high ground north of Charm, and he wondered, once there, what he had hoped to accomplish. He turned around in the driveway and drove to the glade where Ruth Zook had been murdered. A lonely place to die, he thought, seated behind the wheel. He didn't bother to get out.

Out on SR 39, he headed toward Sugarcreek, and with his GPS, he found the residence in town of Earnest Troyer. When a disgruntled Troyer finally opened the door in his pajamas, Robertson invited himself inside and said, "Tell me everything you know about those buses of yours."

36

Thursday, April 7
6:20 P.M.

CAROLINE BRANDEN served chilled crab and pasta salad from the nearby Mar Vista restaurant, and the four sat out on the patio at Ray Lee's beach house to eat while the sun dominated the western sky over the Gulf. The Brandens had opened two large shade umbrellas atop two round tables, and with the tables set edge-to-edge, the oval patches of shade were nearly adequate in size.

Sweating a little under his shirt, Ricky stared out at the green-then-blue stretch of water beyond the white sand and said, "We need this in Ohio."

Orton laughed. "Then who'd come down here to boost our economy?"

For the most part, the conversation that evening had been subdued. The Brandens had waited at home all afternoon, but Jodie Tapp had not come to visit. Niell and Orton had cruised parking lots along the coast for fifty miles, both north and south, and they had not found Tapp's old blue Camry. None of the surfers to whom they had talked had seen Jodie that day, or even the day before. Twice, Niell and Orton had driven past the trailer in Cortez, but Jodie hadn't been home. The neighbors had seen neither her nor her car.

Finished with his pasta, Ricky was rolling a single grape around the edge of his plate with his fork. Orton watched his idle play and then reached across the table to stab the grape with his own fork. He popped it into his mouth and said, "Did your mother let you play with your food?"

Unresponsive, Ricky mumbled, "What?"

Orton said, "She'll turn up, Niell. We just went to all the wrong places. We just missed her out there."

"Wasn't thinking about Jodie," Niell said.

"You got enough sun, out looking for her today," Orton remarked. "You should stay undercover tomorrow."

Niell had loosened his tie and taken off his sport coat earlier that day as they rolled into the second parking lot at Siesta Beach. His arms, face, and neck were cooked to a noticeable pink-but-going-red-tomorrow hue, and his black hair and pencil-thin mustache accentuated the white around his eye sockets, where sunglasses had shielded his skin.

"That's the white-eyed stare of a tourist," Orton remarked. "One day in the sun and all you snowbirds are cooked."

Niell rolled his eyes in protest, but took the ribbing mostly with a smile. "I just wish we had found her."

Caroline gathered up the plates, and the professor followed her inside with napkins and silverware. They brought out a fresh pitcher of tea, and Branden filled the four tumblers on the tables. "She could be out of town," he said as he sat. "Visiting relatives."

"They're all in New Mexico," Orton said. "But that might be the best place for her right now."

Caroline sat. "Did you say there were two unpacked suitcases at her trailer?"

Orton's cell beeped a message, and he checked the display, opened the phone, and clicked to read it.

Branden answered his wife's question. "Two older suitcases. With old leather straps. Like steamer trunks used to be, but small like suitcases."

"Wasn't her place decorated with modern things?" Caroline asked.

Orton closed his phone. "DEA might have something later." He put his phone away and sat back with his glass of tea.

Niell scooted his chair back from the table to stay better in the shade, and Orton remarked, "You're learning, snowbird."

Caroline asked, "Was it all really modern decorating at Jodie's trailer?"

The men looked puzzled. Branden said, "A good mix of colors, I guess. Nice things on the tables and shelves."

Caroline said, "OK," and let it drop.

Orton's phone beeped in another message. He stood to hold his phone display under the shade, read the message, and said, "OK, well the DEA actually has something now."

Ricky stood and finished a hurried last swallow of tea. "Where?"

"Bradenton," Orton said. "They're preparing an entry team at an old house in an eastern neighborhood. Out by the highway, past the trailer parks there. It all used to be ranch country."

Branden rose and said, "I'll ride along," but Caroline said, "Why?" She was up on her feet, now, too.

"We don't even know yet who this is," Orton said. "And they're not gonna let civilians anywhere near this house."

Branden retrieved his tumbler of tea, and Caroline hooked her arm inside his elbow. "No civilians," she said to the professor, and he shrugged a halfhearted apology to the other two men.

Niell was less complacent. "I'll go with you, Ray Lee. If it's the Molinas, then it's my case as much as anyone's."

Orton protested. "They don't know who it is, Ricky."

"That was your own dispatcher, right?" Niell said. "On those two messages."

"So?"

"So he's not going to bother you tonight unless someone thinks they have found the Molinas. Or associates of the Molinas. So I'm going to ride along, Ray Lee."

*   *   *

A Bradenton cop was stationed at the wooden street barricades two blocks from a cluster of DEA agents and city police who had surrounded the old farmhouse with personnel and vehicles. Orton and Niell approached the cop with their badges out.

"Can't let you go any closer," the cop said as they walked up to his position. "They've been negotiating for two hours, and that's an entry team gearing up down there."

Orton put binoculars up to his eyes and studied the distant house. Shades were drawn on all of the windows. The front door had been outwardly splintered by a blast. Orton muttered, "Shotgun," and continued to pan his binoculars across the scene.

"One car, parked under an old carport," he said. "Not a Humvee, Ricky."

"Is it a Buick?" Ricky asked at his side.

"Can't tell. Only the bumper is showing."

"There are other cars on the street," Ricky said. "Should have been towed by now."

"Line of fire," Orton said. "But that's a blue Camry parked there."

He handed the binoculars to Niell and stepped back from the barricade to make a call. Niell legged up to the barricade and used the binoculars. "I'm not sure what they're doing," he said. "They don't act like they're going in."

The cop beside him said, "They think there's only one guy inside, but they don't know. That's what they're waiting for."

Binoculars down, Niell asked, "How are they going to make that determination?"

"Thermal imaging," the cop said. "The DEA has thermal sensors. They're using them now."

Orton came back up to the barricade. "Those are definitely Jodie's plates on that Camry."

Niell looked again through the binoculars. "It's just parked on the street. Like someone got her, and made her drive here."

"They need to know that," Orton said to the cop. "There might be a hostage."

The cop took his shoulder mic in hand, and Orton said, "Jodie Tapp. Five-five and a hundred pounds. If she's in there, she's a hostage."

The cop keyed his mic. "Captain, a Bradenton Beach cop says he recognizes the blue Camry. Belongs to a girl named Jodie Tapp."

Orton broke in, "We've been looking for her all day. If she's in there, she's a hostage."

The cop ignored him, and the captain answered, "We've got that on the sensors, Stone. Stationary person. Laid out flat between the backmost wall and a bed. Hasn't moved, and might be bound."

Stone clipped his mic back onto his shoulder strap and asked Orton, "Friend of yours?"

"Yes, a little Mennonite woman. Someone I know from the beaches."

"That's the worst place for a Mennonite," Stone remarked.

"I think she's a hostage," Orton said, distracted.

Niell said, "They're gathering at the front door," and Orton took the binoculars from him to watch.

"That's the worst kind of place for a Mennonite girl," Stone said again. "Why is she mixed up with this bunch?"

Niell said, "Amish girls from Pinecraft have been carrying drugs up to Ohio on the buses."

"You're kidding," Stone said, eyes wide.

"We don't think they had any choice," Niell said.

"They're all going in," Orton said and took his binoculars down.

Flash-bang concussion charges sounded from inside the house, and men poured into the front entrance with their weapons drawn. Niell and Orton stood beside Stone and could only watch and wait. A cluster of five or six shots popped off, and then it was quiet. One agent came back out through the front door and signaled "all clear."

Then, from the back of the house, even at a distance of two blocks, they heard a girl's terrified screams. The screams reached the front door, and a Bradenton police captain pushed outside with little Jodie Tapp in his arms. Clutching her arms around his neck, she was still screaming as he handed her off to paramedics.

* * *

The cop Stone escorted Niell and Orton through a maze of DEA and police vehicles, up to the front of the old farmhouse. Jodie Tapp was sitting on the edge of a gurney, and a medic was checking her blood pressure with an arm cuff. Orton went up to her.

Niell found the captain who had carried Jodie out and asked, "You found her in the back bedroom?"

The captain stuck out his hand. "Ed Bench. You have credentials?"

Niell lifted his badge off his belt and said, "Holmes County, Ohio."

Bench returned the badge. "Orton told us you were back down here."

"You remember the last time?" Niell asked.

The captain was smiling. "Rumors, is all. You took a swim in Sarasota Bay? With Orton, the way I hear it."

Niell returned the smile, awkwardly. Then he asked, "Who's inside?"

"That's your Dewey Molina, Detective, and he's dead. Never bothered to change the license plates on the Buick you boys have been hollering about."

"What?"

"Some sheriff has been phoning down here about every half hour. For the last three days."

"Robertson."

"That's the one. So, tell him he can pull his BOLO down and stop calling."

"But was there another person in there?" Niell asked. "Teresa Molina?"

"No. Just the one," Bench said. He led Niell in through the front door.

In the hallway leading to the back of the house, Dewey Molina was sprawled lengthwise, face pushed in against the baseboard trim at the floor, one arm pinched underneath him. A pump-action shotgun lay at his feet. Near his outstretched right hand, there was a stainless steel Smith & Wesson model 645 pistol with black rubber grips. Forensics had chalked the floor around three silvered brass .45 casings. Captain Bench stood over the body and said, "He threw three shots with the forty-five. One with the shotgun."

"Did they pull the forty-five magazine?" Ricky asked. "Clear the chamber?"

Bench grunted disgust and nodded. "Black Talons, Niell. I'm glad he couldn't shoot straight."

"Did you have a chance yet to gather any spent rounds?"

"Two are still in the wall, over by the door. One sailed out and hit our truck. Lucky it didn't kill someone."

Ricky eyed the brass on the floor. "I could use one of those casings up in Ohio. We could match the firing pin depression and the pressure marks on the base. The extractor groove, too."

"We haven't processed them," Bench said. "Maybe we could send you one after they've been cataloged and processed."

"Tomorrow morning I need to be on a plane," Ricky said. "Any chance I'd be able to take one back to my sheriff?"

Bench smiled. "Your sheriff is wound a little too tight?"

"He just likes thoroughness," Ricky allowed.

"I'll tell the lab to rush it overnight. But you take only one, Niell. We keep the other two."

*   *   *

Back outside on the front lawn, Niell found Orton still talking with Jodie Tapp on the gurney. She was both shaken and dazed. What little she said sounded hoarse. Constantly she rubbed at her throat and swallowed with difficulty. "I couldn't breathe with that gag," she told Orton. "I thought I was going to die, and then all that shooting. I just wanted to scream."

She stalled, cleared her throat, and drank a sip from a water bottle the paramedic had given her. She was dressed in Mennonite clothes—a muted pink dress and a white apron. Pinned to her apron strap was a nameplate from Miller's restaurant. Niell introduced himself and said, "You left the beach house last night."

Whispering, Jodie said, "I didn't want to be a bother."

"But these people were looking for you," Niell said.

Jodie's eyes spilled tears. "They were waiting for me at home."

"You're lucky," Orton said. "You should have stayed with us."

"I know. But really, Ray Lee, I didn't want to be a bother."

37

Thursday, April 7
8:45 P.M.

CAL CAME back to the Zooks' after dinner to try a second time to talk with Emma. She had refused him earlier.

As he parked on the driveway, Andy and Alvin Zook had two other men positioned at the back of a long wagon with slatted sides. Because they had traveled after dark, the wagon was rigged at its four corners with kerosene lanterns.

Andy and Alvin were up in the bed of the wagon, sliding Ruth Zook's coffin toward the back gate, as two helpers waited behind the wagon. When one end was ready, the Zooks jumped down at the back, and together the four men slid the heavy coffin out of the wagon. Awkwardly, they turned it around beside the wagon, carried it to the front porch, and struggled up the steps. Cal held the front door open, and they took Ruth Zook inside.

Three wooden sawhorses had been placed at the back wall of the parlor, and the men carried Ruth in and set her coffin across the sawhorses. Women gathered behind the men, Zooks and neighbors, too, and Andy Zook hinged the coffin lid open so people could see Ruth. There were tears in every eye, Cal's included, and Irma Zook cried out and stumbled forward, on legs that Cal feared would buckle, to the head of the coffin.

In her Amish clothes, Ruth lay inside, her forehead repaired so expertly that no one could have told she had been shot if they hadn't known before. All around Ruth was packed crushed ice. Crushed ice lay underneath her, too, but nobody would know that unless they were familiar with Amish burials.

Cal realized that people had arrived and were lining up on the front porch to come in, so he quietly asked Alvin, "Is Emma still in her bedroom?"

"Yes," Alvin said. "I sat with her most of the afternoon."

"Does she know you were bringing Ruth home tonight?"

"Yes."

"Is it all right if I go up, to try to talk with her?"

"Yes, Pastor," Alvin said softly. "I think she needs to come down to say good-bye to Ruth. We'll have her in the ground by noon tomorrow."

* * *

Cal knocked on Emma's bedroom door and entered. He found her kneeling at the windowsill, gazing out at the night sky. She turned briefly to see him, then returned to her study of the stars. Cal sat behind her on the edge of her bed and said, "I didn't forget about you, Stratus Flower."

Emma pivoted toward him on her knees, and he saw that she was crying openly. Her eyelids were red and swollen, and she held a hankie at her nose. Cal knelt beside her, and she turned back to the window, sobbing.

Cal remembered how sternly she had promised him that she wouldn't cry and she couldn't pray, and he laid his hand on her shoulder and said, "Next you'll tell me you've been praying, Emma."

Emma nodded. "I'm not good at it," she said through her tears. "All I do is say how much it hurts. I don't think God hears me."

"He hears you, Emma. He is close to you now because you can tell him how it hurts you to lose Ruth."

"I didn't know my heart could be so broken," she said. "I feel like my heart has been crushed and I can't breathe. I wanted to die and be with Ruth."

Cal waited a moment and then said, "The sheriff told me about the truck."

Emma nodded and seemed ashamed. "I won't do it again."

"You are supposed to have a life, Emma. A full life. One of your own."

"Ruth can have mine," Emma said. "Tell God to give my life to Ruth."

"Then who would remember Ruth as well as you can?"

Emma shook her head. "I'm forgetting what she looked like."

Cal weakened on his knees, but held to his place beside her. "You can come downstairs to see her, Emma. They've brought her home."

Emma doubled over in front of the window and buried her face in her lap. Cal planted his forearms on the floor beside her and whispered near to her ear, "God is close to the broken-hearted, Emma."

Releasing her tears completely, Emma cried out and sobbed on her knees, rocking with her arms folded over her belly. Cal embraced her and let her rock and cry in front of the window.

"Tears are all the prayers I have, now," Emma sobbed. "Tears are my prayers."

Something profound broke loose in Cal's heart. Something newly free of burden. Something like the majesty of flight. A celebration of tears set free.

"I miss Ruth," Emma said.

"I know," Cal said, misunderstanding.

"No. *I miss Ruth*," Emma repeated. "Those are the names of my tears."

Mixing his sobs with hers, Cal began to weep at her side, holding her shoulders with one of his arms, holding his eyes under the other arm, because he feared the release of her prayers would break him apart.

38

Friday, April 8
11:15 A.M.

RICKY DROVE up to Tampa Friday morning for an early flight, and Mike and Caroline Branden met Ray Lee for an early lunch at the New Pass Grill and Bait Shop, a weathered bayside shack with a dock where fishermen could buy bait and with picnic tables under trees at the water's edge. They stood in line and bought sandwiches and oranges in Styrofoam boxes, then carried their lunches to the tables painted with a rainbow of pastel colors. Ray Lee chose a po'boy, and, "living local," as Caroline put it, the Brandens each chose a BLT on untoasted white bread.

Ray Lee was taciturn and distracted by his thoughts, so halfway through her sandwich, Caroline asked, "Is Jodie OK, Ray Lee?"

He put his po'boy back in the box. "I've been out most of the morning. Since six, really. She slept in my guest room and didn't want to talk last night. When I woke up, she had already finished half a pot of coffee."

"She's probably still in shock," the professor said. He had finished half of his BLT and was peeling his orange.

Caroline asked, "Was she better this morning?"

"She wouldn't talk about anything, but she got three calls that beeped in. She had her phone set to go to the message box, so she didn't bother to pick up any of the calls."

"Is she still there?" Caroline asked.

"As far as I know," Orton said. "I've been running errands."

Caroline held his gaze and Orton asked, nervously, "What?"

"Those old suitcases," Caroline said. "Do you really think they were Jodie's?"

"Who else's?"

"I don't know. They just seemed out of place to me."

Branden asked, "Because she's a modern decorator?"

"Very modern," Caroline said, "from what you described."

The three sat and thought as boats pulled in and out at the docks. Tables were filling up with locals who knew the grill well. Fumes from a dozen boat motors circled and settled around the grill's wooden docks as more cars pulled into the gravel lot out front.

Ray Lee pulled his phone out and dialed a number, saying, "Jodie's cell." He held a hand cupped over his other ear as an outboard raced away from the bait shop.

"No answer."

He tried the number at his home phone.

"No answer."

He called the phone at Jodie's trailer.

"No answer."

"I don't get it," Orton said as he put away his phone.

"How long has Jodie been a waitress at Miller's?" Caroline asked.

"Ever since I've known her," Orton said. "Years."

"And do I understand it right—that Jodie is the one who gave Fannie Helmuth the old suitcase that she used?"

"Yes," Orton said. "At least that's what Ricky said."

"And Ruth Zook brought home an old suitcase, too?"

"Don't know," Orton said. "All Ricky said was that she brought home an *extra* suitcase."

"But a modern bag would look out of place for an Amish girl on a bus, don't you think?" Caroline said.

Orton paused with his eyes closed. Opened, he said, "You're thinking that Jodie gave an old suitcase to both Fannie and Ruth."

"I'm just wondering," Caroline said, "why Jodie Tapp would keep any old suitcases at her trailer."

Orton shook his head and called Jodie's phone again.

"No answer."

* * *

The Brandens pulled in behind Orton at Jodie Tapp's trailer and followed him down the narrow pathway to her side door. He knocked, but got no answer. When he tried the knob, the door opened. He called out Jodie's name several times, and then reached inside to switch on the lights. Jodie didn't answer.

Ray Lee turned back to the Brandens and said, "I know her, and I believe she's in danger. So I'm going to look around inside."

The professor said, "I'll come with you."

Caroline said, "I don't have a badge," and she watched from the doorway.

Inside, Branden and Orton saw that furnishings, mostly small items, had been removed. Bare spots on the walls showed where pictures had been taken down. Magazines had been left on the large, hammered-copper table in front of the couch, but the smaller end tables and decorator lamps were gone.

In a front closet, there were no hanging clothes and no shoes on the floor. In the kitchen, drawers were empty and the shelves held no plates, bowls, or glasses.

Caroline called in, "Check in the bedroom," and the two men walked back down the narrow hallway of the trailer. When they came back to the front, each was carrying an old, empty, strap-leather suitcase, and Ray Lee said, "All her clothes are gone."

39

Saturday, April 9
3:25 P.M.

IN THE sheriff's office, Ricky Niell made his report. Robertson listened with a spreading frown stretching the corners of his mouth.

They had not captured anyone alive.

The brass casing that Ricky had carried home *might match* the one that little John and Mahlon Byler had knifed out of the horse's hoof at the murder scene.

There would be no way to know, lacking further arrests, who had actually shot Ruth Zook.

Other than Dewey, who was dead, none of the drug-running crew had been captured, either in Ohio or in Florida. No cutters and no baggers. No dealers and no transporters. No bosses and no pirates. No Teresa Molina and no Humvee.

And Fannie Helmuth? Ricky wouldn't even try to guess.

Fuming behind his desk, Robertson paced back and forth, pounding one fist into his other cupped hand, and then switching when one became tender. After pacing and pounding out his frustration for several long moments, he finally lost steam and turned to face Niell across his desk.

"We lost," he said to Niell. "On all the points that matter to me, we lost."

"I know," Ricky said, "but there's more."

Robertson sat wearily down on his swivel rocker.

Niell said, "I was dropping off the brass casing at Missy's labs when Ray Lee called."

Robertson said nothing, waiting with a scowl.

"And," Ricky continued, "Jodie Tapp has pulled out. Moved. Run off, or something like that."

"Not abducted again?" Robertson asked.

Ricky shook his head. "Ray Lee says she cleared her trailer out. And he thinks Caroline might be right. That Jodie never was abducted."

Robertson pulled himself up to his desk and planted his elbows on his desktop, palms flat on the wood and fingers splayed. He thought, glanced up at Niell, and thought some more.

When he looked up again, he said, "She was in on it, Ricky. All along."

40

BY THE time the sheriff got home, Missy had set out dinner on the kitchen table. Robertson pulled off his slicker, hung it on a wall peg, and sat down smiling. "Been out to the Zooks'," he said. "The EPA equipment is a total loss. Completely underwater. And anything they might have found environmentally has been washed away in the flood."

"That'll suit your sensibilities regarding federal agencies," Missy said.

"It does," Robertson laughed. "What's for dinner?"

Missy lifted the lid on her bakeware. "Meat loaf." She served him a plate with mashed potatoes.

The sheriff stirred his fork through his mashed potatoes and said, "Nothing worked out on this one."

"Ricky told me."

They ate together in silence for a while, and then Bruce said, "Cal says Emma Wengerd is going to be OK."

"Good news, there at least."

The sheriff pushed back from his plate. "I've got no idea where Fannie Helmuth is."

"She may never come home, Bruce, but does it matter?"

"She's not safe, Missy, and this isn't over. It won't be over until she can come home. Until Jodie Tapp and Teresa Molina are in jail."

"Why would she come home?"

"I don't know. But she's not safe here if she does come home. She's not safe anywhere, really."

"How would anyone find her?"

"I traced her as far as Memphis, Missy. It wouldn't be that hard for them to look for her. Just start checking Amish settlements to start with."

"What, all across the country?"

"I don't know. I just know she can't come home. Not with Molina and Tapp still running free."

"If her family has all moved out, why would she want to come home?"

"There's her farm just sitting there, Missy. Who's gonna take that?"

"I don't see that there's anything you can do here, Bruce."

"I can send Ricky over there, Monday," Robertson said. "To check on the farm."

"OK, can't hurt."

Unsettled, the sheriff stood and paced in the kitchen. Missy stayed seated and waited. Eventually, the sheriff asked, "Did you compare those casings?"

Missy sighed, stood, and cleared dishes from the table. "They matched, Bruce."

The sheriff sat at the table. "So, Dewey Molina's gun killed Ruth Zook."

Missy sat back down at the table. "Yes, the gun did. Can't say *who* shot her, though."

Robertson got up, carried his cup of coffee into the parlor, and sat on the divan.

Missy joined him and asked, "Are you going to be able to leave it like this? An unsolved murder?"

"I guess I have to," the sheriff complained. "But this case isn't over for me until I know Fannie Helmuth is safe. And that means arresting Teresa Molina and Jodie Tapp. In the meantime, Teresa

Molina's entire outfit is surely going to move somewhere else, so it's the feds' problem, now."

"Pirates and interstate drug running," Missy said. "It always was the feds' problem."

"I suppose so."

"You look tired, Bruce. Frazzled."

"Hmmpf."

"We need a vacation."

"What?"

"I called the Brandens. They're going to be at the beach house for another two weeks."

"What are you talking about?"

"I booked two flights."

The big sheriff shook his head. Couldn't think of a single thing to say.

"We leave tomorrow, Bruce."

"OK, Missy. Who's gonna run my shop?"

"You have Chief Wilsher and several good captains who can *run your shop* just fine."

Robertson frowned.

"And you need another detective, so I think you should use Stan Armbruster."

"I'd already decided that, Missy. Gonna tell him Monday."

"That's a good decision, but we're going to be in Florida on Monday."

"Then I'll just call him tonight. Maybe he can move out of that trailer and stop raising rabbit dogs for half his rent."

Missy smiled and waited while her husband finished his coffee. As he rose with his cup, she said, "Wait, Bruce. Sit a bit."

"What?" the sheriff asked, keeping to his seat beside her.

"Ellie is pregnant, Bruce."

Robertson smiled. "Oh, I know that! Who could miss it?"

"You knew?"

"Of course."

"She's been worried that you'd react badly."

"Well, tell her I didn't."

"Are you thinking about a replacement?"

"Maybe a temp. But she'll come back to work when she's ready."

"What makes you so sure?"

The sheriff stood and spread his arms with a wide smile. "Missy," he said, "it's me, Bruce! How's she gonna walk away from that?"

41

WHEN HE first arrived at the Helmuth farm, Ricky thought it was completely deserted. He knocked on the front door and no one answered. At the back door, he got the same result.

Standing on the gravel patch between the barn and the house, he heard a rhythmic chunking sound coming from behind the barn, so he circled around beside it and found twin Amish teen-agers sinking postholes in the ground near the back of the barn. They continued working on their holes as Ricky walked up. Off to the side, a wagon sat with a load of fence posts and rolled wire fencing. The horse was still harnessed, straining to nip at the top of the pasture grasses.

"Why the fence?" Niell asked. "And where are the Helmuths?"

The boys regarded him skeptically, and Ricky realized he was dressed in a coat and tie, not his uniform, so he showed them his badge and asked again, "Why are you setting a new fence?"

One of the boys stopped digging and pulled his posthole tool out of a deep hole. He dropped it on the muddy ground at his feet and took out a handkerchief to wipe the inside of his hat. Hat and handkerchief back in place, he said, "Our family—we live right there—is going to work the farm, now. We're fencing off pastureland."

"What about the Helmuths?"

"Don't know," the lad said. "Father said we wouldn't need the house."

"Isn't anyone going to live here?" Ricky asked.

"You'd have to ask the bishop."

Ricky started to leave and then turned back. "I'm headed over to see Mervin Byler. Do you know him?"

Both boys smiled, and one said, "You'll be lucky to catch him at home, as much as he's taken to Coblentz chocolates."

* * *

Mervin was rocking on his front porch when Ricky drove up. They sat together and remembered the day, only a week earlier, that Mervin had found Ruth Zook's body in the glade around the corner on TR 165.

"If I never see anything like that again," Mervin pronounced, "it'll be too soon."

"We don't really know who killed her," Ricky said. "Don't know that we ever will."

"Does it matter?" Byler asked.

Ricky shrugged a reluctant acknowledgment and said, "I suppose not, but the sheriff wants me to go down to Memphis next week."

"Whatever for?"

"To try to find out where Fannie Helmuth went. He's not going to give up on this. Not in a million years."

At the far corner of the big house, the brothers John and Mahlon appeared, walking their white pony by its bridle.

"We're never too old," Mervin said. "Never too old to have fun with a pony."

42

Tuesday, April 12
8:30 A.M.

MERVIN BYLER wore a smile with his best Sunday outfit.

Hadn't she given him a wink last Friday? The widow Stutzman?

He was at the intersection with busy SR 39, and he intended to take that road, no matter the traffic. Once he had gone the safe way, and clearly that had been a disaster.

But SR 39 was truly a busy road. Maybe even a dangerous one for an old fool in a buggy. Never mind, Mervin thought. Less chance of finding dead bodies.

Was it a wink she had given him, or just a smile? He clicked his horse out onto the blacktop and pointed her toward Walnut Creek. Underneath him, the clatter racket of his buggy wheels on hard blacktop was music to him, the clipping of his horse's hooves keeping time.

Sure, it could have been just a nod, Byler mused. He wasn't sure anymore. Still, it had been encouragement.

He had stood at the glass to watch her make the chocolates, and she had definitely given him a look.

Or just a glance?

Still, she was the widow Stutzman, and she might have looked his way.

And as much as he had always favored the salty chips, Mervin Byler found that he was developing a taste for fine Coblentz chocolates.

Other Books in the
Amish-Country Mystery Series
by P. L. Gaus

978-0-452-29646-6   ISBN 978-0-452-29661-9   ISBN 978-0-452-29668-8   ISBN 978-0-452-29669-5

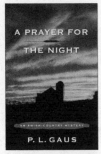

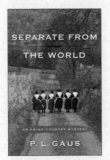

ISBN 978-0-452-29670-1   ISBN 978-0-452-29671-8   ISBN 978-0-452-29671-8

www.plgaus.com

Available wherever books are sold.

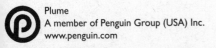
Plume
A member of Penguin Group (USA) Inc.
www.penguin.com